The Tyrant
and the
Squire

Terry Jones

Unbound

This edition first published in 2018

Unbound
6th Floor Mutual House, 70 Conduit Street,
London W1S 2GF
www.unbound.com

Text Design by Ellipsis, Glasgow

A CIP record for this book is available from the British Library

ISBN 978-1-78352-462-4 (trade hbk)
ISBN 978-1-78352-463-1 (ebook)
ISBN 978-1-78352-461-7 (limited edition)

Printed in Great Britain by Clays Ltd, St Ives Plc

1 3 5 7 9 8 6 4 2

For everyone who has enjoyed my books

Dear Reader,

The book you are holding came about in a rather different way to most others. It was funded directly by readers through a new website: Unbound. Unbound is the creation of three writers. We started the company because we believed there had to be a better deal for both writers and readers. On the Unbound website, authors share the ideas for the books they want to write directly with readers. If enough of you support the book by pledging for it in advance, we produce a beautifully bound special subscribers' edition and distribute a regular edition and ebook wherever books are sold, in shops and online.

This new way of publishing is actually a very old idea (Samuel Johnson funded his dictionary this way). We're just using the internet to build each writer a network of patrons. At the back of this book, you'll find the names of all the people who made it happen.

Publishing in this way means readers are no longer just passive consumers of the books they buy, and authors are free to write the books they really want. They get a much fairer return too – half the profits their books generate, rather than a tiny percentage of the cover price.

If you're not yet a subscriber, we hope that you'll want to join our publishing revolution and have your name listed in one of our books in the future. To get you started, here is a £5 discount on your first pledge. Just visit unbound.com, make your pledge and type **squire5** in the promo code box when you check out.

Thank you for your support,

Dan, Justin and John
Founders, Unbound

Chapter 1

Milan 1385

'If only life were as simple as you think it's going to be,' thought Tom, 'it wouldn't be nearly such fun. On the other hand, it wouldn't be nearly as dangerous either.'

And at that precise moment it was the dangerous aspect of life rather than the fun aspect that Tom was experiencing – although he wasn't quite sure which bit of it was more dangerous: the drop that had suddenly opened up beneath him or the animal that was at that moment banging its tusks a few feet above his head.

Goodness knows why the boar was banging its tusks against the trunk of a tree, but there it was – doing it. Maybe it was a case of sheer bad temper – after all, the creature had just been cheated of its quarry, which happened to be Tom. It was one of those curious reversals of roles of which life is full. In one moment, Tom had been the pursuer, hunting the wild boar, and yet

1

the next moment one of his co-hunters had given a piercing whistle, Tom's horse had reared, Tom had fallen off, and the wild boar had started chasing *him*.

It was just possible that the wild boar simply had poor eyesight and had mistaken the tree for Tom. In which case, thought Tom, as he watched large gobbets of bark flying off the tree in all directions, poor eyesight in wild boars was definitely something to be encouraged.

The more he thought about it, however, the more it seemed to Tom that the drop below him represented the most immediate danger. The small branch onto which Tom was pinning all his hopes of a future existence in this world was really more of a twig than a branch, and even that seemed to be in the process of coming loose from the ground out of which it was growing.

As for the ledge, onto which Tom had leapt, as he escaped the wild boar's leading tusk, that was even now tumbling down the cliff face as a shower of earth and stones. It had not, it appeared, been the right thing to leap onto . . . but then he hadn't had much choice – or much time to choose.

Tom was, in every sense of the word, in the middle of a cliffhanger.

At that moment, however, the danger diminished by 50 per cent. A voice rang out:

'Sir Thomas! Sir Thomas!'

And the wild boar turned, without even saying 'excuse me!' to the tree, and charged off into the wood.

Tom tried to yell back but simply couldn't find his vocal chords . . . his mind was too preoccupied with considering whether or not the danger had really been reduced by 50 per cent. True, the wild boar had run off, but the danger from the drop below him was still 100 per cent, since the twig onto which he was holding was now definitely severing forever its connection with Mother Earth.

'Sir Thomas!' It was the voice of his squire, John. 'Where are you?'

'I'm here!' Tom almost yelled, but the awful fascination of watching the last root of the twig pulling itself free of earthly ties stopped the words in his throat. Or was it the loose earth falling from the root and filling his mouth that stopped the words? At all events the only thing he could say was:

'Mgmeurgh!'

'Sir Thomas!'

'Here it goes . . .' thought Tom, watching the root. 'Going . . . going . . .'

'Got you!' Squire John's face had appeared over the cliff edge and his hand had grabbed Tom's jerkin just as the last root came free, and Tom hung dangling from his squire's fingers for what seemed like half an hour but was, in fact, half a second.

John's other hand grabbed his wrist and Tom rammed his feet and hands against the cliff edge as the loose earth tumbled slowly down . . . down into the ravine.

In another thirty seconds, which felt like three hours, Tom had been hauled up to the comparative safety of the cliff edge, and Squire John was dusting him down, as a good squire should.

'The pleasures of boar hunting are rather overrated if you ask me, John,' Tom said. His squire grunted, and went off to find the horse.

It's curious, thought Tom, as they rode back to the great castle of Bernabò Visconti, how you can get something you've always wanted, only to find out that maybe it wasn't really what you wanted at all. Here he was, Sir Thomas English, a knight in the service of a great lord, riding with his squire, and yet nothing about being a knight was quite what he thought it was going to be . . . and the more he thought about it, the more he wondered whether what he used to think was what he now wanted anyway.

*

The Visconti fortress loomed ahead of them, and he turned to his squire and said: 'Do you really like boar hunting, John?'

John shrugged. 'Not that much,' he replied. 'It has its moments.'

'But . . .' said Tom.

'Where does it get us?' asked John, who was a bright lad.

'Exactly!'

'Halfway down a cliff face?' suggested John.

Tom leaned across and cuffed him across the ears. John choked on a laugh. That was another thing Tom liked about his squire – his sense of humour.

They were now within sight of the guards, stationed outside the main gates of the Visconti stronghold. In a few minutes they would have to plunge into the gloomy depths of the palace of the great warlord of Milan. They would make their way to the great hall and then, doubtless, they would have to hang around for an hour or two until the great lord himself deigned to appear, and the dinner could commence.

'The food isn't bad,' said Squire John, as if he were following Tom's chain of thoughts.

'Yes, but the place is so stuffy,' replied Tom.

'Well, nobody dares say anything,' said John. He had a way of serving up the truth without any of the usual trimmings – no garnish, no stuffing, not even any gravy. Just plonked on your plate like a slab of raw meat.

'Well, would you?' asked Tom. 'You never know what sort of a mood my Lord Bernabò is going to be in.'

'Did you hear what he did to that funny-looking chap with the long ears?' asked Squire John.

'The ambassador from my lord the Conte Verde? Yes, I know,' said Tom, 'he said he was as ugly as a bloodhound, and he had him shut up overnight in the kennel with the other dogs. I believe it was a joke.'

'But they were my Lord Bernabò's Great Danes,' gasped Squire John. 'And by the morning all that was left of him was his earring.'

'Some sense of humour, eh?' said Tom.

'I'll tell you what,' said Squire John, lowering his voice even more, so that the guards couldn't overhear, 'my Lord Bernabò may have a sense of humour, but I don't think I've laughed once since we've been here.'

'Exactly my point!' exclaimed Tom. 'That's why we've got to escape!'

Squire John looked a bit nonplussed. 'Escape? I didn't know we were prisoners, Sir Thomas.'

'We're not,' agreed Tom. 'But my Lord Bernabò won't take kindly to people spurning his hospitality. If he gets wind that we're thinking of bunking off, he might turn ugly.'

'That won't be hard,' said Squire John, although in fact the Lord Bernabò was proud of his good looks.

'In fact it's ten to one he'd try and stop us,' said Tom.

'Like how?'

'Like . . . er . . . cutting off our legs?'

'That would slow us down,' agreed Squire John.

'And the great plus is: we wouldn't have to go boar hunting ever again,' added Tom.

'It's overrated anyway,' said his young companion, but he wasn't laughing. In fact, as Tom looked across at him, he looked downright gloomy.

'What's the matter? Don't you want to get away?' asked Tom.

'Yes, yes . . . of course . . . everything you say is true about this place . . .'

'Ah! Don't tell me! The lovely Jenny has her apron strings tied around your heart and you just don't want to cut free?' said Tom.

Squire John went bright red. 'No . . . not Jenny . . . though indeed she is truly lovely of course . . .'

'But only last Sunday you were ready to die for her!' exclaimed Tom.

'Indeed . . . I . . . er . . .' If Squire John could have turned an even brighter red, then he would have done. 'But . . . I met someone . . . someone so beautiful . . . so charming . . . and . . . well . . . there it is . . .'

'And what is your new mistress's name?' asked Tom.

Squire John looked round as if he were searching out a hiding-hole from which to escape his master's queries. But he was duty-bound to reply.

'My lord . . .' he stumbled, '. . . her name is Beatrice.'

Suddenly all Tom's cheery banter dried in his throat. As if to mark the moment, a cloud passed over the sun as Tom let out a low whistle.

'The young Lady Beatrice?' he asked.

Squire John bit his lip and nodded.

'John . . .' Tom sighed. 'It's one thing to make eyes at a serving girl, but to make love to one of my Lord Bernabò's own daughters . . .'

'She is only his natural daughter,' said John.

'Legitimate or illegitimate – you're playing with fire.'

'But what can I do?' asked John. 'She's told me she loves me . . . and . . .'

'That settles it,' said Tom, 'the sooner we get out of here the . . .'

But at that moment they came to the city gate, which also formed the outer entrance to the Visconti palace. Two guards grabbed their horses' bridles and the chief held out his hand for their documents.

Everywhere you went in the domain of the Visconti, you had to have passports and paperwork ever at the ready. Innkeepers had to report each and every person who stayed in their inn. Bridgekeepers kept a record of whoever crossed the rivers. Gatekeepers noted the names of those that entered and left their town. The Lords of Milan knew who was where and when almost every hour of the day. Those whose whereabouts they didn't know were soon sniffed out by the Visconti spies. – and there were a lot of those.

'Every time I come into this place,' whispered Tom in English, so that the guards wouldn't understand, 'I feel like that poor fellow up there.' And he nodded up towards the top of the gatehouse, where a man with his arms held up in horror was being swallowed by a serpent with a wolf's head. The image was scored into the brickwork, and the man was painted blood red against a blue background. It was the emblem of the Visconti lords.

Squire John shuddered, as the guard returned their papers and nodded them in. Tom and his squire kicked their horses forward, and they were quickly swallowed up by the grim fortress.

They were honoured guests of the Lord of Milan. And they were trapped in his world like two flies in the jam.

Chapter 2

Milan 1385

No one could say that Bernabò Visconti, Lord of Milan, did not have a sense of humour. He also had a sense of what was just – so everyone said. But when you mixed these two things together the results were often unpredictable.

For example, when a priest refused to bury some poor man until he'd been paid the correct funeral dues, Bernabò told the priest he'd get his due all right, and promptly had him buried alongside the pauper – alive and upside down.

Another time, when the Pope had sent two Benedictine abbots to pronounce a sentence of excommunication on Bernabò, the Lord of Milan had thoughtfully met them on a bridge over the river Lambro, which in those days raced through the city open to the skies. There he cordially inquired whether the Pope's representatives would prefer to eat or drink. It was made clear that 'drinking' involved being thrown off the bridge into the waters of the river, so the two abbots chose to eat. Their meal consisted of the entire parchment upon which the sentence of excommunication was written – along with its silk cord and seal.

The story had kept Bernabò's court in stitches for days. You see, nobody in that court was particularly worried about divine retribution – although I suppose they should have been . . . particularly Bernabò himself, as he was eventually to discover.

This evening Bernabò appeared to be in a particularly benign mood, which – as far as Tom was concerned – made it all the worse, for as dangerous as Bernabò was when he was in a bad mood, it was his good moods that Tom found more unnerving.

And tonight Tom had an extra cause for worry. Normally Squire John would have been at his side the moment Tom stepped into the court, but tonight he was not there. Tom had been looking round the court for some time, but the young man had totally vanished. It was most unlike him.

What if John had gone to take his leave of his new paramour, Bernabò's daughter Beatrice? What if he'd been discovered? His life would not be worth a fly's. What if he'd told her they were planning to escape?

What if she'd persuaded the young man to stay? What if she'd given their plans away?

In the court of a tyrant you were always treading on eggshells. Now Tom felt as if he were under siege with miners digging away beneath his feet. The whole edifice of his life was – for the moment – propped up by wooden struts in the mines below. Soon they would be fired, whereupon they would collapse and the whole castle would come crashing down about his ears. It was imperative that he find Squire John before anything else could . . .

'Sir Thomas Englishman!' a voice rang out across the great hall. Tom's blood ran cold. It was the voice of Bernabò Visconti, the Lord of Milan. The 'anything' that could happen just had!

'My lord!' said Tom. As he stepped forward he took a quick look at the great man. It never did to stare at him, and eyes were usually averted for most of the conversation. But in that quick glance, Tom could see that Bernabò was in one of his best moods. Goodness knows what that meant.

'Come forward!' commanded the Lord of Milan.

Tom stepped before the great man, and the eyes of the court turned to him.

'Tomorrow you join me on the boar hunt?' said Bernabò.

'Er . . . I joined you today on the boar hunt,' replied Tom in the Lombard dialect. 'I nearly got killed.'

This was, apparently, the funniest thing the Lord of Milan had heard all day. He laughed and laughed and looked round his court so that others started to laugh as well. It was always wise to laugh along with the most ruthless ruler in Lombardy. Bernabò laughed until tears came to his eyes.

'I . . . er . . . fell off a cliff,' explained Tom. Well, if the information that he'd nearly been killed had been funny, this new detail was apparently so hilarious Bernabò practically fell off his seat.

Tom sighed. He would never understand Bernabò's sense of humour.

'Sir Thomas Englishman!' exclaimed the Lord of Milan, 'I love you!'

Now this was the worst news that Tom had heard for all the months he'd been resident in the court of the ruler of Milan. If Bernabò Visconti 'loved' you, it meant you were well and truly in his grip. It meant that – like the viper on his emblem – he had wound his coils around you and was not going to let you go.

But what could one say? 'Oh! My lord, I don't think it's *real* love . . . I think what you mean is that you find me amusing until you get bored with me and then have me shut up in the kennels with your Great

Danes'? No, all Tom could do was make a low bow, which would, he hoped, convey the enormous sense of honour that had overwhelmed him as the great man had pronounced his sentence of undying affection upon him.

At this moment the Lady Donnina whispered something to her Lord. Now it was well known that Bernabò loved the Lady Donnina more than anything or anyone under the sun. And because of this, he found it impossible to refuse her slightest request.

Everyone understood Bernabò's infatuation with the Lady Donnina. Her beauty was so powerful it was almost contagious . . . just by being next to her you felt more beautiful yourself. The golden light from that golden hair of hers somehow reflected on one's own skin and made one feel richer . . . more valuable. The sparkle of her eyes and the jewels around her throat lit up the darker recesses of the heart and made even the most desperate supplicant feel unexpectedly full of light.

Everyone understood why the Lord Bernabò kept the Lady Donnina beside him day and night. His footmen understood. His servants understood. His brother understood. His children understood. Even his wife understood.

And Tom understood. He just hoped that whatever it was the Lady Donnina was suggesting to her lord at

14

that moment, it did not involve him or his squire John.

Bernabò Visconti laughed out loud. (Yes! He was in an insufferably good mood tonight, thought Tom.) It was the best idea the Lord of Milan had ever heard. Yes! The Lady Donnina was absolutely right! It should be done at once! Call the footmen! Call the musicians! Light the oil lamps! Banish the night! We are to have a *carolle* in the garden! Everyone will dance! Everyone will sing! It is a beautiful night! A night for lovers! A night for rejoicing! Come! Let us step out! And Sir Thomas Englishman! Come! And lead the Lady Donnina to the first dance!

Tom's heart sank. If it wasn't bad enough having Bernabò saying he loved him, the last thing he wanted was the Lady Donnina's attentions. The Lady Donnina's attentions were the sort of attentions that could get your head separated from your shoulders and your stomach taken out and burned in front of you.

But it was too late. Tom found himself holding the Lady Donnina by the hand and escorting her out into the garden, where the servants and footmen were already tripping over each other trying to get the oil lamps in place before the court emerged.

In those days, a *carolle* wasn't just for Christmas. It was actually a dance – a dance in which the dancers also sang, usually in a circle. Sometimes the men would

15

be in one circle and the ladies in another, and they would take turns to dance and sing. Sometimes the circle would be made up of men and women alternately, and sometimes they all danced and sang together. Sometimes the men sang one part and then the women another, moving around the circle as they did so.

Tom found himself hand in hand with the Lady Donnina, as the circle of dancers formed around them. The Lord of Milan did not join the dance. He had been drinking spiced wine steadily since he returned from the hunt, and was now inclined to sit out the dancing. He would beat time with his foot, and he would observe the dancers. In fact, he would be watching everyone closely – very closely indeed. It was the Lord of Milan's opinion that you could see into people's heads if you stared at them hard enough. And when you saw into their heads, you could see all their thoughts, clear as if they had laid them out for you on a platter. And the best time for doing that was when their guard was down – such as when they were enjoying themselves.

The Lord Bernabò had not drunk so much spiced wine that he was not prepared to make full use of the Lady Donnina's suggestion of a *carolle* in the garden. He would sit there in his high chair in the garden, under the maples, and try to spot the plotters and traitors that, he was pretty sure, always surrounded him. It was, in fact, his favourite way of passing the time – apart, that is, from the time he spent alone with the Lady Donnina.

As for Tom, he didn't know when he'd been more alarmed. The Lady Donnina had a firm grip of his hand, and – to his horror – kept squeezing it every so often.

Could the Lord of Milan see those squeezes? wondered Tom. If so, Tom was convinced he would be a headless and stomachless Englishman before the night was out. Maybe the Lord of Milan could actually feel the squeezes himself? There was one again! Maybe each squeeze was a test and a secret signal to the great lord from his Lady? Maybe she was testing out which of his courtiers could be trusted with her? And the moment Tom squeezed her hand in return the guards and dogs would surround him and he would be marched off to the darkest torture chamber to enjoy the delights of 'Lent'.

Now Lent of course normally refers to the forty days of fasting that any good Christian undertakes before Easter. Bernabò Visconti's 'Lent', however, referred to the forty-day remission of sentence that the Lord of Milan graciously granted to those he had condemned to death. The only snag was that those forty days consisted of forty days running through the *Torturer's Handbook*, with practical demonstrations and firsthand experience of most of the techniques contained therein.

All this was racing through Tom's mind as the musicians struck up the first bars of the *carolle*. Under the circumstances it was very hard to look cheerful and carefree – both of which were essential requirements for anyone frequenting the court of Bernabò Visconti.

The great lord hated uncheerful people almost as much as he hated ugly people. His reasoning went like this. If anyone didn't look cheerful, it was ten-to-one that they had a problem, and if they had a problem, it was ten-to-one that that problem had been caused by the excesses and arbitrary rule of the Lord of Milan. Thus every careworn face was a silent accusation against himself, and the Lord of Milan did not take kindly to having his evil deeds pointed out.

A lack of total cheerfulness might also be a sign that someone was preoccupied with something, and who was to say that that 'something' might not be about ridding Milan of its great lord? It was the sort of preoccupation that fed into Bernabò Visconti's own chief preoccupation: how to get rid of people who wanted to get rid of him.

At this moment Tom felt his hand squeezed yet again by the Lady Donnina. He couldn't help turning to her, whereupon her eyes instantly locked him in a steady gaze. She was at the same time singing:

> 'My heart is in the hands of one
> Who looks another way.
> I pray he'll turn his eyes on me
> And there that they will stay.'

Tom didn't know where to look. It would be disrespectful to turn away from the Lady Donnina's gaze, and any disrespect for the Lady Donnina might well be seen as disrespect for Bernabò himself. And Tom could feel the eagle eyes of the Lord of Milan watching him as he danced and as he now took up with the other men their part of the song:

> 'She whom I love is far away
> And in another land
> But till we meet another day
> I'll hold another's hand.'

And there he was again – holding the hand of the Lady Donnina! She gave his another squeeze. Was it disrespectful not to return the squeeze? Tom had never felt more like a rabbit in a mantrap. He sort of squeezed her hand with what he hoped could have been mistaken for either a reflex reaction or a deliberate squeeze back, depending on which the Lady Donnina was expecting.

At the same moment, something happened to the Lady Donnina's eyes . . . they slipped to one side of her head and she nodded in the same direction. Tom followed her glance and saw she was indicating a dark corner of the garden.

Sheer unadulterated panic seized Tom and jerked him up bodily so that he nearly tripped over into the Lady Donnina. Was the beloved lady of the Lord of Milan suggesting that he – Thomas the Englishman – should secretly meet up with her in the darkest corner of the garden?

This was the worst thing that had happened to him since he'd been in Milan, and yet the Lady Donnina's eyes once more slid across to the shadows in the far corner, and she gave a meaningful nod. It seemed clear what she was trying to convey to him.

Tom thought he had better give some sort of response, since she was clearly expecting one; her eyes were once again fixed on his. So he started to give a vague understanding nod of response – the sort of nod one might give to someone who had just told you the price of a pair of kippers or who had just informed you that the world was about to end that evening. But before he could complete the understanding nod the music changed, and the ladies stepped forward into the middle of the circle to form a smaller inner ring, and away they danced from their partners. The men, Tom included, meanwhile danced in the opposite direction until the music once more brought them to the verse of the song and Tom found himself next to a dark-eyed lady-in-waiting with a mischievous smile and a prominent nose who was already singing with the other ladies:

'So hold my hand, sweet stranger do,
Until we have to part
And since our days are brief and few
In your hand you hold my heart.'

By the end of the dance, Tom once again found himself beside the Lady Donnina. The exertion of the dance made her breast heave within her ermine-trimmed bodice, just slightly, but her red sleeves betrayed not even the slightest suspicion of sweat at any point. She looked him straight in the eyes as if challenging him to find fault or flaw in her perfect presentation. Tom bowed and before he had regained the upright position she had turned on her heel and left him. But as the musicians reached for their wine, he saw her slip inconspicuously into the shadows in the dark corner of the garden.

So did she mean it? Was she really expecting him to meet her there, in the shadows beyond the gaze of the other folk – beyond the gaze of her lord and master?

Tom quickly looked at Bernabò. He seemed too busy making ribald jokes to his drinking companions to notice what his mistress was up to – although, of course, you could never be sure.

Tom found his mind racing. Should he follow the Lady Donnina? Every sensible atom in his body told him not to. He had told Squire John that he was playing with fire if he courted the young Lady Beatrice . . . what sort of an inferno lay in store for him if he consorted with the Lord of Milan's favourite mistress?

Look what Bernabò had done to his own daughter, Bernarda, for engaging in an affair of which he disapproved! The Lord of Milan had had Bernarda subjected to icy showers for days on end, and then walled up in a dungeon in the Porta Nuova with just enough food to keep her alive for seven months. If that was the sort of thing the Lord of Milan could do to his own daughter, what might he do to Tom?

On the other hand, if Tom did not go into the shadows of the dark corner of the garden to join the Lady Donnina when she had so clearly invited him to do so, he would surely incur the Lady's displeasure. In which case might she not seek some sort of revenge? She could easily go to the Lord of Milan and accuse Tom of whatever crime she felt like dreaming up. As far as Tom could see, his goose was cooked whatever he did.

So he decided take his fate into his hands and, making sure he was unobserved, he slipped into the shadows and made his way round to the darkest corner of the garden.

By the time he reached the spot that the Lady Donnina had seemed to be indicating, the musicians had struck up another melody, and the dancers were taking up their positions for a new dance. Tom stood in the darkness for what seemed like an interminable time. He was quite sure the Lady Donnina was there, looking at him. He could feel her presence, although he wasn't sure where or how close she was. However, he was determined to let her make the first move, whatever that might be.

But nobody spoke. Nobody moved. Nothing. And the longer he stood there, the more convinced Tom became that he was wrong. The Lady Donnina was not there . . . she must have slipped off somewhere else. A spasm of relief passed through Tom's body. He must have been imagining the whole thing. What a wonderful and blessed and utterly joyful deliverance from the jaws of the Visconti monster! Tom's heart slowly climbed up from its hiding place in his boots and once more settled itself in its proper place, under his jerkin.

'Englishman!'

A woman's voice, low but commanding, suddenly came out of the darkness.

'My lady?' whispered Tom, and his heart plummeted back down to his boots.

'Come here,' ordered the imperious voice.

Tom stepped forward in the direction that he thought the voice had come from, but a hand came from behind and touched him on the shoulder, spinning him round ninety degrees. The light from the distant torches just caught the side of the lady's face. She smiled slightly, but it was not the Lady Donnina. It was Regina della Scala, the wife of Bernabò Visconti, Lord of Milan.

'Englishman,' said Regina, 'you should leave. My husband suspects you of treachery.'

'Of course! That's why he was being so nice to me!' thought Tom.

'I tell you this because there is something you can do for me in return. Otherwise I would leave you to your fate,' said the regal mistress of Milan.

'My Lady Regina,' said Tom, 'I am at your service day and night.'

'Do not be flippant with me, young man, or I will tell

my husband that you have tried to make advances to the Lady Donnina here.'

Tom suddenly realised that the Lady Donnina was indeed standing behind Regina della Scala. It was well known that despite the one being Bernabò's wife and the other his mistress, the two women looked after each other's interests. Moreover they both did their best to mitigate some of the worst aspects of their lord's rule.

'What service can I provide the two most beautiful women in Lombardy?' asked Tom, bowing to each in turn.

'You are to go to Gian Galeazzo. Enter his service. Become his familiar. Find out all you can of his plans and return here to inform us.'

The silence hung in the air like a sheet on washday – flapping in the gale of thoughts that were now rushing through Tom's mind.

'You want me to act as a spy against my Lord Bernabò's nephew, Gian Galeazzo?' asked Tom carefully. He could barely grasp the enormity of what was being asked of him.

'As you know, the rule of Milan is supposed to be divided equally between Bernabò and his nephew Gian Galeazzo. But Gian never sets foot here. In his father's day the two palaces were equally full of life, but since

that illustrious man's death his nephew has been
co-ruler of Milan in name only,' said Regina della Scala.
'We know Gian Galeazzo must be plotting something
against my Lord Bernabò. But my husband is so convinced that his nephew is a weakling and a coward that
he refuses to take anything about him seriously.'

'But he's up to something,' added Donnina. 'He must
be. My lord is blind to it.'

'But . . . why me?' asked Tom.

'You are an outsider – an Englishman,' said Regina
della Scala with what might have been the merest trace
of contempt in her voice. 'You have no commitment
either way. You can tell us the truth.'

'And what makes you think I will return once I have
left the court of Milan?'

'We know you are a man of honour,' said the Lady
Donnina. 'If you say you will do something, you will
do it.'

And suddenly there it was again! She was squeezing
his hand. Tom couldn't stop himself snatching his hand
away as if it were touching the fire.

'Besides,' the Lady Regina cut in more prosaically,
'your squire – what's his name? – Gian? John? – he
will remain here with us. Should you fail to return by
the Feast of All Saints, your squire's infatuation with
the young Lady Beatrice may well have become

common knowledge, and then who knows what my Lord Bernabò will do for him?'

'Ahh . . .' said Tom, as if he'd just been told the state of the weather or the name of a particular dog. 'And if I refuse to go at all?'

'You remember you squeezed my hand?' said the Lady Donnina. 'It would be most unfortunate if my Lord Bernabò ever got to hear about it.'

If there had been any doubt in Tom's mind before, now there was none. He knew he had to find his squire immediately, and they must escape that very night – before dawn rolled across the plain of Lombardy to light up this viper's nest of intrigue and secrecy.

'Oh, and by the way,' said the Lady Regina, 'I hear that your squire was thrown into prison earlier this evening – some trifling business that I'm sure will be sorted out when you return.'

So that was it.

Tom turned to her and bowed both to the two women and to the inevitable. 'My ladies, I am honoured by your commission,' were the words that crossed his lips, but in his thoughts he heard another voice saying: 'The flies never get out of the jam . . .'

Chapter 3

Milan 1385

'I didn't steal that ring . . .' began Squire John as soon as Tom approached the bars of his cell.

'Nobody thinks you did,' replied Tom.

'Then why have they put me in . . .'

'Listen,' said Tom. 'The Lady Regina della Scala and Donnina de' Porri know about the Lady Beatrice and you.'

'But how on earth . . .?'

'It is they who have put you in here, but they say they will release you once I return from some business they wish me to conduct.'

'It's all my fault!' said John. 'I have put you in jeopardy by loving the Lady Beatrice.'

'They would have found some other way to make me do what they want.'

'But I am ashamed,' whispered Squire John. 'What do you have to do?'

Tom regarded his squire with some affection, and then said: 'John? Do you always tell the truth?'

'I do, my lord!' replied John instantly.

'I know you do,' said Tom. 'And in this place that is a problem.'

'But surely it's right to tell the truth?'

'What if my Lord Bernabò or – more likely – one of his torturers quizzes you about where I've gone and what I'm up to? You would tell him the truth – you would have no choice.'

John thought for a bit and then said slowly: 'In that case, Sir Thomas, it would be best for me not to know.'

'But if you say you don't know, they won't believe you. They will never believe that I haven't told you where I was going.'

John was silent, waiting for his master to continue.

'I am going to Ferrara to claim a ransom that has suddenly come available.'

'Really?' asked Squire John.

'So if you are asked where I have gone,' continued Tom patiently, 'it will be no lie to say that is what I told you.'

Squire John nodded. It amazed him how Sir Thomas seemed to think of every eventuality. But then suddenly the image of his lady-love blotted out all else from his mind's eye.

Terry Jones

'Can't I just say goodbye to the Lady Beatrice?'

'No! You must never go near her again! Not if you value your life.'

'Can't I just send her a note to tell her . . . I don't know . . . that I'll wait for her forever or something?'

'John . . . the duke's wife and his favourite mistress are both watching your every movement. For the moment you are useful to them alive, but they will not hesitate to dispose of you as soon as they want to. All we can do is play along with them until we can find a way out – and that means not doing anything more to inflame their anger against you.'

'Sir Thomas?' Squire John was looking down at his shoes, as he stood in the filth of the dungeon floor.

'Yes, John?'

'May I ask you something?'

'You may,' said Tom.

'I don't mean to be impertinent . . . Sir Thomas . . . but I was wondering . . . I mean talking about my Lady Beatrice . . . I was wondering that you don't have a lady . . . at least I've never heard you mention her name . . .'

Squire John looked up anxiously to see if he had offended his master. But Tom was staring into the darkness, as if he were searching for a memory there . . . as if he expected to see some image from his past step out of that dungeon blackness to greet him with open arms and smiling face.

'My lady?' murmured Tom. 'My lady is . . . I don't know where she is . . . that is . . . I don't know where *they* are. There were two ladies I served . . . I loved them both . . . both . . .'

Squire John waited . . . but that appeared to be all that Tom was going to say on the matter.

'Time's up!' said an oddly falsetto voice, and instead of a precious memory, it was the jailer who stepped out of the shadows. He was the most unlikely jailer. He was as pleasant looking an individual as you could possibly find, elegantly dressed in particoloured hose and a pink tunic. He seemed to bear no affinity with the heavy and gloomy dungeons through which he passed.

The jailer smiled affably at Tom. 'I'm afraid it's time to go. Sorry and all that, but I'm under orders not to let anyone speak to the prisoner. I was only doing you a favour because I love England.'

'You love England?' said Tom in amazement.

'Yes, it's odd, isn't it? Most Italians hate the English – they call them "devils incarnate". After all, they infest our country and burn our farms and kill our people and steal from us and destroy our crops and vines and nowhere is safe from them – not a cottage, not a village. And yet I once went to England and it was very nice. I stayed with a family named Philipot. They were very nice.'

A silence descended on the dungeon. No one quite knew what to say. In the end Tom held his hand out to John. 'Goodbye,' he said.

'Uh uh!' said the jailer. 'No touching!'

Tom shrugged and with a last glance at his squire, he retraced his steps towards the stone stairway that led back up to the world of the living.

Chapter 4

Milan 1385

As Tom rode up to the great gates of Milan, he reflected once again on how nothing was at all the way he'd imagined it would be when he was young. He'd always imagined himself dressed as a knight in brightly coloured coat armour, emblazoned with his own coat of arms, a plumed helmet on his head and a vivid shield on his wrist, displaying the same arms. And yet here he was, riding out in a battered old brown jerkin that bore the marks of his mail coat and nothing else . . . no *chevronels braced*, or *bend sinister* . . . no *unicorn passant*, or *wolf salient* . . . just a brown jacket with a black cloak over his shoulders. He hadn't even chosen himself a coat of arms yet. It seemed that irrelevant.

His horse's harness was serviceable but not decorated. And he didn't carry a shield. Only the sword at his side indicated a man-at-arms – although not necessarily a knight.

Another thing that was not at all the way he'd always imagined it was the weather. As a youth, he'd always imagined the future in sunshine, with a clear blue sky above. Today, despite the fact that it was already May, it was cold. The sky was dreary and there was a fine mist of damp – you couldn't even call it rain really – but it drifted down from the clouds making everything wet and somehow unheroic. The day was as drab as Tom felt. But then this wasn't the future – this was now.

The gatekeeper was examining the papers that had been provided for Tom by the Lady Regina della Scala.

'What's your business in Ferrera?' demanded the gatekeeper.

'Oh, it's a debt I have to collect,' said Tom.

'Usual thing,' grunted the gatekeeper, and handed the papers back. 'Avoid the Lodi road, there are reports of bandits,' he muttered, and Tom was through the gate and heading away from the court of Bernabò Visconti at last.

But instead of feeling relieved of the burden of the Visconti serpent that had been coiled around his heart and spirit for so many months, he felt more ensnared by it than ever.

What of Squire John? The Visconti ladies said they would release him as soon as Tom returned. But would they? In his heart of hearts Tom felt he knew that the Visconti would never suffer an insult to their pride to go unpunished; for an insult is how they would regard the love of a humble squire like John for one of the daughters of the great Bernabò.

Bernabò looked after all his children with the zeal and care of a doting father. It was quite a feat, when you considered the malignance of his own character, and even more so when you considered that he had no less than thirty children.

He certainly looked after them, but he looked after them to his own advantage. In Bernabò's view, the marriage of every child was a business opportunity: his sons would be married off to the daughters of the wealthy, who would bring with them handsome dowries to swell the Visconti coffers, while his daughters – offered complete with lavish portions of the Visconti wealth – would be married only into the royal households of Europe, thereby extending the influence of the Visconti name. In this way, for example, he had seen his daughter Violante married off to one of the sons of the king of England.

In Bernabò's eyes, his daughter Bernada's sin was not a moral failing, it was far graver than that: it was bad for his business. In dallying with a courtier of low rank, she had been squandering whatever marriage potential she might have had. To put it plainly, she had been consorting with someone who was of no political or economic advantage to her father. Her fate was a warning to all the other twenty-nine children.

So would Regina della Scala and Donnina de' Porri *really* let Squire John out of his prison? Would they be content with simply giving him a ticking off? Tom had to believe it for his squire's sake, but it was an act of faith.

Then there was his own situation. Wasn't that was just as bad as Squire John's? Here he was travelling to the court of Pavia to spy on its lord, Gian Galeazzo Visconti – a man whose father had been not only as ruthless as his brother Bernabò but even more scheming. If his son followed in his father's footsteps, what chance did Tom have of concealing the true purpose of his visit? Surely the eagle eyes of Gian Galeazzo would be watching him, and his mind (which was far more truly devious than Tom's could ever hope to be) would be weighing up the deceits that Tom would be forced to employ.

And to tell the truth, Tom was really no better than Squire John when it came to deception. He had learned to employ it to survive but it did not come naturally, and a deceiver who does not truly enjoy the art of deception will, one day or another, be caught out.

One false step, one contradictory story, and Tom knew he would find himself under torture in the dungeons of Pavia, unable to rescue his squire from the dungeons of Milan. Tom knew that for the next month he would be treading a tightrope over an invisible pit of hell. The stench of the dungeons, of course, never rose up as far as the refined and lavishly furnished public rooms of the court.

At this point, his reverie was interrupted by a drop of water that had trickled somehow inside his hood and now suddenly made its way down his back. Tom shivered and tried to concentrate his mind on the journey ahead.

Pavia was an easy day's ride from Milan, but Tom had set out on the Ferrera road into order to give the impression that that was where he was going. He had planned to curve down south when he reached the river Adda, but now the gatekeeper's warning meant he would have to make an even wider sweep, adding a few hours to his journey.

On a bright sunny day that would have been no great hardship, but in this miserable, dripping day of mist and wet, every hour on horseback was like a day in purgatory . . . or an hour in the dank dungeons of the Visconti.

Tom wrapped his cloak around himself and pulled the hood over his head, trying to blot out as much of the irksome world as possible. At least the steam that rose from his wet horse surrounded him in a comforting cocoon of horse smell and damp warmth. But otherwise it was a cheerless journey, and long.

Bucephalus, the horse, kept grunting in a most un-horse-like way. He appeared to be groaning, as if he too wished he were anywhere else. Tom's mind seemed to be doing the same thing. It refused to stay in the tedium and discomfort of the here and now, and kept sneaking off back to another time and place.

Images kept rising in his mind's eye: a river in full spate, the wind snagging up the waves as they slammed into the piers of a bridge . . . a bridge across a wide expanse of dangerous water . . . and on the other side of the river – a grim square-walled fortress . . .

The horse stumbled and Tom's attention was dragged back to the uneven road. The rain was now falling in heavier droplets and running off his hood and down his face . . . he would need to find shelter.

But as Bucephalus regained his regular gait, Tom found himself jogged back again into his memories . . .

He saw a cart crossing a bridge . . . no! Now it was

falling . . . the oxen stamping thin air . . . a cart loaded with great tree trunks falling slowly and below the cart he could now make out two figures: one a fat man in a blue surcoat, the other a giant with a moon-face . . . Anton the Giant . . . it had all happened so long ago . . . but for Tom it seemed so recent it could have happened this morning.

What had they been doing? Oh yes . . . Anton's village, like so many French villages, had been devastated by the English soldiery who had been slashing and burning their way through France on their routine of terror, until the villagers had been forced to sleep in underground dens.

And the French nobility? Instead of protecting the poor village people, they had demanded their cut. If the villagers could afford to pay off the English soldiery, they said, they could afford to pay off their own aristocracy! It was only fair! And then the Church demanded its tenth . . . which is why Tom had been despatched with Anton the Giant to take a letter to the Pope begging him to waive the money due to the Church.

In Avignon – that grim fortress in which the Pope daily counted his treasure – Tom had realised that his mission was futile. Although he succeeded in putting the villagers' request to the great pontiff, the great pontiff's only response had been to call the guards.

Tom had rescued his best friend Alan (who was actually a girl by the name of Ann disguised as a boy). He had also rescued the beautiful Emilia de Valois, who was desperate to escape marrying her uncle, Jean de Craon, Archbishop of Reims.

Together the three of them had jumped from the top of the Pope's palace into a sheet held by Anton the Giant and Sir John Hawkley. Chased by the palace guards, they had tried to escape across the bridge of Saint-Bénézet at Avignon, but halfway across, Tom, Ann and Emily had turned to watch in horror as Anton the Giant and Sir John Hawkley had been swept to their deaths by an out-of-control cart.

Tom blinked. The image of a house was looming out of the curtain of rain ahead of him. A canal ran alongside the building, and the rain was now pitting the surface of the water like the hoof prints of a million tiny water-borne horses galloping down its length into the increasing murk descending from the skies.

It took Tom a moment to realise that this was not in his mind's eye: this was a real house that actually existed here and now. It was a real house that represented real warmth and real shelter and perhaps real food.

He dismounted and tied his horse to a post.

Chapter 5

The Road to Pavia 1385

A girl came to the door with feathers in her hair and a cross smile on her face.

'How on earth can you look cross and be smiling at the same time?' wondered Tom. But before he could come up with an answer, the girl had said:

'You're soaked to the skin.' She said it in a way that indicated annoyance and yet at the same time sympathy. 'You'd better come in.'

The cross-yet-smiling girl showed Tom into a simple room. A faint suggestion of a fire was smouldering in the grate, and a pot hung hopefully over it – as if there were the slightest chance of any heat reaching up that far.

Tom dropped his bag, and stood there, a pool of water forming at his feet.

The girl leaned against the wall and looked at him with that same expression on her face . . . or rather now she looked half-amused by the sight of Tom and yet irritated by his presence. Tom simply could not work her out. So he just stood there, dripping.

'You'd better take your clothes off,' said the girl. 'You can dry them by the fire.'

Tom looked at the sorry excuse for a fire that lay, gasping its last, in the cold sepulchre of the fireplace. The girl followed his gaze and stared at the ailing fire too. She frowned and the furrows across her brow made her look momentarily old. Yet, as soon as she stopped frowning, the youth returned to her face and she looked almost beautiful, thought Tom.

And so they both stood there looking from the sick fire to each other and back again, as if the absurdity of the suggestion that you could dry anything there – let alone cook something – had wiped their minds blank.

At last, the girl stood up and walked across to the fireplace. She bent down and took a stick from the small pile and placed it very carefully and gently on the embers, as if she were laying a penny on a dead man's eyes.

'Well?' she said. 'Are you going to stand around and catch a fever?'

'No,' mumbled Tom. 'Where shall I hang my clothes?'

'Give them to me,' said the girl.

And so Sir Thomas English took off his wet cloak, in the house of a girl whose name he did not know, and handed it to her. Then he took off his sodden doublet and his wet hose and finally he removed his outer breeches and handed them over to the girl, who scowled in an amused and friendly way.

She hung his clothes from iron hooks around the fireplace and then she prodded the stick with her toe. It almost burst into flame, but then died immediately, as if the effort were too much for a patient who was so far gone.

The girl suddenly looked round at Tom defiantly.

'We have to be careful with our wood!' she said, as if he had just accused her of unforgivable and flagrant niggardliness. 'The duke makes us pay for every stick. His officers come and poke their stinking noses into our woodshed. He would make us pay for the blood in our veins, if he could get at it.'

Tom stood there in his under breeches. 'Perhaps you have a blanket?' he suggested helpfully.

But the girl didn't answer. She turned away and put another stick on the fire . . . then another . . . then another . . . then she turned back to Tom.

'I expect you can burn your fire all day and never think twice about it?' It was an accusation, and she narrowed his eyes as she waited for his defence.

'Why should you think that?' asked Tom.

The girl got up from the fire, and strode across to a chest. She unlocked it and pulled out a worn old blanket, then she came across to Tom and began to drape the blanket across his naked shoulders.

'It's obvious,' she said.

'What's obvious?' asked Tom, as he gratefully wrapped the blanket around himself.

'You,' she said.

Tom pulled a stool up beside the fire – yes! You could actually start calling it a fire now, thought Tom. It had crossed that indefinable threshold where non-combustibility and flammability meet. The non-fire had become a fire . . . like life and death . . . it's such a thin line that separates them, thought Tom.

'Why am I so obvious?' he asked. 'What is so obvious about me?'

'It's obvious you're used to good things,' she replied. 'You should have seen your face when you first saw our fire. You went like this . . .'

And the girl put on an expression of eagerness and expectancy that suddenly turned into total dismay. Tom couldn't help laughing. But the girl scowled before she smiled.

'And then another thing,' she said. 'You took off your hose like this . . .'

And suddenly she was doing a pantomime of a man balancing on one leg and having trouble removing his stockings from his legs . . .

'It's obvious you must usually sit down to take them off . . . and I'll bet your man usually pulls them off for you . . .'

Tom laughed out loud.

Yes, she was probably right. He'd never even thought of it. And yet he had grown up in a house not so very different from this. And the fires that he and his little sister Katie and old Molly Christmas had huddled round, ever since his parents had died of plague, all those years ago, were not so very different from the sorry-looking excuse for a fire that this girl had been keeping alive when he arrived.

In those days – more often than not – he went unshod, he wore coarse cloth and ate the plainest food and little enough of that. And yet now? Perhaps he was not dressed in silk or scarlet at this moment, but he was used to fine clothes and to living surrounded by luxuries, to sweetmeats and dainties, baths and music, and, of course, books.

When did he cease to notice all those things? he wondered. At what point did he get used to them? And did that mean he had lost something?

Tom frowned.

'I like your laugh,' said the girl.

Tom looked up. 'It's the only one I've got,' he replied. 'No . . . I tell a lie . . . when the Lord Bernabò commands it, I laugh like this . . .' and he gave a courtly chortle that rang with as much sincerity as a friar's sermon. 'When my Lady Donnina de' Porri makes a joke, I go . . .' and he gave the sort of low snort that people give when they've heard the kind of story they shouldn't.

'When my Lady Regina della Scala tells a joke, I laugh like this . . .' and Tom scowled . . . rather like the girl was scowling now.

'That's not laughing,' she said.

'My Lady Regina della Scala never makes jokes,' replied Tom.

The girl didn't laugh out loud but she scowled her smile with more of a sparkle in her eye. 'My name is Niccola,' she said. 'I'm usually called Nicca . . .'

Tom gave her a slight bow. 'My name is Tom,' he said.

'Tom,' she repeated, as if disappointed by the brevity of it. 'Would you like some soup, Tom?'

Tom ate the lukewarm soup gratefully in the gathering gloom of the cottage. When he'd finished, he felt his clothes. They were as wet as ever. So was his horse. Tom had poked his head out of the door to find the rain was coming down harder than ever. What was more, night was beginning to fall with it . . . as if the darkness were being washed out of the sky onto the sodden ground.

Tom turned back into the house. The girl had lit a candle and was rearranging the wet clothes closer to the fire.

'I need to stay the night somewhere,' said Tom. 'Do you know of anywhere nearby?'

'You can stay here,' she said. She stood up and looked at him with a frank gaze that held no apology, and at that moment she seemed to embody nothing but kindness and generosity – at least to Tom.

'I will pay for the fire and the food,' said Tom.

The girl shrugged. 'You can have my father's bed upstairs,' she said.

'What about your father?' asked Tom.

'He died,' she replied, 'last Lent.'

'I'm sorry,' said Tom.

'You can put your horse in the barn,' said the girl. 'You can borrow some of my father's clothes.'

Some time later, Tom was sitting by a reasonably lively fire. Since he was now paying for the wood, he had put more on, and he reflected, his clothes now had a fair chance of being dry by the morning. In the meantime, he had been fitted out from the dead man's wardrobe: he sported an old brown tabard that came down to his knees, but which was rather tight on him, and dirty brown hose.

Suddenly, he became aware that the girl had been staring at him for some time. But as he turned to look at her she dropped her eyes.

'How old are you?' Tom asked.

'I am eighteen,' she replied. 'I should have been married last spring.'

'What happened?'

The girl did not reply but she raised her eyes and they made contact with Tom's. In the candlelight her face had become softer and the frown seemed to have been brushed out. She looked like . . . who was it? A memory stirred in Tom's mind . . . but he couldn't pin it down. Her eyes were grey-green and she had shaken her dark hair out from the tight roll in which she'd been wearing it.

Suddenly he realised she was smiling at him. He smiled back. 'You look like my father,' she said.

Now I don't know whether or not any romantic feelings had just then been creeping up upon Sir Thomas English, but – if they had been – they now suddenly turned tail and scuttled out of the door like naughty hens caught raiding the larder.

'What happened to your marriage?' asked Tom. 'Or would you rather I didn't ask?'

The girl's smile dropped for a moment. 'No, I will tell you,' she said, but then fell silent.

'Well?' asked Tom. The girl sighed and stared into the fire.

'Piero – the man who was to be my husband – was tortured and killed by my Lord Bernabò.'

'I'm so sorry,' said Tom. Then he waited until he found himself forced to ask: 'What for?'

'He was *not* a handsome man – Piero,' she said.

'Well, that's not a crime,' smiled Tom.

'He was lame – he had a shrivelled leg – and one of his eyes sort of looked the wrong way.'

'It's all still perfectly legal, as far as I'm aware,' said Tom.

'But he was a good man. I loved him well enough.'

'So?'

'One day, Piero caught a fish,' said Niccola.

'He caught a fish?' It was as if every statement she made was the end of the story, so Tom felt he had to keep prompting her or she would never get to the end.

'Cursed to God the day he did,' said the girl.

'What are you talking about, Niccola? He caught a fish? So?'

49

'It was a big fish. A very big fish. Such a fish had never before been pulled out of the river.'

'And . . .' Tom coaxed her, for she had stopped again.

'It was so extraordinary a fish, that he was afraid to sell it in the market.'

'Why should he be afraid?'

'Because if my Lord Bernabò were to hear that such a fish had been caught, and had not been offered to him, he would be angry.'

'Ah ha . . . so Piero didn't give it to him and the Lord Bernabò put him in prison?'

The girl shook her head.

'No. Piero decided to go to the court of my Lord Bernabò and give the duke the fish himself.'

'A wise move.'

'Was it?'

'Er . . . well . . . why don't you tell me what happened,' said Tom in a kindly way.

'Piero, in his simplicity, went to Bernabò's court, and when they saw the fish they allowed him into the great man's presence. It was indeed a very big fish. Piero went down on his knees and said: "Great duke, please accept this gift from a simple man."

'Well, my Lord Bernabò looked at the size of the fish, and then he looked at Piero, and then he suddenly flew into a rage. "Who allowed this freak into my court?" he screamed. "Look at him. He looks like a fish himself!" Then the great duke turned on my poor Piero and yelled at him: "Do not ever presume to think that I would accept any present from an abomination of nature like you! I'll flay the man who let you into my court!"

'Well, my poor Piero just knelt there and said: "My lord, I am sorry if my looks offend you. Could I change them I would do so – only too willingly."

'And then do you know what the great Duke of Milan said? He said: "In that case, I'll give you a hand! Guards! This misbegotten creature has one leg longer than the other – even him up! And do him another favour by making both his eyes the same!"

'And that is what they did. They cut off his good foot and they put out both his eyes. He died a few days later from loss of blood.'

The girl stopped, and looked Tom straight in the face, dry-eyed and open. There was no emotion in her voice. It was as if all feelings had been strained out of her by the press of cruelty.

'Such a man is the lord you serve, sir,' she said. 'But then you probably know that better than I . . . as well as you know that if you were to report these words of

mine, I should doubtless meet the same end as Piero
. . . or worse.'

It was Tom's turn to drop his eyes.

That night, Tom lay in bed, Niccola's words jangling in
his ears. He knew the Lord Bernabò was cruel and
arbitrary. He knew the Lord of Milan acted without
constraint – mutilating and killing wherever his whim
fell. And yet because you could not smell the dungeons
from the state rooms, because you did not see the killing and the mutilation, it was so easy to forget that it
was all going on all the time . . . so easy to convince
yourself that the marble-tiled floors and the gaily
painted walls and the gorgeous dresses were the whole
reality . . .

And, for all that he felt that the whims and out-
rages of the tyrant were nothing to do with him, Tom
suddenly felt he had been – no! still was – a party to
them. It was true that he had not thrown anyone into
a dungeon on Bernabò Visconti's behalf, but he had
drunk his wine. He had not tortured anyone for
Bernabò Visconti, but he had danced with his mistress.
He had not murdered anyone at Bernabò Visconti's
behest, but he had made the great Lord of Milan laugh.

Tom suddenly felt that anything he did for the
Visconti made him implicit in the evil that had plagued

this girl's life. And that went for the Lady Regina's spying mission on Bernabò's nephew – and yet, if he did not see it through, how was he to rescue his squire, John?

He opened his eyes, and found that he was staring at the blank wall of night. He could see nothing and that pitch-black room might just as well have been his future. Either was equally impenetrable.

Chapter 6

Mende 1361

Tom had no idea how long she had been lying there. He must have fallen asleep, but now he was aware of her breathing gently beside him. Tom lay absolutely still, and listened. Was she asleep? Did he dare wake her up? Or should he turn over and go back to sleep himself?

He tried to make out her silhouette but could see nothing in that absolute dark. Eventually he reached out his hand and touched Ann's shoulder. She didn't stir but the words came immediately – as if she had been waiting for the signal to release them.

'Do you think Anton's dead?' she asked. 'Do you think he drowned? Or was he crushed beneath all those huge trees?'

'He couldn't have survived,' whispered Tom, 'either way.'

They were lying in a barn somewhere near the small

town of Bagnols. It was two days since they had fled across the bridge at Avignon and had watched as the giant Anton, whom they had come to respect and even love, had been flung into the angry river Rhone beneath a cartload of sawn tree trunks.

'It's too terrible,' whispered Ann.

'But what can we do?' asked Tom.

'Maybe we could turn time backwards . . . maybe we could make some magic . . . ah . . . no . . . we saw what we saw . . . there is no magic that can undo what we saw . . .'

'Ann,' whispered Tom. 'This Peter de Bury . . .' He fell silent. The blackness also fell silent. Everything fell silent for some minutes and Tom could think of no way of going on.

'That's a very difficult question to answer,' said Ann eventually. 'For a start there's no verb. Then there's no question mark. In fact it isn't really a question. "This Peter de Bury . . ." Hmm. It isn't even a statement. I wonder if you could elaborate a little bit – just to give me some hint about how to reply?'

'I know I asked you before, but do you love him?' breathed Tom.

'I suppose I do,' replied Ann.

'How do you know?' asked Tom.

The question hung in the air like a falling star that had got stuck.

'I don't know how I know,' replied Ann. 'I could list all the things I like about him, but there are lots of people about whom I could list the things I like. Like you, Tom.'

'But you don't love me, do you?' asked Tom.

'Of course I do,' said Ann.

'But not like you love Peter de Bury.'

'No,' said Ann, and the star went out. 'I don't love you like that, little Tom.'

Tom turned over. Why did it matter? Why was he asking Ann these questions? He was in love with Emily. He was to become her knight in shining armour. Even though Emily was not in love with him, Tom was going to win her hand. And they were going to ride off together and live forever in a grand house with a chimney.

The next morning Emily was extremely cross about something or other. But then she tended to be these days. Ever since she had discovered that Alan was not a boy but a girl in disguise whose name was Ann, she had been in a vile temper. She would kick anything that was remotely kickable, including Tom.

'So have you decided yet?' she demanded, as Tom

laid some breakfast in front of her. It never ceased to amaze him how – no matter how hard he tried – he always ended up feeling like her servant.

'Well, it seems to me that Brittany is on the way to England. So why don't we all go along with Alan . . .'

'Ann,' snapped Emily with a certain bitterness.

'Ann . . . to find Sir Robert Knolles's army and then . . . maybe . . . you and I could . . . possibly . . . get a ship to England from there.' It seemed a perfectly reasonable plan, but Emily frowned.

She wanted to get to England to find her brother, Guillaume de Valois, who had been languishing in an English prison ever since the Battle at Poitiers, waiting for his ransom to be paid. Emily had learned that her uncle, Jean de Craon (who also just happened to be Archbishop of Reims), was plotting to have her brother murdered so that he could control the family fortune. What's more, the archbishop was planning to marry Emily – just to make his control complete. She had escaped the archbishop's clutches at Avignon, thanks to Tom, but now she wanted Tom to accompany her to London to try and help her brother escape.

'What's all this "maybe" and "possibly"?' Emily demanded.

'Well . . . you know . . . I mean you never know . . . things change, and . . .' Tom felt himself running out of words. It was always the same when Emily looked at him in that way she had. He could never quite make out whether it was the perfection of her straight nose . . . the whiteness of her skin . . . the blackness of her hair . . . or those long lashes that framed her grey eyes . . . or maybe it was the smile that played around the corners of her mouth even as she pouted her displeasure at Tom . . . but whatever it was, Tom knew he had no defence. Whatever it was that made him, he would do whatever Emily said.

'We're going to England,' said Emily. 'We decided.'

'Of course we're going to England,' said Tom. 'But it's sensible for us all to keep together as far as Brittany.'

'Ann seems to be able to manage pretty well for herself,' said Emily.

'Yes . . . but . . . look! It's better to all keep together.' Tom couldn't understand why Emily had a problem with that. It was obvious really. Together they were protection for each other and company and . . . and . . . he couldn't bear the thought of leaving Ann to make her way all on her own – even though she was disguised as a boy, and even though she was going to find this Peter de Bury whom, apparently, she loved in some way that she didn't love Tom.

'We've got to stick together, until she can find this

Peter de Bury chap!' exclaimed Tom. And then one of
the weirdest things happened . . . well, it seemed weird
to Tom. It certainly took him totally and utterly by surprise. The commanding and demanding Emily, whose
imperious voice could make the toughest palace guard
touch his forelock and the most truculent gatekeeper
open up his gate, suddenly burst into tears. And they
weren't gentle, ladylike drops that merely wetted her
beautiful cheek and no more . . . these were great
heaving sobs that shook her to the root of her elegant
body.

At first Tom was so taken aback, he couldn't think
what was going on. He thought for an awful moment
that the breakfast he had just given her must have been
poisoned. How was he going to feel if he'd given the
most beautiful creature in the world a poisoned breakfast? He would never have forgiven himself.

When he realised that the paroxysm was, in fact,
grief – albeit unaccountable grief as far as Tom was concerned – he sat beside her and put his arm around her
heaving shoulders. She immediately leaned her head
heavily on his chest, and they sat like that for some
time.

Yet even in this situation, thought Tom, I'm simply
providing a service. You see, no matter how much the

lovely Lady Emily relied on him and needed him, he still felt like her servant.

But so it was the three of them set out to cross the immensity of a France ravaged by war and plague.

Chapter 7

The Road to Pavia 1385

Sir Thomas English awoke with a start. There was the sound of laughter coming from downstairs. For a moment he thought he was back on the floor of a little inn room, with Ann and Emily asleep on the bed. But, as the light broke through the sleep in his eyes, he saw the russet smock of Niccola's father hanging from a peg above his bed – the same bed in which, Tom assumed, her father had died some months before.

Gradually Tom's present situation came back to him: how he was travelling from Milan to Pavia to spy on Gian Galeazzo, nephew of Bernabò Visconti, the ruler of Milan. He had to find out the nephew's intentions towards his uncle, and report those intentions back to Bernabò's wife and mistress to save his squire John from death in a Milanese dungeon.

Suddenly he yearned for the comradeship of those former days – for the company of Ann and Emily, with whom he could discuss what to do. But those days were long gone now. Tom mentally shook himself free of the past and fell with a jolt back into the present.

The laughter from below was not happy laugher. It was the sort of laughter that spelled trouble. And, from the sound of it, whatever that trouble was, it involved more than one intruder.

'If I go down the stairs I'll walk into the thick of it,' thought Tom, 'Better to approach from the outside. I might even get a chance to see what I'm up against.' For he knew, beyond a shadow of doubt, that he was up against something.

Hastily he scrambled into the old man's clothes, and grabbed his sword. There was no window, so he cut out a square of thatch with his sword and pushed it upwards. Mice and birds, whose place of residence the thatch had been for many years, protested and scuttled from their homes as Tom lifted himself up through the roof and dropped quietly down to the ground.

That is to say, the dropping was quiet, but the landing, unfortunately, was not. Glancing down, Tom had thought he would be falling onto a muck heap up against the house.

'Odd place to have a muck heap,' he'd thought, but was then too busy doing the dropping to take the thought any further. It was only as his feet went clear through what turned out to be a roof, and as the chorus of grunting and squealing instantly hit deafening level, that he realised he had, in fact, dropped straight into the pigsty.

The noise that his silent getaway created was almost gratifyingly loud. 'It's loud enough to be heard back in England,' he thought. And he couldn't prevent a stupid question occupying his mind when it should have been thinking about other things: if he could get these pigs to squeal a message home to England for him – to Katie and Old Molly Christmas – what would he have them squeal?

'Help!' was the first word that came to mind, for from round the corner of the house three men had just appeared. They were holding swords and grinning in a rather stupid sort of way as they approached the pigsty.

'Well! Well! Well!' said one of them in a thick accent that Tom found quite difficult to understand. 'What a fine little piglet we've got here, boys! Whassay we roast him nice 'n crisp?' The difficulty of the accent was compounded, Tom suddenly realised, by the fact that the man was slurring his words.

'There's plenty of crackling on him!' said another, swaying just ever so slightly from side to side.

'They're drunk,' thought Tom. 'That'll even things up a bit!'

Tom didn't move. He crouched with his back to the wall and watched the three men closely.

'One of them is going to make a lunge,' he told himself. 'The one on the right I think . . . yes . . . I bet he's the one who's going to go first . . .'

'Well, well,' said the man on the left. 'Three against one . . . now that just ain't fair, is it?'

'No,' said Tom quietly. 'It's three against three.' And he suddenly kicked out with his right leg, so that the door of the pigsty flew open and the great sow, who all this time had been squealing and turning round and round in circles, now leapt away, bowling over the attacker to the right. At the same time, Tom kicked down the left-hand wall of the sty and the old boar charged at the other two men. Meanwhile Tom lunged at the one who been knocked over by the sow, thrusting his sword right through his ribcage and pinning him to the ground.

Then he grabbed the man's sword and swung it across the assailant to the far left, slashing his forehead so the blood streamed down over his eyes, instantly blinding him in a hot stream. The man cursed, and, dropping his sword, clutched his face with both hands.

The man in the centre, who seemed to have consumed the largest share of whatever it was they had been drinking, lunged forward at Tom, but misjudged his thrust. It was a simple matter for Tom to slice clean through the man's sword arm and then through his right leg, so the man pitched forward with a cry of outrage and fell head first into the sty.

Before the man had managed to utter another curse, Tom had stabbed the sword into his back and out again so the air in his lungs rushed out sounding like a gasp from hell, and Tom had turned to the man still trying to wipe the blood from his eyes. A second later, to the man's unutterable surprise, his hand suddenly no longer encountered any head . . . it was rolling on the ground and he himself was toppling soundlessly backwards onto the pigsty floor.

Tom leaned back up against the wall, panting, the blood rushing round his brain and body.

It had taken so little time. One moment there had been three mocking men standing there, full of drink and malice. The next, there were three corpses.

Back in the days about which he had just been dreaming, the young Tom would have hesitated. He would have wondered who these men were. He would have wanted to ask why they were attacking him . . . if indeed that was what they were about to do. But fifteen years of action had taught Sir Thomas English not to ask such questions.

But nothing, thought Tom, took away this terrible-ness . . . this sickness that increasingly came upon him . . . this realisation that he had just taken away that which could not be replaced . . . turned life into non-life . . . fire into non-fire . . .

Tom shut his eyes and breathed deeply. So fast. He had become so fast. The men had been drunk, of course, but he had done it all so fast that even he had not had time to realise what he was doing. He had become a killing machine.

He staggered over to a full water butt that stood beside the house and peered down into the surface. There was his face. The same face he had looked at countless times, and that now looked no different. But, he thought deep inside himself, he knew it was the face of someone different. This couldn't really be him – this man who took the lives of others so quickly and with such authority; who asked no questions, who acted with economy and consummate skill, and – in the heat of the moment – without pity.

When he entered the house, he found the fire had returned to its former pathetic state. Without saying anything, Tom lifted the girl, Niccola, up from the floor and laid her down on her bed. He then fetched a bowl of water from the butt and washed her face and shoulders. Then he threw some more sticks on the fire and warmed up the porridge that was to make their breakfast.

'I was told there were bandits around Lodi,' he said, as he watched her eat. 'At least there are three fewer now.' Maybe the words were an attempt to reassure himself about what he had just done, but they provided as little comfort as yesterday's fire provided warmth.

Niccola looked up at him. 'Why is there so much evil in this world?' she asked. It was as if she expected Tom to come up with the definitive answer then and there . . . as if she expected him to know . . . as if he weren't part of the evil himself . . .

'The churchmen will say we brought it upon ourselves . . . when Adam took the apple from Eve . . .' Tom felt he had to attempt some sort of response, but the girl snorted.

'The churchmen blame everybody but themselves. They live in luxury and ease while they incite men to kill other men. That was never God's intention.'

Tom fell silent. This uneducated girl, who'd lived out here on the edge of a canal alone with her poor father and had been engaged to marry the lame, wall-eyed fisherman from the village, how did she see so much? Was it those grey-green eyes of hers that allowed her to see through the sham of the world so clearly?

And then it was that Tom realised who she reminded him of . . . the smile that never left the corners of her mouth, even when she was frowning . . .

'What are you looking at?' she asked.

'Nothing,' said Tom, looking away. 'I was just remembering someone.'

Chapter 8

Pavia 1385

Tom paused as he caught his first sight of Pavia. It lay straight across the horizon, blotting out any view of the future. It was literally where his road ended. That distant line of wall also marked the limit of his escape from the Visconti web. He would get no further.

The previous day, he and the girl had stripped the dead brigands of their arms and clothing and buried the bodies on the other side of the canal.

He had then ridden with Niccola into the town of Lodi, and there, in the harsh sunlight that had replaced the rain, they had sold the bandits' gear and horses, bargaining with strangers in front of the great cathedral that dominated the Piazza Maggiore.

The men may have been bandits, and their horses and harnesses as like as not all stolen, but such things still fetch a good price. Tom could tell that the girl had never seen so much money in her life. She probably had no idea that so many soldi and golden florins could possibly exist all together in one place at one time.

For a moment he envied her the simplicity of the life she must have led with her father in that house beside the canal.

'You owe me only for the wood and the food,' said Niccola as Tom pressed the money into her hands. But Tom had kept her hands around the money.

'From now on, you can burn your fire as you want,' he said.

Niccola looked at him, with that frank gaze of hers.

'Will you ever come back to me?' she asked simply.

Tom shook his head: 'I don't know . . .'

She stepped towards him and put her hand around his neck and kissed him on the mouth – but as you might kiss a holy relic or a bishop's ring. Then she turned and was lost in the market crowd.

But that was yesterday and might as well have happened in a previous life. Today, Tom was currently staring at the walls of Pavia, trying to work out what it was that he found so disturbing about them, for there was definitely something very odd . . . something wrong . . . something missing perhaps . . . but he couldn't put his finger on what it was.

He had arrived at a corner of the city wall, which was high and a rosy red. It did not seem to be crenellated. Maybe that was what was disturbing him? No . . . there was something else . . .

A feeling of foreboding started to creep up Tom's legs, like wading into a cold pond . . . if his first view of Pavia was so disconcerting, what on earth was it going to be like living there? What's more – living there as a spy? He hardly dared think about it.

The gatekeeper, however, was reassuringly surly. He examined Tom's papers as if they held a clue to the secrets of the universe. 'I hope he lets me in on whatever the secret is,' thought Tom to himself.

The gatekeeper scowled . . . 'Uh oh!' thought Tom, 'Regina della Scala's scribes must've slipped up!' Tom started to look around for the nearest escape route, but then realised that the man was scowling because he could find nothing wrong with the papers.

He tried to make up for it by looking Tom over, from head to foot, with such distaste that if Tom could have borrowed another body, he undoubtedly would have. 'Maybe it's just the clothes,' thought Tom. 'I knew I should have worn the bright pink.'

And then suddenly the man was grunting with some incalculable pain – his frame was wracked with agony that forced the groans and gasps from his throat . . . or could it possibly be that he was speaking?

'I'm sorry?' said Tom. 'I didn't catch what you said?'

'You should've gone to the other gate,' growled the gatekeeper's voice – as if it were coming from his entrails.

'Oh,' said Tom. But before he could wonder what the man meant, he was nodded through, and he found himself riding into the realm of Gian Galeazzo . . . the famous city of Pavia . . .

Except that there wasn't any city there.

Suddenly Tom realised what it was that had been so odd about the view of the city walls; what had been missing was the sight of church spires, a dome, perhaps, and tall towers, and now the reason became clear. There were no spires or domes or towers because there were no churches or, indeed, buildings of any sort whatsoever – except for that shepherd's hut over there beside the wood.

Otherwise the city of Pavia appeared to consist of nothing but gently rolling fields, dotted with groves and copses. There were plenty of trees and bushes and flowers but no people . . . oh, except for an old man ploughing a field over towards the wood.

'For a great city this place could do with a bit more town,' Tom muttered, as his horse made its way under a line of elm trees that bordered the main path. And then he heard the first blast of the horn and the thunder of hooves and the baying of hounds.

The old man threw his plough down, and ran away as fast as his wobbly legs could carry him. The oxen stood in their traces, and looked round at him as if to say: 'Hey! What about us?'

The next moment, a wild boar burst out of a thicket and charged across the field, with hounds baying and snapping about its ears, blood pouring from its already torn flesh. As it reached the field its hooves sank into the newly ploughed earth, and the hounds took their chance. Some leapt at the boar's throat, while others buried their teeth in its flanks, and the rest yelped and bayed – one or two turning round and around trying to bite their own tails in the frenzy.

The next moment the hunt itself appeared, and the field was churned up by the hooves of the horses and the feet of the men, who ran brandishing their pikes and yelling and blowing horns, every bit as excited as the dogs.

But there was one figure there who did not seem to be excited at all.

And quite a remarkable figure he was. He was dressed in a gown of blue and silver, and wore a silver collar round his neck. But the most remarkable thing about him was that he wasn't carrying a sword or a spear, or anything that he could have used for hunting. What he was carrying was the most beautiful lady sitting behind him, on the crupper.

By now, the huntsmen were calling off the dogs, while two horsemen prodded the boar with their swords, as if to see how much life it had left in it. The answer was not much, so they slid their swords into the creature like two King Arthurs returning their Excaliburs into the rock.

The boar was gutted and the offal thrown to the dogs. The carcass was then hoisted onto a pole and the whole hunt began to move away from the blood-splashed furrows, down across a sward of grass towards a shining lake.

As soon as they had gone, the ploughman emerged from his hiding place in the wood and stared at the careful furrows – now heedlessly churned up and broken down. But he didn't shrug his shoulders in despair or sigh, or lean heavily against a tree. He didn't even raise his eyes to heaven. He simply stood there for a moment and then walked back to the plough, and took up where he'd left off.

'As mundane as that!' thought Tom. Like death on the battlefield.

He wheeled his horse round and followed the hunt.

The Captain of the Guard, accompanying the hunt, was as reassuringly surly as the gatekeeper. 'They're busy,' he said. 'They won't want to be interrupted.'

'I am the Lord Gian Galeazzo's guest,' said Tom. Apparently that is what his papers said he was, although how he was going to carry it off Tom had no idea. 'I mean, the moment I show these papers to Gian Galeazzo himself, he's bound to say: "Well, who invited you? I never did!"'

And now here he was. These were his papers. And there was nothing he could do about it . . . not if he were to have any chance of rescuing his squire, John.

The papers, however, seemed to work with the Captain of the Guard.

'All right,' he said. 'Pass on.' And Tom made his way towards the courtiers who were now stretched out in their flower-embroidered robes on the flower-embroidered lakeshore.

The food had stilled the baying of the hounds. The horses had been led away by the grooms, and a buzz of civilised conversation and genteel laughter had descended over the lords and ladies of the hunt.

A table had been set up and covered with a chequered cloth, and a whole forest of servants now appeared as if from nowhere, scurrying about to bring chairs and stools to the board, and pouring wine into

75

silver goblets. The fire was already red and ready, and the cooks were sharpening their knives. It was all happening with the speed and precision of a well-rehearsed routine.

Gian Galeazzo was sitting at the table next to his lady companion, whose face was framed in a headdress that consisted of nothing but a thousand frills. Tom kept his eye on the Master of Pavia, waiting for his opportunity. Eventually he accosted the great man's steward and presented his credentials. 'I am a guest of the Lord Gian Galeazzo,' he said with as much conviction as he could muster. 'May I speak to your master?'

The steward glanced through the papers and then nodded. 'Wait here,' he said.

Tom watched as Gian Galeazzo listened to his steward and then stared straight at Tom without apology. That was the prerogative of these great rulers, thought Tom. They do not need to bow the knee or avert the eye – it was almost their duty to show that the normal rules of politeness simply did not apply to them.

Tom, for his part, bowed and waited to see what would happen. Gian Galeazzo was frowning now . . . now he was shaking his head . . . 'I never invited any "Sir Thomas Englishman" to anything!' That's what he'd be saying. No! He was ordering more food . . .

now he was speaking to his frilly companion . . . oh! Oh! Now he was looking over towards Tom . . . this was it . . . was he about to call the guards? 'Arrest the imposter!'

No! He was smiling! And now he was beckoning to Tom.

'Sir Thomas Englishman!' called out the great Lord of Pavia. 'Come! You are welcome. Sit and eat with us.'

Tom bowed gratefully. 'Thank you, my lord. Pavia is indeed blessed with a wise and benevolent lord.'

'So she is,' agreed the wise and benevolent lord. 'She is lucky, for he is very wise and very benevolent indeed.'

The arrogance left Tom almost speechless, but he managed to stutter: 'I am very much indebted to you,' said Tom.

'For what?' asked the great man. Alarm bells started to ring in Tom's head.

'For having me here as your guest,' he vaguely gestured towards the papers, which the steward still held in his hands.

'But . . .' said the wise and benevolent ruler of Pavia, and the alarm bells became deafening . . . '*I* didn't invite you here,' he said.

So the encounter was exactly as Tom had predicted it would be. Gian Galeazzo would now beckon a guard and Tom would be dragged away through the smirking faces of the court, to be strung up by his heels in the deepest dungeon and subjected to all the unspeakable things that they did down there in the dark, and that could scarcely be imagined in the light, airy rooms of the court above.

'I didn't invite you,' Gian Galeazzo was repeating, with a hint of menace in his voice.

'Forgive me, my lord.' Tom had practised this answer many times in his head. 'But I was given to understand that I had been invited here by you personally . . . of course I shall leave at once if that is not the case . . .'

'My name is Pesquino Capelli,' said Gian Galeazzo.

For a brief moment, Tom thought: 'Typical Visconti! They're so devious they can't even admit who they are . . .'

'You won't catch my Lord Gian Galeazzo out hunting!' continued Pesquino Capelli. 'He is more careful of his person.'

'Then he should take more care of his knees,' smiled the be-frilled companion. 'He is in danger of wearing them out!'

This caused a good deal of laughter round the table, and, although the point of the joke was not clear to Tom, the moment did give him the chance to pick his wits up off the floor where they'd fallen.

'My lord, please forgive the ignorance of a stranger,' he murmured.

'Why should you recognise someone you have never seen before?' asked Pesquino Capelli. 'However, since you have apologised we shall exact a penance – it shall be to sit here beside the Lady Bianca and myself and drink our health together.'

And that is what Sir Thomas English did. He joined in the laughter and the feasting, but he never forgot that he was in the court of a Visconti lord, and that nothing was probably what it seemed it was. Moreover he kept reminding himself that he had made a classic error on his very first encounter in the court of Gian Galeazzo. If he were to survive the coming weeks, he would have to keep his wits sharp and his eyes open and never let down his guard.

Chapter 9

Pavia 1385

The hunters were in an expansive mood as they made their way through the park back to the castle.

'My Lord Gian Galeazzo seldom goes out of the castle these days,' said the young man riding on Tom's right. He was sporting an elaborate red headdress with a gold motif embroidered on the front, and had been drinking generously from the silver goblets.

'Is he unwell?' asked Tom.

'No . . . he is just cautious . . .' said the young man, dropping his voice. He too, it seemed, would prefer to be cautious, but unfortunately the wine had imbued him with an irresistible urge to err on the side of incaution.

'Cautious of what?' persisted Tom.

The young man glanced around and dropped his voice so low that Tom thought the horses would trip over it.

'He does not trust his uncle, Bernabò,' whispered the youth, and then shook himself as if rid of a great secret. He started to whistle a tune that was popular just then.

However, the news that Gian Galeazzo did not trust his uncle was scarcely news, Tom reflected. He had known all about that before he had set out for Pavia. Indeed it was the common talk of Milan how young Gian Galeazzo lived in daily fear that his uncle would poison him, or have him arrested or secretly murdered at any moment. And there were few that did not think that was a perfectly plausible scenario, even if they said the opposite.

Certainly no one doubted that Bernabò had eyes on Gian Galeazzo's half of the Visconti dominions. It would be a pleasant thing to be able to add that half to his own when the time came to divide the state between his five sons.

Ricardo, which was the young man's name, seemed to be so hell-bent on imparting forbidden information to Tom that he kept leaning across and almost toppling from his horse as he did so. At this moment he caught Tom's sleeve – more as a means of preventing himself hitting the ground than of attracting Tom's attention.

'It's embarrassing,' confided Ricardo. Tom was just about to ask him what was embarrassing, when they passed once more through some city gates, and once

Terry Jones

again, instead of houses and shops, Tom found himself surrounded by yet more bucolic countryside.

'You see?' exclaimed Ricardo.

'Not really,' replied Tom.

'Walls!' said Ricardo, rather more loudly than he intended. He lowered his voice. 'He's put walls around the entire hunting ground . . .' and at this point his voice became a hissing whisper 'It's all because *he*'s afraid!'

'Gian Galeazzo?' asked Tom.

'Sh!' whispered Ricardo fiercely and extremely loudly. 'I'm not saying who I'm talking about . . . but look around you . . . Is someone who's afraid to hunt in the open country a man fit to rule a city like Pavia?'

'But where *is* the city?' asked Tom.

'We'll be there soon,' said Ricardo, and even as he spoke, Tom could see yet another wall looming up ahead of them, and this time he could also see spires and towers, peering up and waving at him from over the wall.

The castle of Gian Galeazzo formed part of the walls of the city of Pavia. The whole was surrounded by a good-sized moat, and the hunters were only allowed to pass over the drawbridge after a thorough inspection of their papers.

'I mean, can you believe it?' Ricardo was seething. 'We can't even go hunting without our papers, we can't go anywhere . . . he's spying on us all the time!'

Tom winced at the mention of spying, but he managed to inquire innocently: 'He employs a lot of spies, does he?'

Ricardo had suddenly produced a flagon of wine from the folds of his rich vestments, and now took a long swig from it, before handing it to Tom.

'Thick as cockroaches . . .' he whispered. 'You can't move without treading on them!' The far-from-humorous laugh which followed this observation was accompanied by an irritated gesture that Tom took to mean that he should hurry up and drink so he could pass the flagon back. Tom put it to his lips and took a long slug – at least he pretended to, for in truth he didn't want to be fogged by wine; his first few hours as a spy might prove to be the most dangerous he would ever have to live through. He handed the precious object back to its anxious owner.

Where the Porta Nuova di Milano opens onto the narrow streets of the city, there was, in those days, a small apothecary's shop – almost a lean-to, built against another building of brick. A man dressed in particoloured hose, who might have been a servant or a squire, was gazing into a small phial that the apothecary was holding, while the apothecary was explaining something in great detail. As the hunt approached, the two of them glanced up quickly and moved inside as if at a pre-arranged signal . . .

It was such a well-rehearsed movement that Tom couldn't help speculating about what the two were doing. Perhaps some great lord wished to rid himself of an unloved spouse? Or perhaps his mistress hoped to remove a rival in love? Or, and this may have been the most likely scenario, the scion of a powerful house wished to eliminate a rival to his inheritance?

On the other hand, of course, it could just have been indigestion powder that was being handed over, but somehow in the scheming cities under the Visconti yoke, poison seemed as likely a purchase as camomile and rhubarb.

As the boisterous party of hunters moved down the street, the equally boisterous town dogs began barking at the hunters' hounds, and the hounds whined and looked up at their masters as if pleading to be let loose on those low-class mongrels.

At this moment the hunt rounded a corner and for the first time Tom saw the castle of Gian Galeazzo. The sound of his jaw hitting the road would have startled the finches from the trees if there had been any.

The *castello* was red, which was pretty extraordinary.

It was bright red, which was also pretty extraordinary. And it was immense, which was not necessarily so extraordinary, but for one factor: it didn't look like any other immense building that Tom had ever seen.

Immense buildings generally fell into one of two categories: castle or cathedral, but the *castello* of Pavia fell into neither. Houses were houses – some bigger than others, but once a building passed a certain size it was either dedicated to worship or dedicated to war. Soaring spires and elaborately decorated windows or crenellations and arrow slits, drawbridges and massive walls. You could not mistake a cathedral for a castle or vice versa, and most certainly you could not mistake either for a house.

But the *castello* of the Visconti was built on a scale so immense that it most certainly could not be a house. And yet nor had it been built for either war or worship . . . unless you were talking about worship of the Visconti dynasty. No! The building was clearly built as a *residence*, and that was what was so extraordinary about it.

It was three storeys high, with row after row of windows – but not the sort of windows you get in churches, with coloured glass and bright patterns. Nor were they the sort of windows you got in most houses, which tended to be square openings in the brickwork,

85

with a couple of wooden shutters to close them off. These windows had glass in them – but glass that you could see through! And there were so many windows: it was a building that wanted to view the world without feeling it; a safe place from which the observer could watch the storms and tempests outside those protective walls, without a single hair being blown out of place.

As if to reinforce the notion of security, each corner of the house was guarded by a tower, and around the whole edifice ran a moat, across which a single drawbridge gave the only access to the town.

It was the sort of building that must have intimidated other buildings, for not a single other construction had dared to intrude on the grand vista offered by the façade of the *castello*. The shops and houses of the town hung back in awe of the power and wealth of the man who lived in such a house, and whose hair would never be blown out of place because of the glass in the windows.

As Tom gazed over the vast structure, something in one of the windows caught his eye. It was a figure . . . a woman, standing at the window watching the returning hunt, and who stepped back into the shadows as soon as she saw Tom look up at her.

But there was no more time to think. The column of

hunters were peeling off now for the stables; some were dismounting at the main doors to the *castello*, and Tom had to begin his new life as a spy . . .

He sighed. It had all been so much simpler when he and Ann and Emily had made their way across France in the wake of the English army, back in the old days. And yet it hadn't seemed that simple at the time . . .

Chapter 10

Marvejols 1361

Emily had been behaving in a very peculiar way ever since they'd left Avignon. And today, as they made their way out of the town of Mende, she had grabbed hold of Tom's arm as they were crossing the narrow packhorse bridge across the river Lot – and she still had hold of it by the time the half-built cathedral of Mende had disappeared behind them in the morning haze.

In one way, Tom was only too happy to have the beautiful Emily holding tightly onto him just as a lady should hang onto her knight. On the other hand she kept leaning on him and that threw his balance out. And when you take into account the fact that he was already carrying her huge bundle of clothes, you can see the problem he was having in walking straight.

'It's an odd thing,' thought Tom, 'how when you

wear clothes they don't seem to weigh anything, but as soon as you try to carry them – they're lead weights!'

Ann, on the other hand, was now fully into her role of Alan the Jaunty Squire, and she was striding off ahead without a backward glance.

For some miles they followed the river, but by the time they came to turn their steps up into the hills, Tom decided that he had been chivalrous enough for one day.

'I'm sorry,' he said, finally shaking Emily off, 'I just can't walk like that – with you leaning on me.'

'All right!' said Emily. 'Go ahead and join your friend. I'm sure you'll be much happier with her.'

Unable to think of a suitably chivalrous retort that would at the same time express his feelings, Tom didn't reply, and the pair toiled on in silence, watching Ann's figure as it diminished in the jumping haze of the day's rising heat. Eventually she disappeared altogether, and once again, Tom felt Emily clinging onto him.

'We ought to catch Ann up,' said Tom. 'The whole point was to stay together.'

'Go ahead, if you're so worried about her,' said Emily.

'No . . . let's just you and I go a bit faster, and we'll go faster if you don't keep leaning on me.'

'I can't go another step,' said Emily suddenly, and she sat down in the middle of the path.

'Oh look, come on!' said Tom. 'We can't afford to fall further behind.'

'You go on ahead. Leave me here, if you want to,' said Emily. 'I've got to rest.'

'But . . . but . . .' What would the true knight in shining armour do in a situation like this? Tom wondered. But, as far as he could recall, the manuals of chivalry omitted to mention what the would-be knight errant should do if the object of his adoration sat down in the middle of the road and pretended to be a pig-headed, selfish brat.

Not, of course, that Tom considered the beautiful Lady Emilia de Valois to be any of those things, you understand, but there was something about her behaviour that did not seem consistent with what he had heard in the popular romances.

He would have to work out his own code of chivalry. So, after a moment of consideration, Tom threw the Lady Emily's clothes down, strode over to her, grabbed her by the shoulders and yanked her to her feet.

'Now look here!' he said. 'I'm doing my best to help you. I don't want to go to England. I don't want to carry your clothes. But I'm doing it as a favour to you. So if you don't try and do your bit to help, I'm just going to throw your clothes down into the ravine there and you can jolly well go and look after yourself.'

He knew this was not really how a knight in shining armour should address the lady whom he loves and serves, but then, he wasn't one – not yet anyway.

Emily jerked herself upright, and her eyes went round as two bowls of cream with a plum in the middle of each. 'You wouldn't throw my clothes down there!' she exclaimed.

'I would!' said Tom – now forgetting any thoughts of gallantry.

'You thief!' shouted his companion, and – quite out of the blue – the gracious Lady Emilia de Valois punched Tom squarely on the nose. Again it was scarcely text-book behaviour for a true heroine of romance.

'Ow!' said Tom in a most un-knight-like voice.

'You villain!' screamed the beautiful and usually ladylike Emily. 'You wretched turncoat!'

'Look! I haven't done anything!' squealed Tom, still holding his nose. 'I just said I *would* if you didn't buck your ideas up!'

'But how could you even say such a thing!' demanded Emily.

'It was a threat!'

'Villain!' And she punched him again on the nose,

and because he wasn't expecting it, she caught him another beauty and he squealed again.

'Stop it!' shouted Tom, and he caught hold of her arms. She struggled and wriggled but he held her firm. 'Just follow me!' he said. 'And stop leaning on me!'

And he picked up the bundle of clothes once more, and strode off after Ann without another backward glance at Emily. 'If she wants her clothes,' he said to himself, 'she can jolly well keep up with them.'

Ann was now so far ahead that Tom could not see her. And when he came to a fork in the path, he stood there for some moments in a state of ditheration (which was a word he'd just made up). At the same time he was thinking: 'This is it! We're going to lose each other! I know it!'

It was then that he noticed a few twigs lying beside one of the paths. They weren't particularly interesting twigs *per se*, Tom said to himself, but then there isn't a lot that a twig can do to make itself interesting *per se*. Except these twigs looked as if they just might have been arranged on the path by an absent-minded jackdaw with no particular artistic talent . . . and, if that is indeed what had happened, the artistically handicapped jackdaw might well have intended the arrangement of twigs to form an arrow.

Of course! Tom reflected, Ann wouldn't have left

him without any indication of which path she'd taken. Tom took courage and boldly turned on to the right-hand path as Emily caught him up.

'Oh look,' she said brightly. 'There's a pile of twigs in the form of an arrow!'

'I know,' said Tom.

'Oh,' said Emily. 'I just thought . . .'

'Come on!' said Tom.

The path took them into a deep valley and at the same time turned itself into a stream – nothing much to write home about – but enough to slake their thirst and cool them off. They struggled along the stream for some way, towards a high flat-topped hill.

'Are you sure this is the way?' asked Emily at last.

'You saw the arrow,' said Tom.

'Yes,' said Emily.

'So?'

There was a silence.

'Let's keep going,' said Tom making an effort to get back into chivalric spirit. 'It's getting to be dusk and if we can get up to the top of that hill we should see Marvejols any minute.'

'Right,' said Emily.

They trudged on with the sun now long lost behind the surrounding hills. A chill of future darkness brushed against them and made them walk closer together. Eventually Tom took Emily's hand in his, and Emily didn't object. The tide of darkness was rising continually up the sides of the valley. Soon they would be drowning in it.

The sky had clouded over some time ago and their way would be lit by neither moon nor stars. And now, in the failing light, the flat-topped hill, from which Tom hoped to see the next town, was beginning to look more like a mountain: a bare and pitiless mountain.

Neither Tom nor Emily spoke. But their silence did not indicate a convergence of thought, as such silences so often do, especially in books. As it happens, Tom was wondering why he felt so annoyed with Ann for running off ahead like that. Of course she'd left him with the object of his affections . . . the lady whose hand he would one day win jousting against the other knights of Anjou and Burgundy, Brittany and Germany . . . and yet he'd felt irritated.

Emily, for her part, was thinking . . . but then who knows what the daughter of the brother of the king of France might be thinking?

By now the tide of night was up to their chests . . . and they were wading through the rising flood of darkness, hoping against hope to see the realm of candlelight. But there was nothing. The gates and walls of

Marvejols were still out of eye's reach . . . over the hills and far away . . . and with every passing second they were being sucked further into the gullet of blackness.

Tom and Emily found themselves walking closer to each other. And Tom could hear Emily's breathing in his ear. And suddenly all the problems between them vanished. He was there to protect her. And protect her he would – until the last breath in his body . . .

Suddenly her breathing stopped. Tom's reverie stopped at the same moment. 'Look!' whispered Emily. 'A light!'

They had been climbing for some time now, and the moment Tom looked up to see what Emily had seen, the absurd rush of hope that he would see Marvejols stretched out below them, fell with a splash into the sea of night behind them.

They were still a long way from that strange flat top, but there was a slight glow over to their left. So they turned towards it – away from the cheerful sound of the stream that had become their reassuringly garrulous companion, gabbling into their ears for the last hour or so. They stumbled and fell over rocks and into the holes of unnamed animals, staggering towards that faint glimmer of hope, that seemed so fragile in the immense darkness, and then suddenly went out!

Tom knew that tears had sprung into Emily's eyes,

but she didn't say anything. She simply gripped his hand a little harder.

'I can't see anything!' said Emily.

'It can't have been far away,' whispered Tom. Though why he was whispering he had no idea . . . perhaps he didn't want to wake the night.

'Maybe we didn't really see a light?' suggested Emily helpfully.

'You mean, maybe the light we both saw a few moments ago wasn't really there at all?' asked Tom.

'Yes!' breathed Emily, a note of drama creeping into her voice.

'Oh!' said Tom, mustering perhaps slightly more sarcasm that a true chivalric knight ought to when addressing the lady whom he loved and served. 'You mean it might have been a will-o'-the-wisp or a jack-o'-lantern . . .' and even as the words left his lips and were swallowed up by the smug, all-knowing darkness, he realised that that might very well have been the case.

It was Emily who found it first. 'Ow!' she cried.

'Ow!' agreed Tom. They both picked themselves up from where they'd fallen backwards. 'I think we're there,' said Tom.

He reached out and could feel the wooden sides of a hut. There was a shingle roof at head height and as he followed the line of the wall he discovered a doorpost.

At the same moment that the wall hit them, the realisation also hit them that whoever had extinguished that light was most probably still here in the hut . . . and yet there was no sound . . . no greeting . . . no 'Who's there?' Just silence . . . not even the sound of someone looking at them – which is of course the slightest of all sounds.

'Well? Is anyone there?' demanded Emily in a loud voice.

'Sh!' said Tom, even though they'd already made enough noise to wake a hibernating bear.

'We need shelter for the night!' said Emily again in her most authoritative voice. 'Will you let us in?'

Silence.

After fumbling around for some moments, Tom found the door latch. 'I'm opening the door,' he said, and he lifted the latch.

'We're coming in,' said Emily, and she suddenly kicked the door and the latch flew out of Tom's hand. If it was pitch black outside the hut, it was even blacker inside, and neither Tom nor Emily felt like taking the first step into the unknown.

'We're lost,' went on Emily, 'and we need shelter for the night. May we come in?'

Something stirred in the black. Tom and Emily instinctively took a step backwards.

'We're sorry to intrude,' said Tom.

They waited and listened . . . something was definitely moving inside the hut. They could hear scrabbling sounds . . .

'Hello?' said Tom.

The reply was a series of short sharp blows, like stones banging together . . . and then suddenly there it was again . . . a flare . . . and then a glimmer and then the soft glow of candlelight reflected on the rough planks of a shack . . . but the candle itself and whoever was holding it were still hidden behind the door.

'Come in,' said an old voice that cracked like a rusty hinge that hadn't been used for a long time.

The interior of the hut was almost bare. There was a pile of rags up against one corner, however, and it seemed to be speaking to them. It was certainly holding a stub of candle in a broken pottery holder.

In amongst the rags, Tom could make out the features of an old woman. The lines on her face made it look as if her skin had been thrown onto her in bits and pieces – just like the pile of rags around her.

'You are lucky,' she said.

'Yes, we thought we might have to stay the night in the open.'

'Few people survive,' creaked the old woman's voice.

'I wouldn't have thought it got that cold at this time of year?' said Tom.

'No, not the cold,' said the woman. 'The Beast.'

Chapter 11

Pavia 1385

For some reason, Tom found those words, spoken so long ago, rattling around in his head as he crossed the courtyard of the *castello* of Gian Galeazzo the morning after he arrived. 'It wasn't the cold that would get you . . . it was the Beast . . .' Could the Beast be a serpent with a wolf's head? he wondered.

He had spent the night in Ricardo's room, but he had not slept very well owing to the rather lively sleeping habits of his new friend. Ricardo had ended the day having got the better of so many bottles of wine that he'd lost count. He must have decided to check how many, because he suddenly regurgitated them all onto the floor of the chamber . . . it was certainly a lot.

Tom, who happened to be trying to sleep on the floor where all this took place, had to leap out of the way to avoid being part of the accounting process. Ricardo, meanwhile, collapsed back onto his bed, where he disappeared under an impenetrable blanket of heavy-duty snoring interspersed with a sort of low moaning. The moaning may have kept Tom awake, but it also became a valuable indicator of future accounting activity: the moans would gradually get louder and louder until they invariably climaxed in another generous deposit on the floor.

All in all Tom had had better sleeping companions.

But now he was thankfully up and out of the chamber and heading for his first meeting with the illustrious Lord of Pavia.

That morning, the great man's captain general, Jacopo Dal Verme, had appeared, wrinkling his nose up at the stinking room, and informed Tom that his lord would receive him in the small chapel that lay on the south side of the palace courtyard, which in those days formed a complete square with a tower at each corner. Jacopo had then accompanied Tom across the courtyard, which was surrounded by an elegant colonnade where gentlemen and ladies could stroll, shaded from the midday sun, but halfway across the captain general had remembered some important business, and had hurried off after pointing out the way to Tom.

Tom stood there, gazing at the chapel. It struck him as a curious place to hold a meeting, but nevertheless here he was, standing outside the door, with its ornate terracotta surround. Above the lintel, an amazingly lifelike painting of Christ beckoned the viewer to step out of the violent world of wars and men and into the peaceful world of God within.

Tom accepted the silent invitation, and stepped into that serene interior, where he was immediately grabbed by four heavily armed soldiers and propelled backwards towards the door.

Tom was about to explain that he was reluctant to leave the peaceful world of God so quickly when a voice – which could well have been the voice of God, even though it was no more than a murmur really – eased itself across the chapel and rapped the military types on the shoulders: 'Let him approach,' said the voice.

The guards froze, as if they'd been caught drinking the blood of babies, and fell back to allow Tom through. He could see a figure in grey, kneeling in front of the altar, but the face was turned away and the eyes closed once again in prayer. It seemed so unlikely that this could have been the owner of the voice that Tom found himself looking round for someone else. But the chapel was otherwise empty.

Tom approached the kneeling man, and as he reached him, the figure in grey – without so much as a glance at Tom – indicated for him to kneel as well.

The next hour was the longest in Tom's life. In fact maybe it wasn't an hour. Maybe it was six hours. It couldn't have been six days, because the sun didn't rise and set during the course of it, but it might just as well have been. In fact it actually *felt* more like six weeks.

Tom studied the floor in tremendous detail for about a week. Then he studied the altar, with its embroidered blue and gold cloth, for another week.

There was also a painting, in three folding sections, standing on the altar. The central section depicted a religious theme that was, currently, extremely popular with the devout: it showed a mild-looking man with a tonsure having his entrails pulled out. The poor fellow had a gash in his abdomen through which his greater intestine was hooked onto a windlass operated by two dubious-looking characters, while four elegantly dressed courtiers were shown watching the operation with the expressions of true connoisseurs.

Tom realised that the picture represented the martyr-dom of St Erasmus – patron saint of children who suffer from colic. What Tom didn't know, however, was that the account of St Erasmus's martyrdom, upon which the painting was based, was the result of a mis-understanding.

St Erasmus was originally celebrated for preaching during a thunderstorm and for refusing to stop even when a lightning bolt struck nearby. His bravery in the face of the elements also made him the natural choice as the patron saint of sailors. That crucial piece of naval gear – the windlass – was therefore chosen as his emblem.

The idea that the windlass represented some form of torture came of someone not reading their history book properly, but once the mistake had been made, it became embedded in the legend of St Erasmus. Part of his gut was shown coming out of his abdomen, to re-assure children with stomach problems, and then attached to a windlass and wound out from his body, to give heart to those at sea.

Tom knew nothing about this, but even so he couldn't help thinking that the painting was a curious thing to be an object of veneration. And he couldn't help wondering why the figure in grey should be spending what seemed like a month kneeling in front of it.

At last, however, the figure in grey murmured: 'Amen' – as if he'd been engaged in one long, unbroken prayer – and rose to his feet. Tom, who had almost forgotten how to stand up straight, struggled into a more or less vertical position and found himself staring into the grey-green eyes of a man of his own age.

'Welcome to Pavia,' said Gian Galeazzo in that soft

yet strangely compelling voice. 'Sir Thomas English, I have heard you are a man of learning.'

'Scarcely that,' replied Tom. 'I have a facility with language. More than that I cannot claim.'

Gian Galeazzo nodded, but his eyes never left Tom. Those eyes seemed to be searching into Tom's soul . . . 'He knows why I'm here,' thought Tom in a panic. 'He can tell that I have been sent as a spy as clearly as if it were written in large letters on my forehead,' and he could not stop himself wiping his hand across his forehead as if to remove the offending inscription. 'Any moment now he'll call those guards over,' Tom's thoughts continued, 'and I'll end up like St Erasmus, with part of my stomach . . .'

But the gentle voice of authority cut his thoughts short.

'I want to show you something,' said Gian Galeazzo. And Tom found himself being swept out of the chapel, with the soldiers snapping to attention and bowing to him as he went.

Gian Galeazzo appeared to be a man of few words. He certainly had few words to say to Tom as they strode across the courtyard towards one of the corner towers. In fact he didn't have any words to say at all. The soldiers, Tom noted, were keeping close behind them, as they entered one of the towers overlooking the deer park.

Gian Galeazzo still had not added another word to the six he'd already said by the time they'd climbed up to the first floor. Here, however, he broke his silence by telling the guards to stand outside the room which they were now entering.

It was a long time since Tom had been in a real place of books. His mind flashed back to the great library of Laon, with its thousands and thousands of volumes, and the terrible fire that had consumed it. That had happened so long ago, when he was just starting out on his adventures. At the time it had seemed the most dreadful calamity that had ever happened in the history of the world, but since then Tom had witnessed so much destruction and devastation that the event had begun to diminish somewhat in his mind.

Now, however, confronted by this smaller but equally beautiful collection of books, the shock of that distant disaster suddenly jolted him.

'You are surprised to see so many books?' asked Gian Galeazzo.

'Yes . . . that is . . .' murmured Tom. 'I was just remembering something.'

Gian Galeazzo's heavy-lidded eyes rested on Tom and

remained there as if testing the truth of this statement, until Tom felt bound to explain.

'I was once in a library . . .' he began, 'when some-one set fire to it . . .' and suddenly he found he couldn't go on. The memory, now he came to confront it, was still too raw.

Gian Galeazzo curled his lip slightly, but that was the only clue as to what he was thinking, and Tom had no idea what it meant.

'These . . . these are beautiful books,' Tom finally managed to say, as he gazed around the shelves that rose from floor to ceiling all the way round the room. Most of the books were chained to the wall, and there was a reading shelf running all the way round, with benches and stools.

'See!' exclaimed Gian Galeazzo, seizing a book off its shelf and opening it in front of Tom. The page was solid with colour: it showed a bright blue sky and green, green grass and figures robed in white. A man crowned with laurels was sitting against a tree, pen in hand and a book upon his knee. Another man was pulling back a curtain and pointing the writer out to a man-at-arms.

Below, a peasant was chopping down a thorn bush while another sat milking sheep.

'Have you ever seen such painting?' asked Gian Galeazzo eagerly. 'The people are alive, aren't they?'

Tom was speechless.

'This book belonged to our great poet Francesco Petrarca. He ordered many of the books in this library. He helped my father organise it.'

'He was a man of genius,' said Tom. He had read some of Petrarch's poetry, and actually found it a bit pompous, but the Latin was very fine, and surely it took a man of genius to write pompous poetry in fine Latin.

'Perhaps you will help me expand this library, Sir Thomas Englishman?' said Gian Galeazzo.

'There's nothing I'd rather do in this whole world! How did you know?' Tom was about to say, but something inside told him not to reveal everything he felt to this great lord, no matter how benign he might seem. So instead Tom bowed rather formally and merely said: 'It would be a tremendous honour.'

'Then stay here and look around, if you so wish,' said Gian Galeazzo. 'The Lord be with you.' And the ruler of Pavia swept out of the library without more ado.

Tom sat down on the nearest bench. He could hardly believe his luck.

And yet twenty years ago, if you'd asked him to help build a library, he would have told you he was too busy . . . he had other things in mind . . . he was off to see the world . . . to explore the far-flung corners of the earth . . . he was going to become a knight in shining armour . . .

And some of those things he had done, and some he had not. But in almost every single case, his assessment of those things had changed. And so it was in this case. As a child he had turned his back on the world of books. When the Abbot of Selby had wanted to train him to be a clerk, a priest, to be able to read and to write, he had run away from home. But that was then and this was now . . .

Tom looked around at all those books sitting on their shelves. They seemed to be jostling against each other with excitement. 'Look! There's someone who can read us! Someone to choose one of us . . . me! Me! Oh please let it be me! I haven't been read for so long!'

It made him almost dizzy to think of them . . . each one a distant voice from the past . . . and now the great Lord of Pavia had actually asked him to add to their number . . . to swell the choir of knowledge. It was beyond his wildest dreams.

Except . . . how could he? Of course he would love to serve the Lord Gian Galeazzo, to be his librarian, to travel the courts and towns of Europe buying books for him – to catalogue them – to arrange them on their shelves in their correct order – perhaps even to read them aloud to the nobles and ladies . . . but it was impossible. Tom had to rescue Squire John, and once he had done that, neither of them would be safe anywhere in the dominions of the Visconti.

No. Gian Galeazzo's suggestion was a mirage. Tom had been offered the phoenix's egg, the golden fleece, something which no matter how much he desired it he could never possess.

And a gloom would have settled over his spirit, had it not been for all those voices calling to him from the shelves, and also another voice that was calling to him from the past – from years ago – that he could not quite identify . . . until suddenly he could hear it quite clearly . . .

Chapter 12

Marvejols 1361

'A wolf the size of a cow,' croaked the old woman. 'That's what those who have seen it say. Though there are few enough that have looked at it and lived.'

Tom and Emily were sitting with their backs against the hut, while the old woman blew a few bits of charcoal into life under a pot. The prospect of a little food had cheered them slightly less than the old woman's story had alarmed them.

'And what does this Beast do?' asked Emily, although she was pretty sure of the answer.

'It leaps out of the dark night on lonely travellers, and tears them limb from limb. It steals babies from their cribs and devours young and old alike,' said the old woman. It was exactly what Emily had been expecting.

Tom thought back to the black impenetrable night

they had just walked through, and felt his throat constricting.

'But whereabouts does it live, exactly?' he asked.

'No one knows,' said the old woman, ladling some thin soup into the one bowl that she possessed. 'But they say that its lair is somewhere in the great forest of Gévaudan, some miles north of here.'

'Surely it hasn't attacked anyone round here though?' asked Tom nervously. He was thinking of Ann.

'No one knows where the Beast will strike next,' replied the old woman. 'It has killed over at Saint-Amans, and they say it has been seen as far south as Millau. Farmers and farmer's wives, shepherds in their cots and merchants stepping out of town, young men on their way to the wars and milkmaids carrying the cheese to market . . . the Beast will strike at anyone at any time and anywhere. I expect one night to hear it sniffing outside this very hut and then all I shall be able to do is pray that Mary in her mercy keeps me safe from its claws and teeth.'

Tom looked down into the bowl of soup he was holding and saw the reflection of his face was white even in the flickering candlelight. But it wasn't his face he was seeing – it was Ann's. Where was she? Had she got to the town? Or had she ended up like them, lost on the mountainside?

All that night Tom could not sleep, even though he was as tired as a miller's donkey. The moment he started to fall asleep he saw Ann staggering back as the great slavering Beast of Gévaudan leapt towards her . . .

By the time the sun had lit up the first thistles on the highest rocky outcrops of the Truc du Midi, Tom had become so inured to the idea of Ann's death under the claws of the terrible Beast that he quite expected to find her half-devoured body lying outside the old woman's hut. Instead he found a glorious morning, with the sun cuffing the terrors of the dark out of the light to creep back into the holes and hollows of the earth.

The Truc du Midi no longer seemed so daunting. Even its name seemed comical, now Tom came to think of it. Roughly translated it means 'The Thing in the Midi' (which is an area of France).

'You must return back along the path you came, for there is no way through to the town from here,' the old woman told them.

But Tom insisted they must carry on . . . for they had to find Ann before they could turn around.

'But why are you so sure she came up this way?' asked Emily.

'Because she left an arrow!' Tom felt slightly exasperated. 'You remember? You saw it too!'

'Yes, but it was pointing up the other path,' said Emily.

In the silence that followed, Tom watched the mist that still clung to the lower slopes drift across the mountain and brush over the forest firs. The mist seemed as opaque and hard to grasp hold of as the mind of his companion.

'What do you mean, "It was pointing up the other path"?' asked Tom.

Emily looked rather hurt. 'Well, I kept trying to ask you why you decided to go this way when the arrow was pointing the other way, but you wouldn't listen,' she said. 'I thought you knew something I didn't.'

'But the arrow was pointing *this* way,' replied Tom. 'Otherwise I wouldn't have chosen to come this way!'

'It was pointing the other way,' said Emily.

'Look! Why would I have taken this path if the arrow was pointing up the other one?'

'Well, that's what I wanted to ask you . . .'

'Look! We have to find Ann!'

'But if she left the arrow, she went up the other path, and there's no point in looking around here.'

'But she didn't!' exclaimed Tom. Once again, Tom

couldn't recall any instances of a chivalric knight arguing with the lady whom he loved and served, but here he was doing it.

The old woman, who had been following this exchange with some amusement, shook her head.

'Listen, you two,' she rasped. 'Go back to the fork in the road – it will only take you half an hour in daylight. There you will see what you will see, and then you can decide what to do.'

It was two against one, so Tom hoisted Emily's clothes onto his back, thanked the old woman for her goodness, and the two of them set off down the mountainside and into the morning mists which seemed to vanish as they entered them.

When they reached the fork in the paths, there was no mistaking the arrow. It was a large clear arrow, formed out of twigs, which pointed the way as clear as daylight. But it wasn't on the ground, it was arranged boldly and confidently on a large boulder.

Tom realised that he had been so busy looking at the ground that he simply hadn't raised his eyes up high enough to see the real arrow on the boulder. And when he looked at the random pile of twigs that he had somehow made into an arrow he had simply shut his eyes. How is it possible that one's mind can do things like that?

'Why did you want to go the way we did?' asked Emily, quite reasonably.

'Er . . . well . . . never mind . . .' said Tom. 'Let's find Ann. At least she'll have reached town and won't have been eaten by the Beast.'

The town of Marvejols, then the capital of the whole of the Lozère region, was entered by three imposing gates, each set between two tall towers. Tom and Emily entered through the Porte du Soubeyran and found themselves immediately swallowed up in the busy streets. They had been on top of the world, and they both now lowered their heads as if the buildings that here loomed over them were crushing their spirits.

But it wasn't the buildings that crushed their spirits . . . it was the fact that as they tramped through the narrow streets and round and round the narrow marketplace and through the even narrower back-streets they found not a single trace of Ann. They asked at the inns and they asked people in the streets, but nobody had seen a clean-shaven young man in a short blue jerkin with brown hose carrying a bag on his shoulder.

'They say the Beast was on the prowl again last night,' a butcher reassured them. 'I pity anyone who didn't make it into town before nightfall.' He shook his head and shuddered as he sliced through a piece of steak. 'The Beast has claws that can rip through the hide of an ox,' he added for good measure, as he separated the two bloody halves of steak and cleaned his knife.

But the old woman selling eggs by the fountain shook her head. 'I never heard the Beast was in these parts last night. Oh, sure enough, it's out there somewhere . . . but no . . . not last night . . . not here, my dears . . . I never heard nothing . . .'

'Thanks,' said Tom.

'What's that you say?' asked the old egg woman.

'She's deaf as a post,' said Emily in a loud voice.

'Sh!' said Tom.

'That's right,' said the old woman. 'The big ones are duck eggs.'

'I heard it last night, howling sure enough!' said the blacksmith. 'It was out beyond the walls, sure enough. I lay there shivering in my bed, sure enough.' And sure enough, he didn't look like the kind of man who would be frightened easily.

'We saw its prints as we drove our animals here this morning,' said a shepherd. 'They were as far apart as the length of my crook . . . the creature must be huge . . . God save us!'

By the end of the morning, Emily and Tom found

themselves sitting in the marketplace, staring blankly at each other, until finally Emily burst out:

'The Beast ate her!'

'Don't jump to conclusions.' replied Tom sensibly. 'Just because she didn't reach town last night, doesn't mean she got eaten by . . .' But no matter how sensible he tried to be, Tom couldn't shake off the same thought, and all the sensible words died in his throat.

'*You* think the Beast ate her too! You do, don't you, Tom?' said Emily. For once all her innate superiority seemed to have deserted her. She sounded almost lost . . . which was something unthinkable for the Lady Emilia de Valois.

'No!' said Tom. 'I don't think anything at all about what happened to Ann. And I won't have any opinion until we find out for sure.'

'But how can we do that?' asked Emily.

'We're going to look for her,' said Tom.

Chapter 13

Marvejols 1361

When you know that you've got to walk across the whole of France, and then cross to England, and then walk to London, it takes a surprising degree of determination to retrace your steps, but then Tom was surprisingly determined, and so that is what Tom and Emily did.

Emily naturally insisted on a proper meal before they set off, and so Tom found himself sitting with her at a table in the grandest inn in town, confronted by some mutton chops and a flask of wine. At any other moment, Tom would have been more than happy to sit with the beautiful Emily eating a splendid meal, but right now he could hardly bear it. His mind was racing ahead to discover Ann, digging into fox holes, trampling down the undergrowth, searching every nook and cranny for any trace of his best friend.

Every minute lost in getting on with the search

might be the difference between life and death for Ann, he kept telling himself. And yet nothing he could say or do would shake Emily from her determination to eat. She had dressed herself for the day's business but still managed to look elegant and cool, as she allowed Tom to pour her a little wine.

'You cannot function properly,' Emily told him, 'unless you have had a proper meal at the proper time in the proper place. Nobody can. That's why the poor are so hopeless at things: they don't eat properly – or regularly enough! How can you think straight if your tummy's rumbling? Or concentrate on anything if your mind's running ahead to the next supper? One should always eat when one has the opportunity and time.'

'But we haven't the time!' pleaded Tom. 'Ann may be in trouble . . . she may be needing us . . .'

'And she may not,' said Emily . . . the implication of which was just too awful to contemplate.

So in the end, Tom suffered himself to sit at the table and play with his chop, while Emily managed to scoff a quite remarkable quantity of meat and bread – goodness knows how she fitted it all into her slender frame.

The moment she'd done, however, Tom leapt up and grabbed her bundle of clothes. 'Come on then! Let's go and find Ann!' he said, and was halfway out of the inn before the innkeeper stopped him.

'Sir!' he said. 'Take care out there today, for they say the Beast has been seen in these parts not many hours ago.'

'Don't worry,' said Tom. 'We'll be back by nightfall.'

'The Beast don't respect neither night nor day,' said the innkeeper. 'You'd best wait for a party of travellers before you go on your way.'

Tom lowered his voice, for he didn't want Emily to catch this conversation. 'We can't wait. We're looking for someone . . . someone who should have been here last night.'

The innkeeper shook his head and gazed at Tom as if he were looking at him for the last time. 'The Beast is full of evil – head to toe. It has taken folk in God's daylight. I urge you, young sir, think twice before you set out with this young lady.'

'What was the old innkeeper bending your ear about?' asked Emily, as they strolled towards the city gates of Marvejols.

'Oh, he was telling me some joke or other . . .' said Tom, considerably more breezily than he felt.

'I didn't hear you laugh,' said Emily.

'I'd heard it before,' replied Tom.

'Oh,' said Emily.

Although it may not have sounded like it, that

exchange was the first true piece of gallantry that Tom had performed for the lady whom he loved and served since they'd set out on their walk across France.

They walked on in silence for a few paces, and then Tom stopped.

'Emily,' he said, 'I don't really believe in all this "Beast" stuff . . . but . . .'

'I believe in it,' said Emily.

'Well, I don't . . . but at the same time it's best that we're careful, and I don't think you should come looking for Ann. I'll do it.'

The look in Emily's eyes was all Tom needed for a reply.

'All right!' he tried to anticipate her. 'I know it sounds like I'm playing the hero, but . . .'

'Do you realise who you're talking to?!' exclaimed the Lady Emilia de Valois. 'Perhaps we haven't been travelling around the countryside together for the last few months?'

'No, of course I . . .'

'Or have you perhaps grown an extra pair of hands last night? So you can deal with whatever's out there all on your own?'

'I didn't mean . . .'

'Think you've suddenly grown up, do you? Well you haven't! You're still a little shrimp of a boy!' Emily knew where to punch and how to make her punches land – even on a knight in shining armour. Tom had experienced her punches already, but these hurt more.

'We are both going looking for Ann,' said Emily, and although she didn't stamp her foot, she certainly wiggled her hip.

'All right. But we'll have to be really careful – we haven't any weapons.'

'I assume you are joking?' said the Lady Emilia de Valois in her most scornful voice.

'I'm sorry?' said Tom.

'You don't think I was intending to go out there and hunt for a fearsome beast without weapons, do you?' Emily replied.

To tell the truth it hadn't occurred to Tom that Emily might have been thinking about anything other than digesting her lunch.

'The armourer has a place by the main gate,' said Emily. 'I noticed it on the way in, and I assumed that that was where we were going.'

'Oh,' said Tom, feeling like a little shrimp of a boy.

In his imagination, Tom had always received his first sword from the hands of the king – it didn't really matter which one so long as he was a king. He'd always seen himself, in his mind's eye, kneeling before His

Majesty, King Whoever-It-Was, and receiving the weapon while the other courtiers and knights stood around him smiling their approval. He never in his wildest dreams thought he would be bought his first sword by a beautiful damsel or have it bestowed on him in a dingy armourer's shop on the edge of a French town that he'd never heard of.

Also, in his imagination his first sword was going to be shining and new – the latest and best weapon of its day. But the only sword that the armourer could offer was a decidedly old-fashioned affair. The armourer told them that the blade was of fabled Damascus steel, but even Tom could see it was pattern welded. A modern sword would be fashioned from a single bar of high-quality steel that meant its surface could be polished like a mirror. Pattern welding, on the other hand, produced a dull surface of densely packed whorls, where the alternate strips of hard and soft iron had been endlessly hammered together until they fused.

The blade was also straight, for cutting and slashing, rather than the more fashionable pointed blade for thrusting that everyone seemed to favour these days.

The hilt was also a little disappointing: a wooden grip with plain iron quillons and an undecorated pommel.

Still, it fitted him, being a *corta spada,* or short sword, and Tom felt a surge of confidence as the armourer pushed it into the scabbard that now hung from his belt.

Emily for her part furnished herself with a *berdona* – an elegant, slender-bladed dagger that seemed as if it had been made for her.

But as soon as the two friends stepped out through the town gate of Marvejols, Tom found that the feeling of invulnerability that his new sword had given him started to evaporate into the heat of the afternoon.

As they looked about the granite hills that sur-rounded them, they both realised that Ann could be anywhere . . . and so could the Beast . . .

Chapter 14

Le Truc du Midi 1361

The mountains to the south of Marvejols, that in yesterday's sunlight had seemed remarkable for their beauty, now appeared equally remarkable – but for entirely different reasons. The sweeping hills and flat tops were still there to admire, but all Tom could see now were the thousands of nooks and crannies where a Beast might happily lie, ready to pounce on any unsuspecting person who came looking for their friend . . . a friend whom the Beast had most probably consumed the day before. Every rock was a hiding place, and every fold in the ground had become a monster's lair from which Tom expected at any moment to see the great creature rear up.

At which point Emily screamed: 'Look!' and Tom froze. A horned creature was indeed rising up from the tall grass ahead of them – a creature whose devilish eyes seemed to glare straight at them but who almost at once turned away and started chewing the grass again.

'*That*,' agreed Tom, 'is the most terrifying goat I have ever seen!'

Emily's fingers still held on to Tom's sleeve.

'But what if it wasn't a goat?' whispered Emily.

Tom tried to think of an answer but couldn't. There was a logical conundrum involved, but he couldn't quite put his finger on it.

'We've got to keep our eyes peeled,' said Emily.

'Right,' agreed Tom. 'So let's keep our eyes peeled for things that aren't goats . . .'

'Ahhhhhh!!!' cried Emily, pointing again at the horizon.

'Or sheep,' added Tom.

'Can you use a sword?' asked Emily. It was not the sort of question the Lady Whom He Loved and Served usually asked her knight errant, but then the whole conversation was not really typical of the romances.

'Well . . . er . . . I've practised, and . . .' Tom began, but the words tripped over his teeth and fell onto the stony ground where, as it happened, Tom's eyes were already focused. There lay something that he'd hoped he wouldn't see, and yet it was what he was looking for.

'It's hers,' breathed Emily.

'Are you sure?'

'Look at it . . . it's from her tunic – blue – see?'

Emily picked up the cloth-covered button and held it out for Tom's inspection. There was no doubt in his mind. And if only a little round button could speak or point, instead of lying there mute and still in the palm of Emily's hand, it could have told them which way Ann had taken . . . or – more likely perhaps – which way had she *been* taken . . .

'I think it took her off in that direction,' whispered Emily, pointing towards the hill.

'What did?' asked Tom.

'The Beast!' said Emily.

'We don't know for certain it was the Beast – or even that she was carried off!' exclaimed Tom.

'Well it's pretty obvious, isn't it?' muttered Emily. 'I mean she didn't get to town, she's lost a button and she's disappeared.'

'But . . . her button could have just come loose . . .' said Tom hopelessly. 'Maybe she was hot and undid her tunic or . . .'

He was aware that Emily was looking at him sceptically. 'Anyway, what makes you think she went in that direction?'

Emily shrugged. 'I don't know. Female intuition maybe?'

Tom felt another surge of irrational irritation. 'But it could have been any direction!'

'That's true,' said Emily.

'So it hardly helps having "female intuition"!' said Tom.

'Well, which direction do you suggest we go then, Solomon?'

'Er . . . well . . .' Tom looked around for quite a considerable while.

'No male intuition?' asked Emily.

And in truth Tom didn't have any opinion about which way they should go. Eventually he shrugged. 'I suppose that direction's as good as any,' he mumbled rather ungraciously, and they set off in the direction that Emily's intuition took them.

They climbed an escarpment and found themselves on the flat-topped hill they had tried to climb the previous evening. Even though it was now broad daylight, the place had taken on an even more sinister aspect. To their left a forest crept nervously up the side of the mountain. The thistles and high grass petered out before they reached the top. It seemed as if all living things were shunning that spot on God's earth for some reason that could only be guessed at.

Suddenly Emily clutched Tom's arm again and pointed. This time she did not cry out.

'Emily,' said Tom. 'Are you going to grab my arm every time you see a sheep?'

'It's not a sheep, Tom,' whispered Emily.

'Of course it's a sh . . .'

The word died on Tom's lips.

'Look! It's miles away!' whispered Emily. Indeed, Tom *was* looking, and he could see that what he had thought was a small creature a few hundred yards away was in fact much further away and therefore much larger. That was the point.

Whatever it was, it was moving fast from rock to rock, with a sort of swooping, loping motion quite unlike any animal Tom had ever seen.

'The Beast . . .' breathed Emily.

Without a word, she and Tom flung themselves behind a boulder, and then peered round to see where it was heading. At least the creature was not coming in their direction, but that was hardly any comfort, seeing how fast it seemed to be travelling. A moment later, it disappeared behind a rocky outcrop. Emily and Tom took to their heels and ran as fast as those heels could carry them towards the only shelter they could see: the forest.

There they lay with their hearts beating like masons' hammers. Finally Tom poked his head above the undergrowth and looked through the trees towards the slopes where they had seen the creature. But he could see nothing.

'It probably wasn't the Beast,' whispered Tom – more for his own comfort than for Emily's. 'Maybe it was a farmer's dog.'

'But you saw the size of it!'

'Perhaps it was closer than we thought. You can never be sure about these things.'

'Tom,' said Emily, looking him straight in the eyes, 'whatever that thing was, it made the hair on the back of my neck stick up on end.'

Tom didn't argue the toss. The hair on his neck had done the same thing.

'Shall we just leg it back to town?' Tom whispered. 'Or keep out of sight?'

'Let's run for it,' breathed Emily. 'The Beast would smell us out if we hid. Town's the only place we'll be safe.'

But Tom didn't reply. He was looking at a tree branch that overhung the path through the wood. Something was hanging from it. And suddenly all thoughts of the Beast evacuated his mind, as he strode across to it. He knew what it was, even before he was able to recognise it, and when he pulled it off the tree he saw that it was stained with something dark. If this was indeed Ann's hood, he knew that the dark stain must be Ann's blood.

'The Beast must have dragged her to its lair,' said Emily, pointing to where the bracken had been broken down. 'She must have put up a terrific struggle.'

'You can see the trail,' whispered Tom, and he was off, following the line of broken bracken that led into the heart of the forest.

Deeper and deeper they went, and as the forest grew darker and grimmer, so the doubts began to crowd in on Tom's mind. What use could he and Emily be? If the Beast really had taken Ann, all they could do was to view her mangled remains, and he wasn't sure he was strong enough for that.

'She may be still alive,' said Emily. It was almost as if she was listening to the same doubts.

They'd seen the Beast in the distance. Sooner or later it would return to its lair, and – if that was where they were heading – what then?

The trail led them into a clearing. There they scrambled across some rocky ground to find themselves confronted by a cave. If Tom had tried to imagine what a Beast's lair would be like, this would have been it.

Emily swallowed. Tom swallowed. They stood still and listened. The forest swallowed . . . or it felt like that. Then they could hear nothing save a soft rustling of the trees, as if the leaves were murmuring amongst themselves about the foolishness of these two young people, who voluntarily approached so close to the abode of the Beast of Gévaudan.

But if either Emily or Tom had felt at that moment like turning tail and running back the way they'd come, the sight of a shoe lying in the entrance to the Beast's lair wiped all such thoughts from their minds.

They peered into the darkness of the cave, but it was impenetrable. They listened but could hear nothing coming from within . . . Tom looked at Emily. Emily looked at Tom and shrugged. It was a small gesture but Tom knew what it meant. It meant: 'Well . . . we've come this far. Maybe we're going to get eaten by the Beast. Maybe we're not. But we've got to finish what we came for. We've got to find her . . . or what's left of her.'

Suddenly Tom found himself shouting in a whisper: 'Ann!' – as if he were afraid to disturb the Beast or whatever else dwelled in that darkness. But Emily had no such compunctions.

'ANN!' she screamed at the top of her voice.

Tom glanced around, as if expecting the Beast to leap out at them there and then, tearing at their throats and ripping with its claws. But nothing happened. Emily's cry echoed from within the cave . . . but it was just an echo. The Beast did not respond, but then neither did

Terry Jones

Ann. All was silent again, save for the rustling of the forest trees: 'Tss! Tss! What a foolish pair!'

Tom felt the knight in shining armour within him rear his head above the parapet.

'I'm going to run in there and take a quick look around,' he said. 'If anything happens to me, promise you'll run straight back to town. Don't try and help me.' Tom had been holding his unsheathed sword for some time now, but he suddenly became aware of it for the first time.

'I'm coming with you,' said Emily.

Tom opened his mouth. But whatever it was he was going to say never came out, and the knight in shining armour ducked back behind the parapet.

'I didn't think you wouldn't,' said Tom.

Emily shrugged: 'There's no point in being cautious. Let's just do it as fast as we can.'

And with that Emily plunged into the dark interior . . .

Tom put down Emily's clothes, and for a few moments rummaged around in the bundle before finally producing a tinderbox and a tiny stub of candle that he had managed to keep. Then he heaved a sigh and followed.

Chapter 15

Le Truc du Midi 1361

The air in the cave was fetid as Tom followed Emily into the gloomy interior, and there were bones on the stony floor.

'Ohhhh!' said Emily and Tom at the same time. Their knees went slightly weak – also at the same time. It seemed like the natural reaction.

'That must be where it sleeps,' whispered Emily. She was pointing to a hollow depression in the ground that was strewn with rags and sacking.

Tom found himself kicking some bones apart and wondering if they were Ann's.

'This is pointless,' he muttered. 'She's not here. Or if she is – there's not much of her left by now . . .'

Gradually their eyes were getting used to the gloom. It was then that Tom saw it on the floor. His heart missed a beat, and he put his hand onto a rock to steady himself. Then he bent down and picked it up.

'Emily!' he whispered.

Emily turned to see Tom holding out Ann's other shoe.

'She's here!' whispered Tom. 'She's in the cave. Somewhere . . .'

'Maybe we should look through there,' said Emily without enthusiasm. Tom could make out a hole no more than two feet high in the back wall of the cave, and he could see why Emily didn't relish the idea of going through it. But that was exactly what Emily was doing.

'Wait!' said Tom, and he pulled out his tinderbox and began the business of making fire.

'We haven't time for that!' whispered Emily. 'The Beast may come back at any moment!'

'There's no point in going any further into the cave if we can't see,' Tom pointed out quite reasonably, as he positioned a small piece of charred rope close to the steel.

'Well, hurry up!' said Emily. Tom was already striking bright sparks off the steel with his flint. He used short, sharp strokes and the sparks began to jump across onto the char.

'Hurry!' hissed Emily.

Tom actually reckoned himself as a pretty proficient fire-maker. Sometimes, of course, it took longer than others, and this looked like it was going to be one of those longer times – or perhaps it was simply the fear that made every second they delayed in the Beast's cave seem like an hour.

For minute after minute, Tom kept striking the flint on the steel and the sparks flew across without catching the char . . . but eventually one did, and then another, and the next minute Tom was blowing the end into a red ember.

'Right! Now light the candle!' cried Emily.

'It won't light from that,' said Tom. 'Haven't you ever you done this?'

'Of course not! My maid does that sort of thing!'

'Well, then stop telling me what to do.'

'Just hurry!'

Tom kept blowing the red ember until he was satisfied with it, and then he applied it to the dried leaves in his tinderbox.

'Oh come on! The Beast's coming! I know it is!' moaned Emily. 'Do you really have to do all that?'

The tinder finally burst into flame, and Tom was able to light the candle stub. He then smothered the flaming tinder.

The whole process must have taken five minutes or so, and all that time Emily had been hopping about from one foot to the other. Now they both bent down

Terry Jones

to inspect the hole. By the light of the candle they could see a tunnel running several yards through the rock and then beyond that there was just blackness again.

'Well, let's go!' said Tom. Once in the narrow tunnel, a strong current of air threatened to extinguish his candle, and Tom had to crawl forwards on his elbows, holding the light in front of him with one hand, the other cupped around the fragile flame to prevent the wind extinguishing it. It was an awkward, slow process, and he hadn't gone many yards before he felt a hand grabbing his ankle.

'What is it?' he yelled. But there was no reply. Just another tug at his foot. 'Emily? Are you all right?' But still there was no reply.

Tom reached the end of the tunnel, and found himself in a larger chamber than the first. He was still trying to make out the dimensions of the new cave by the feeble light of the candle when Emily emerged. She was speechless and white as a sheet.

'What is it?' he asked.

'Sh!' said Emily, and she beckoned Tom back to the opening of the tunnel. 'Listen!' she managed to whisper.

And Tom knelt, and heard the wind whining through the narrow passageway. Then he heard a crash! Then another. Then what sounded like claws on rock. And then – very faintly – the heavy breathing of a large creature – a large creature returning to its lair . . .

'The Beast!' whispered Emily.

Tom instinctively shaded the light of his candle.

'What do we do?' hissed Emily.

But before Tom could think of a halfway reasonable reply, something else made both of them spin around so fast the candle almost went out altogether.

'Ann?' whispered Tom, and the next second he was running towards a pile of rubble, from the other side of which he could hear muffled groans.

'It's coming!' cried Emily, who was now peering down the tunnel. 'The Beast! It's coming through!'

'It's us! Ann! It's us!' cried Tom as he tripped over an inconsiderately positioned rock. The candle flew out of his hand and was extinguished as he fell heavily onto the ground.

In the silence that followed, the only thing they could hear was the shuffling and grunting of the Beast as it forced its way towards them through the narrow passage. Emily screamed. Tom screamed in sympathy and began scrabbling around in the pitch black, trying to find the tiny stub of candle.

Emily kept screaming. Maybe she was trying to drown out the sound of the approaching creature as it reached the end of the tunnel. The shuffling and the grunting had stopped. The creature must have emerged from the hole, and must now have been standing waiting for its eyes to get used to the dark. Any moment now, they knew, it would leap through the blackness and be upon them.

At this moment, however, by sheer luck Tom found his hand upon the candle stub. The next second he was striking sparks onto his char – desperately hoping to make the quickest fire in the history of fire-making. Fortunately the tinder was still warm, and it exploded into flame, lighting up the cave.

In the same instant, he saw Ann lying in a corner bound and gagged. Emily screamed again and this time her scream was accompanied by a strange guttural growl. Tom span round to see the Beast leap upon Emily . . . except that it wasn't the Beast. It was a man.

Chapter 16

Pavia 1385

'I know you have been sent as a spy, Sir Thomas Englishman.'

The words, though spoken quietly and calmly, sent a shudder through Tom's frame. His head swam slightly and even though his blood had more or less frozen in his veins, he broke out in a sweat.

Tom was sitting in the library of Gian Galeazzo, in the corner tower of the *castello* of Pavia that overlooked the park. He had decided to try and catalogue the books, but was fast coming to the conclusion that the task was a bit beyond him.

The library contained books by Frenchmen, by Germans, by Bohemians, by Englishmen, by Castilians, by Aragonese and Flemish writers, by Poles, by Hungarians and, of course, by Italians. Yet they were all as readable as each other because they were all written in the same language. And Sir Thomas English, with his facility for languages, had been able to read Latin ever since the priest in his home village back in England had taught him the language of the Church.

So here he was in the great Lord of Pavia's library, making a note of as many of the books as he could. He had thought of listing them in different categories: poetry, geography, philosophy, devotion, Bibles and so on. He'd never heard of such an arrangement, but it suddenly seemed a good way of helping you find your way around a large number of books such as this.

The only trouble was that the books of those days were not so easily categorised. A single volume would often cover many different subjects, and each book was more often like a collection of different books, rather than being devoted to a single subject.

Nor was it possible to categorise the books under their authors, since writers tended not to put their names to their works. In the past they never did, and it was only in the case of a great man, like Thomas Aquinas, that one would be in the slightest aware of who the author was. But that was changing, for the modern writers, like Dante Alighieri, Francesco Petrarca and Giovanni Boccaccio, were for the first time signing their names to their own works. These writers had become notable men, celebrated figures . . . heroes, in fact.

But the majority of the books were old and anonymous, so Tom decided the best thing he could do was simply make a list of them, giving the volumes names if they didn't already have them, and then, at a later date, he could decide what sort of order to put them into.

He must have been working away for most of the morning and a large part of the afternoon . . . certainly he had no idea of what hour the day had reached. The sun, which had been slanting in at the window behind him when he started, would soon be struggling in with its evening rays through the window opposite.

His tummy had just started rumbling, and his mind had wandered back to the distant past, as it always did when his tummy rumbled. He always thought of Emily – the Lady Emilia de Valois – and how she lectured him once when he was young on the importance of eating proper meals at the proper time. And the thought of Emily had led on to the memory of Ann . . . and the thought of past adventures.

It was at this point that the door of the library opened and an imposing figure in a crimson gown edged with fur entered the library. She walked in without a word of apology, and for some moments, strode around the shelves not so much like someone choosing

143

a book as like a general reviewing his troops. Her head was held erect and her aquiline nose went before her like a royal herald.

At length she finished her inspection of the assembled ranks of books. They all seemed present and correct. So she dismissed them, and turned her gaze upon the only other occupant of the room: the handsome, ginger-haired Englishman sitting at the table in the east window.

Tom stood and bowed to her. He had already recognised her as the figure he had seen in the window of the palace when he had arrived with the hunting party two days before. Since then he had learned that she was no less a person than Caterina Visconti, daughter of Bernabò Visconti, Lord of Milan and Gian Galeazzo's uncle. For four years now, Caterina had been the wife of Gian Galeazzo.

Caterina was a handsome woman. Her father, Bernabò, was a handsome man. And Caterina did not look unlike her father, so it was only to be expected that she would be a handsome woman.

Bernabò, it has to be admitted, was a man's man: a heavyset ox of a fellow who would have no more been seen in maidenly pursuits than he would have pulling a brewer's dray (which he could easily have done) in his underwear.

And in some ways Caterina took after her father. Certainly you would never catch her in her underwear.

Now she was staring right through Tom, waiting for his reply.

'A spy?' was all Tom could think of saying for the moment. He was aware that it wasn't the most convincing way of allaying her suspicions, but then could he really be certain of what he'd actually heard her say? Maybe Caterina had said, 'I know you have sent me a pie,' or 'I know a way to play I Spy,' thought Tom desperately. But Caterina Visconti, daughter of Bernabò, wife of Gian Galeazzo, was not someone who made light conversation of that sort.

'Why else would my father have sent you?' she said.

'I can assure you, my lady, your father does not even know I am here,' said Tom, hoping against hope that he could say the truth while at the same time avoiding incriminating himself.

Caterina narrowed her eyes and was silent for some time. She turned and plucked a book at random from the shelf. Then she seated herself on the bench and opened the volume, again seemingly at random. Without looking at Tom, she read out: 'Choose a prudent man to write down your secrets . . .' and then her finger ran down the page and across, and she read again: 'You must understand that a messenger shows the wisdom of he who sent him.'

She looked up and into Tom's eyes, and at that moment Tom realised that Caterina Visconti seldom did anything random.

'You know these books well,' said Tom, bowing his head in acknowledgement.

'The *Secreta Secretorum*,' replied Caterina, holding up the book. '*The Secret of Secrets* – they say it contains the advice of Aristotle to princes – the secrets of how to rule.'

'I have heard of it,' said Tom. 'You are well read.'

'I have been a wife for four years now. Until I present my lord with an heir, I have precious little else to do with my time. I spend the waking hours alone in here with these books for company.'

'If I am in your way . . .' Thomas made as if to leave, but a wave from the large and undoubtedly majestic hand of Caterina stopped him.

'You cannot escape so easily, Sir Thomas Englishman,' she said. 'You are a spy. I know you are.'

Tom could not look her in the eye.

'I am here on the business of the king of England,' he mumbled. Somehow the cover story that seemed so plausible when he was inventing it now lay exposed on the polished boards between himself and the Lady Caterina like a stillborn infant.

Caterina laughed . . . or rather she snorted and flung her sleeve over the bench on which she was sitting.

'If it was not my father that sent you, then it must have been that witch, the Lady Donnina. Or perhaps my mother.'

'My Lady Caterina,' said Tom, picking his words carefully. 'I am no spy.'

'That's perfectly obvious,' retorted the Lady Caterina. 'Anyone can see you are not used to that sort of work. But . . .' and here Lady Caterina stared at him with a look that was more like a stranglehold than something done with the eyes, 'someone has sent you as a spy.'

Tom said nothing, for he could think of nothing to say.

Caterina stood up and replaced the *Secreta Secretorum* on its shelf. She then reached for another book and thrust it towards Tom as far as its chain would permit.

'Will you swear on this that you are not a spy?' asked the Lady Caterina.

Tom looked from the Bible up to the black pupils of Caterina's eyes – pupils that seemed so dilated that one might imagine they could suck in every image that they gazed upon and swallow them up for good. At length he whispered: 'What do you want of me, Lady Caterina?'

Caterina put the Bible down and made a face towards Tom that was – he was almost certain – meant to be a smile. But it seemed the Lady Caterina did not have much practice in smiling, for it was a smile such as a corpse might make – or a ghost that had long given up hope of happiness.

'It's all right, Sir Thomas Englishman. I shall not give you away to my husband. Your little secret is safe with me.'

'Little secret'? It didn't seem that little to Tom. He frowned. He knew the sensible thing was to deny it all: to say she was mistaken . . . but – proficient as Tom had become at riding a war horse and wielding a sword – there were some knightly accomplishments that he had never truly mastered, deception being the first on the list.

He sighed. 'Tell me what you want,' he said at length.

'I shall tell you,' replied the Lady Caterina, 'when the time comes. For now I just want you to know that I know who you are and what you are doing here.'

She rose and swept towards the door. 'Welcome to Pavia,' she said, and was gone.

Tom sat there like a stone dog. The Visconti serpent had just wound another coil around him.

He was not in the least deluded by the calm way in which the Lady Caterina had said everything or by her reassurances that his secret was safe with her. Her voice had that steely tone that made her father's pronouncements so dreaded – especially to a cottager whom he was condemning to death for failing to feed one of his hunting hounds.

No, there was no doubt – she was threatening him . . . but what did she want? Perhaps she was going to blackmail him into carrying out some devious plan she had devised . . . maybe against her husband or – even more alarming – against her father?

Tom tried to rid his mind of the thoughts that kept popping up like jack-in-the-boxes. He tried to read through his list of books again, but the titles kept jumping about from one place on the page to another and he soon gave up.

He went to the window and watched the sun now dipping towards the west . . . within the hour it would be dark. Did an incompetent spy stand more chance of staying concealed under cover of the night? Or was the night the time when secrets were revealed? When the inner truths were stripped bare for all to see and understand?

When he looked back into the room, he realised how truly dark it had already become without his noticing it.

Chapter 17

Pavia 1385

The same day that Sir Thomas English had first encountered the Lady Caterina Visconti, he found himself being entertained by her husband. The great man had invited him to take supper in his private apartments. There were just the two of them, but, even so, Tom couldn't help feeling there was more than one conversation going on.

'You are welcome to use the library as much as you wish,' said Gian Galeazzo, but Tom couldn't shake off the feeling that what he was actually saying was: 'I'd rather have you in the library than prowling around the palace, poking your nose into things that don't concern you.'

And when Gian Galeazzo made the generous offer that 'Tom was welcome to use his messengers whenever he had letters to send,' Tom was certain the duke was warning him that all his correspondence would be scrutinised.

In a way it didn't matter whether or not the Lady Caterina had told her husband of her suspicions about their English guest; the more Tom thought about it, the more likely it seemed that if the Lady Caterina could see through his guise, so could her lord.

And, even though Gian Galeazzo was as polite as the Pope on Sunday, everything he said took on an ominous ring. 'Won't you try a little minced quail?' sounded more like a threat than an invitation. And once, when Gian Galeazzo happened to say: 'This fish was caught this morning, Sir Thomas,' Tom nearly choked.

Then – quite suddenly – the great man lurched forward, peered into Tom's face and murmured: 'My uncle Bernabò is a cruel and vicious man, is he not?'

It was the sort of trick question that Tom had been dreading. He gazed at his host, as if trying to gauge the exact degree of cruelty and viciousness that Gian Galeazzo had in mind. Meanwhile his tongue stuck to the roof of his mouth, while his mind raced through every possible combination of cruelty and viciousness that could be applied to the Lord of Milan without sounding like criticism. Eventually the words stumbled out almost of their own accord:

'He is a formidable man.'

There. That should do it. But Gian Galeazzo was not to be fobbed off so easily.

'You know he intends to kill me?' he whispered conspiratorially.

'I . . . I . . . know nothing of such matters . . .' stuttered Tom.

'I am so scared,' whispered the great man. 'I expect my every waking hour to be my last. You see how I dare not leave my palace with less than three hundred men-at-arms. I do not sleep soundly in my bed and you can see I have no appetite . . .' He pushed his plate away from him at this point. 'My life is wretched, Sir Thomas Englishman. All I do – every day – is pray to God to shield me from the malevolence of my uncle.'

Tom didn't know where to look. But Gian Galeazzo kept peering into his eyes as if trying to read the solution to his life's problems there and Tom didn't dare look elsewhere. He had to offer his eyes up to Gian Galeazzo for inspection, as a small child might offer up its hands to show they are clean.

At this point-blank range, Tom could see that Gian Galeazzo's irises were grey-green with little flecks of brown. He could also see how those brown-flecked, grey-green eyes flicked this way and that . . . probing . . . searching . . . doubting . . .

To be faced, at these close quarters, with the private anxieties of such a great and powerful lord was unnerving, terrifying and almost terminally embarrassing.

'My lord,' said Tom after a prolonged and disconcerting silence compounded by the intimate eye-scrutiny, 'I am only too aware of my inadequacies, but if by chance I may be of any service whatsoever to your lordship, you have only to ask.'

Gian Galeazzo sat back and relaxed. It was as if a torturer had extracted the information he wanted from his victim and was now able to put his feet up for the rest of the day. The spell was broken for Tom too, and he took the opportunity to glance around the chamber.

It was fairly dark, since the Lord of Pavia did not like extravagance and would only allow a couple of candles to illuminate the table. When servants came and went with the dishes, they did so either in the dimness of the outer edges of the room or else carrying a small oil lamp in one hand.

'He claims it's to avoid unnecessary expense,' Tom found himself pondering, 'but perhaps the darkness suits him too?'

Several servants stood by, almost lost in the shadows, ready to do the great lord's bidding the moment he lifted his finger. Gian Galeazzo may have had a reputation for frugality, but it didn't quite add up, thought

Tom. The food was excellent, the wine was choice, and there were servants to spare . . . if this was frugality, Tom wished he could be as poor. There again, it was true that Gian Galeazzo himself ate very sparingly.

But the great man was addressing him once more: 'Sir Thomas Englishman, you are reputed to be an honest man, and I feel that I can trust you. You know I have no taste for war. Nor do I have ambitions that would move me against my uncle. All I desire is peace in which to worship the Almighty.'

'Your piety is renowned,' murmured Tom. The great lord bowed his head in acknowledgement. Then he went on:

'You will return to my uncle's court in Milan very soon. When you go perhaps you could ask certain questions on my behalf – without of course revealing that it is I who have asked you make such inquiries. All I would need to know is if and when my uncle plans to move against me. For move against me I am convinced he will. And when that happens, if I am far away from Pavia I can come to no harm. All I shall need is a little warning which, perhaps, Sir Thomas Englishman, you are in a position to give me?'

Tom laughed and laughed and laughed. In fact he was hysterical. Except of course that he kept a perfectly straight face and nodded very seriously at Gian

Galeazzo's proposal. But inwardly he wanted to roll on the floor and howl. The whole thing was a joke! Here he was – already employed by Regina della Scala, wife of Bernabò Visconti, and the Lady Donnina, mistress of Bernabò Visconti, to spy upon Gian Galeazzo – now being recruited by Gian Galeazzo to spy upon Bernabò Visconti.

'My lord,' said Tom. 'I have no immediate plans for a return to Milan . . .'

'I have some messages I would like you to deliver,' replied Gian Galeazzo, adding under his breath: 'Stay three or four days – or however long it takes to find out what it is necessary to know – and then come back and report direct to me . . .'

It seemed as if Tom had no choice. He was being commanded by the Lord of Pavia. He was not in a position to say no.

Chapter 18

Pavia 1385

Sir Thomas was working his way through the library, taking books off the shelves and carefully writing the titles on a wax tablet. But his mind was elsewhere entirely. It was only the night before that Gian Galeazzo had asked him to return to Milan to act as his spy, and to find out what he could about his uncle Bernabò's intentions towards him. And yet he was already engaged to spy upon Gian Galeazzo by Bernabò's wife and mistress.

On the one hand Tom thought, he would not be doing such a great evil . . . after all, his information would not be used to harm anyone. On the contrary, it might save Gian Galeazzo's life, and when you considered it, Gian Galeazzo's life was altogether a lot more worth saving than his uncle's. So there was even a moral argument in favour of undertaking the mission.

On the other hand, there were some pretty strong

arguments to the contrary, which had precious little to do with morality. Tom had been convinced that he would make the world's most hopeless spy, even before the Lady Caterina had told him she could see right through him. And now he was being asked to act as a double agent. Surely that would more than double the jeopardy he would be in. How could he be a double agent when he found being even a single agent difficult enough?

There again, the chance of returning to Milan could prove very useful. He already had sufficient information to keep Regina della Scala and the Lady Donnina happy. Perhaps they would release his squire John, and then the two of them could escape both these nests of intrigue. They could leave Lombardy and the domain of the Visconti, and never ever return.

Tom put down the book he was holding, and gazed out of the window towards the great park of Pavia. He could see a hunting party setting out from the lodge, surrounded by their hounds. He did not look for the figure of Gian Galeazzo, for he knew that the ruler of Pavia would not be amongst them. The great man seemed to spend all his waking hours praying in his private chapel, or talking to holy men. Prayer, devotion, study, contemplation . . . the Lord of Pavia could hardly have been more of a contrast to his uncle or to his father – neither of whom had anything but contempt for churchmen. Both lived for war and hunting and women and drinking. How such a family could have produced a flower as delicate and sweet-smelling as Gian Galeazzo was a botanical mystery.

Yet there was another mystery here in Pavia. For though Gian Galeazzo appeared to have no taste for the dangers of the hunt, yet he still kept up his father's park . . . some said he'd even improved it. And though he professed no interest in battle, he still spent a fortune on military matters – it was said he maintained a thousand men-at-arms . . .

At this point Tom became aware that he was no longer alone in the library. He turned to find the Lady Caterina standing at the door, looking at him. Tom bowed.

'You may carry on,' was all the Lady Caterina said, as she took her place at a table in the great window to the south. Tom reopened the book he had taken down and diligently copied the title onto the tablet which served him as a notebook.

When he'd finished he glanced up at the Lady Caterina. To his surprise she was not reading. She was sitting perfectly still with her hands in her lap, staring at him. Tom shut the book, replaced the volume on the shelf and took down the next.

'You are to return to Milan tomorrow?' said the Lady Caterina.

'As soon as that?' Tom hadn't realised it was all so cut and dried. A great lord like Gian Galeazzo didn't wait for the likes of Tom to decide whether to go or not.

'I have a letter I wish you to take,' said the Lady Caterina. Tom bowed.

'It would be an honour,' he said.

Caterina ignored him, and took out a piece of paper from a locked drawer. Paper was often more expensive than parchment or vellum, but clearly Caterina was used to using it. She sat down again and began to write.

Tom pretended to read the titles of several more books and to write them down on his wax tablet; indeed he copied them in but, if you had asked him afterwards what those names were, he would not have been able to tell you. He was too busy worrying about what it was that Caterina had in store for him.

Finally Caterina finished. She dusted the ink with a little fine sand and when it had dried, she folded the letter up and took out a length of wax. This she melted onto the folded pages and then pressed her ring into the molten blob of wax to seal it.

She then wrote the name of the recipient on the outside of the letter, and turned to Tom.

'You will oblige me by saying nothing of this to my lord,' she said in her commanding voice. Tom bowed his compliance.

Secretly his heart was sinking. He saw it all too clearly now. He was about to become the go-between in a love affair between the Lady Caterina and some member of Bernabò's court – perhaps an old flame of her youth. Were these Viscontis deliberately making life as dangerous for him as they possibly could? What had they all got against him? He'd never done them any harm!

But then how could he deny the Lady Caterina anything without her denouncing him as a spy to her lord? And here she was – not only standing in front of him but placing the letter into his hands.

The heavy folded paper felt like a death warrant, but he bowed to the Lady Caterina as she turned on her heel and strode out of the library.

Tom shut his eyes. But he knew when he opened them he would still be holding that fatal piece of paper.

He could see it all: he'd get caught red-handed with the letter either passing through the gates of Pavia, or else he'd be waylaid on the road by Bernabò's men, or else they'd pick him up entering Milan . . . it didn't matter which side caught him with it, the result would be the same. He could look forward to a nice spot of torture to loosen his tongue and then a leisurely and painful death. The lords of Lombardy did not take kindly to their wives or sisters or daughters being enamoured of the wrong men.

That was precisely why he was so worried about his squire John.

But then, he thought ruefully, the lords of Lombardy probably felt even less kindly towards the go-betweens in these affairs. Go-between! The word stuck in his throat. There was no getting away from it – that's what he had become, as well as a spy and a double agent . . .

Tom opened his eyes and turned the letter over. As he read the name of the recipient, he felt as if a comet had struck the library. He was engulfed in a fiery explosion that wiped out all other problems in one all-engulfing calamity. Just a few moments ago, he'd thought that life simply couldn't get any more complicated or dangerous. But it just had.

The name on the letter was his own.

Chapter 19

Le Truc du Midi 1361

When he'd relit his candle in record-breaking time, back in that cave within a cave, Tom had expected to find the Beast of Gévaudan devouring the beautiful Lady Emilia de Valois, so in one way he was relieved to find that she was in the arms of a man. The man, however, looked as near to a Beast as a man could get without actually being one.

He had grabbed Emily around the throat. His face was marred with dirt and dust from the road, and his black beard looked as if it could have provided a good home for all manner of wildlife. In fact, thought Tom, the man must have had some sort of interest in ornithology, for he was muttering in Emily's ear:

'What are you after, my pretty bird?'

Tom, however, was in no mood to listen to small talk about the Wonderful World of Nature. He drew his sword. The moment he did, however, he felt ridiculous.

He tried to hold the sword in a suitably aggressive way. But it was no good. No matter what he did he simply couldn't make it look anything near as threatening as the man was now making his fist. It was, Tom felt, something to do with belief.

Belief and maybe aptitude and possibly practice . . . and from the look of him, Tom reckoned that the fellow had had a considerable amount of practice with his fist and possibly with swords as well.

'Let her go!' said Tom, but speaking just made it worse. His voice simply didn't carry any sort of authority. He might just as well have been saying: 'Can you pass the marmalade?' or 'Let's go and play tiddlywinks!'

This was confirmed by the fact that the man simply ignored him as he leered into Emily's contorted face: 'You're a pretty one, and no mistake!'

'Let her go!' Tom tried saying it this time in a deeper register and frowning as he said it. But it still came out sounding like he was demanding his marbles back. The bandit (which is what he must have been if he wasn't an ornithologist) turned and sneered at Tom.

'Run along, little 'un!' he said. He was carrying a crossbow on his back and a quiver of bolts over his shoulder, but he made no attempt to reach for them.

Tom pulled himself up to his full height, even though, as the man had so unkindly pointed out, his full height wasn't all that impressive, and prepared to lunge at him, but at that moment the tinder – which all this time had been flaring in the tinderbox – sputtered and started to die. Tom dived for the candle stub and thrust the wick into the dying flame. He just caught it and the candle hesitated into life as the tinderbox fire died.

The man, in the meantime, had pulled Emily into the tunnel and was dragging her back towards the daylight. Tom dived after them, grabbing one of Emily's ankles, but a sudden kick from the man threw him back and Emily was dragged still screaming through the tunnel.

At that moment Tom heard another moan from behind the pile of rubble. He ran back to Ann and was soon undoing her gag and desperately trying to loosen her bonds.

'He was going to leave me to die!' said Ann. 'He said he'd enjoy hearing my cries getting weaker.'

At that moment a far-from-weak cry split the air . . . Emily's scream must have been loud enough to burst the bandit's eardrums. They heard him curse her.

'I can't undo this knot!' exclaimed Tom.

'Then leave it!' yelled Ann. 'Go and help Emily!'

'I can't leave you!'

'Yes, you can!' urged Ann. 'Hurry! She's in trouble!'

So Tom grabbed his sword, and – leaving the candle beside Ann as she struggled to free herself – he leapt across to the tunnel. He emerged into the front cave in time to see Emily bite the bandit's arm.

'You little vixen!' the bandit yelled at her, grabbing her throat in his bare hands. 'You venomous snake! I'll throttle the life out of you!'

But Emily fought back, punching and kicking the man as they fell together and started to roll around on the floor of the cave. The crossbow fell off his back and the quiver of bolts scattered across the floor of the cave.

Tom raced towards them, lifting his sword in the air as he did so, and fell flat on his face yet again.

'Idiot!' he screamed at himself. He'd tripped over the crossbow.

Emily, meanwhile, was still furiously pummelling the man's face and chest as the two of them twisted and rolled over and over on the ground – making it impossible for Tom to strike at the man without being in danger of hitting his friend.

After some moments of this, however, Emily managed to get her finger into the bandit's eye. He yelled and fell back for a second, which was all Tom needed. He lunged forward and thrust his sword into the man's arm.

The bandit looked up at Tom and snarled, and before

Tom had time to pull his sword back, the bandit had grabbed his arm and yanked him off his feet. Suddenly the sword was flying out of his hand and the man's knee was on his chest.

'So much for my career as an expert swordsman!' thought Tom, as a stunning blow across the jaw made his head whirl. And the next minute the bandit's knife, which had miraculously appeared in his hand, would have slashed across his throat, had it not been for Emily, who crashed a rock down on the man's head. He groaned and slumped forward on top of Tom.

Tom pushed him off and leapt away, but the man was only momentarily stunned. He staggered to his feet, and before Tom could repossess himself of his sword, the bandit had grabbed it and was slashing it in front of Tom's face. Tom turned and ran towards the mouth of the cave, and so did Emily, while the bandit, who seemed to have become quite crazed by the blow on the head, whirled around slashing the air and cursing and shouting, the blood running down his sword arm and over his hand.

'He's crazy!' exclaimed Tom.

'He stinks!' yelled Emily.

'Look out!' The bandit was upon them, brandishing the sword and describing in surprisingly exact detail the size of pieces into which he was intending to cut them.

It only took Tom and Emily a second to decide they'd heard enough, whereupon they turned and fled from the cave. The bandit, however, seemed determined that they should hear him out. And he was in a position to carry his point, for not only was he extremely large but he also happened to be extremely fast on his feet.

Now in those days athletic events usually involved men assaulting other men on horseback with large lances or swords, but if they'd held plain and simple running events, such as we do today, I have to tell you that this bandit would have been a champion sprinter. Of course, living in the fourteenth century, he was to live out his life without ever knowing how well he could have done in the 2012 Olympics. He knew he was fast, of course, but never having been entered for the 100 metres sprint or the 4 x 400 metres relay he could have had no idea of just how fractionally much faster he was than any other runner of his time. It was one of those instances of a desert flower blooming unseen . . . although a desert flower is not an image one would have readily associated with this particular bandit.

All this, of course, was bad news for Tom and Emily, for it meant that in just a few strides, the man had caught up with them and grabbed Emily by the sleeve

of her dress. He yanked her hard, and she went sprawl-
ing in the thistles.

Tom felt the blade of the sword slice both the air
above his head and the hair above his head, as he
ducked and ran, praying that this time he wouldn't fall
over. But, I'm afraid, that is *exactly* what he did.

'Damn!' was all Tom thought as he too sprawled into
the thistles and saw the bandit looming above him. The
man swung the sword up in the air. Tom shut his eyes
and waited to find out what it was like to have one's
head severed from one's body. The usual thoughts
came into his mind, such as: 'How long will my head
go on thinking when it's off?' and 'If I can see my body
as my head flies away from it, how will I know it's
mine if it hasn't got a head?'

But he never found out. Several seconds after he had
thought he should have found the answer to both
questions, he hadn't. So he opened his eyes and saw
the bandit still standing there above him, with the
sword above his head, ready to strike.

'Well go on,' Tom shouted. 'Get it over with!'

It was then that Tom noticed a curious look on the
man's face. It was the sort of look you might expect
to find on a young frog's face when it learns that some
humans eat amphibians – or the look on a princess's
face when she kisses the prince and realises he's a

frog after all – a sort of cross between disbelief and horror.

Before Tom could turn to see what had produced this interesting facial expression, Emily had regained her feet and had begun lashing at the man from behind. But he just stood there, and Emily too gradually stopped hitting him and adopted a facial expression that was very closely akin to the bandit's. In her case, perhaps, it was more the look of a high-born lady who feels she has been grossly assaulted by someone far below her station but who suddenly realises there could be worse things in store. Which, come to think of it, was almost exactly the case.

A snarl swung Tom's attention round to the object of their interest. And there it was! Edging slowly out of the forest – the size of an ox but the shape of a wolf – a creature with malice in its eyes and saliva dripping from its huge bared teeth.

Without even realising what they were doing all three humans were instinctively stepping backwards, as if they thought they could escape those jaws and those razor-sharp claws by simply backing away. They stepped backwards carefully, deliberately, never taking their eyes off the creature, trying to assess each glint in its eyes as those cold and hungry pupils flicked from Emily to the bandit to Tom . . .

And the bandit kept that sword above his head ready for that terrible moment when the Beast would spring . . . which was surely about to happen . . .

Tom thought: maybe if he turned and ran in one direction and Emily ran in another the Beast might go for the bandit in the middle. But before he could work out the logistics, it all happened.

The bandit's heel caught a tree stump and he pitched backwards, and that was the trigger they'd all been waiting for. The Beast sprang. It arched through the air so effortlessly it might have been a scarf of silk. Tom could hardly believe the height it leapt. In fact, talking about the 2012 Olympics, the Beast could easily have set a new world record, if super-wolves had been eligible.

As it flew through the air it roared, and then it roared again as it hit the bandit. The next moment its muzzle was covered in blood and it was shaking the man like a rag doll.

Why Tom and Emily stood there watching, rather than running away, would be hard to explain. Perhaps they thought they could help the man. Perhaps they knew there could be no escape from a creature of such power and speed. At all events, instead of getting out of danger's way they just stood rooted to the spot – a couple of mice fascinated by the cat who is destined to kill them. But, as the Beast turned its huge head to snarl at them, something even more extraordinary happened.

The snarling suddenly died in the Beast's throat. Its eyes widened and it opened its bloody jaws as if to roar, but no sound came out. It swayed and then keeled over, and the next moment it was lying there as lifeless as the man whose life it had itself just taken.

For several moments Tom couldn't work out what had happened. Then he heard a voice shout: 'Are you two all right?'

He turned and there was Ann standing at the cave entrance with the bandit's crossbow in her hands. And when Tom turned back to the Beast that had terrorised that region for so many years, he could see a crossbow bolt sticking out of the middle of its forehead.

All he could think of saying was: 'Great shot, Ann!'

Chapter 20

Pavia 1385 / Marvejols 1361

Ah! If only Ann were here now to cut through the Gordian knot of his current situation – to solve the current tangle of problems with one simple, unexpected stroke. That was what she was so good at . . . or used to be . . .

Sir Thomas English smiled to himself as he rode out of the north gate of Pavia to take the direct road to Milan. The smile meant he was recalling to mind the evening that followed those events outside the bandit's cave so long ago.

Word of the slaying of the Beast got back to Marvejols before Tom, Emily and Ann did. How such news can travel faster that those who are carrying it is one of those mysteries that will probably never be resolved. But get back before them the news certainly did, so that by the time the trio walked in through the fortified gate of the town, a small crowd had gathered. The people didn't cheer, or shout out, 'Well done, you three!' or anything like that. No. They just stood and stared.

Perhaps they were just in too much awe of the mighty Beast-slayers to dare to say anything? Or perhaps they just didn't quite believe what they had only heard had happened.

Tom, Emily and Ann walked through the silent crowd and then, without any warning, Emily fainted.

Theatrically speaking it was a perfect piece of timing. The crowd snapped out of their enchanted silence and thronged around the young people. They lifted Emily up and bore her to the main inn. Tom and Ann also found themselves picked up bodily by many hands and as the excited bubble of chatter began to swell around them, they too were carried aloft to the inn. There the landlord poured them mazers of wine, while the townsfolk crowded in ready to hear the story.

Emily was revived. Food was set before them. And for the next hour they were quizzed and questioned about how this wonderful thing had happened.

Sometime later, there was a roar from the people outside who had been unable to fit into the inn, and the landlord led his star guests to the door in time to see the Beast itself, being carried on two stout poles by a dozen men.

Dead, it seemed even larger than it had alive. Its inert mass, hanging from the poles, seemed to impose itself on the world of the living – daring folk to touch it, to try and lift its huge paws, to imagine what the death it brought was like.

The men flung the vast carcass down in the market-place, under the light of two flaming torches. And the crowd was once again mute, as they gathered round that terrible thing and wondered . . .

Sir Thomas English shook the memory out of his head. That was all many years ago. Today, as he set out upon the road back to Milan from Pavia, his problems could not be resolved simply by slaying a Beast – at least not by slaying one Beast alone.

When he had last left Milan, he had hoped that the coils of the Visconti serpent would have been loosened from around him. But he had found instead that he was tighter in their grip than ever. Now he felt that in place of one Visconti serpent, there were two, winding themselves tighter and tighter around him until they would squeeze all the sense and life out of him.

What was it Ann used to say? 'Situation, Alternatives, Action'? Well, the situation was simple enough

. . . no, wait a minute! It wasn't at all! The situation was far from simple. That was the whole point. The situation was so mind-bogglingly complicated that Tom couldn't even get his head around it. The alternatives didn't seem to exist, and the action was being dictated to him.

But would Ann have seen it like that?

And what would Ann have said about the letter which he had been given by the Lady Caterina? He ran it through in his mind, for he had been careful to memorise every word:

'Sir Thomas,' it had said. 'Take care in my father's court. Beware the man they call "Il Medecina" – he may seem to be your friend and may hint that he would be happy to see my father undone. But in truth my father has no more loyal servant, and Il Medecina is cunning and intelligent beyond the normal run of men.

'Donnina de' Porri is not to be trusted. She is totally devoted to my father, and does nothing but at his behest.

'My father, as you know, is capricious and violent. Keep out of his way as much as is possible. Likewise his sons, Ludovico and Rodolfo; both are devious and untrustworthy no matter how they may present themselves to you.

'If my Lord Gian Galeazzo has sent you to divine my father's intentions towards him, the only person to whom you may speak with some safety is my mother, Regina della Scala. But take care. She, too, is loyal to my father and will never act to harm him. What is more she has no love for my Lord Gian Galeazzo. However, she loves me. She may be prepared to save him for my sake. It is not certain, but it is the best you can do.

'Burn this letter the instant you have read it.

'Caterina.'

It was not exactly a cheering letter, but at least it wasn't asking him to act as a messenger between the Lady Caterina and some secret lover. And in addition it gave him some good advice . . . at least it seemed to.

There were, however, still two major problems. First, he would need to get Regina della Scala on her own, and she always seemed to be in the company of Donnina de' Porri. Secondly, Regina had told him that Bernabò already suspected him of treachery. Of course, this might have just been to get Tom on side to do her bidding – but then Bernabò probably suspected *everyone* of treachery, and the likelihood was that she was right. In which case, Tom was running a considerable risk by showing his face back in the court in the first place.

Tom sighed. Why was nothing simple and straight-forward in the land of the Visconti?

Tom's horse agreed and snorted: 'Those Visconti people . . . yeurghh!' it said, although to you or me it might have sounded like a whinny.

Tom looked down at the animal. They had been together for many years now, and Tom knew the horse's moods and feelings almost as well as the horse knew his. In fact, if the truth were known, Tom often spoke to his horse – and he didn't just say things like 'Whoa there!' or 'Giddiup!' but sometimes he directed more intellectually challenging questions at him, such as: 'How are you doing today, Bruce?' or 'We'll soon be there, Bruce . . .'

Sometimes – and now I'm telling you things that Tom himself would never have admitted to – he even carried on conversations with his horse. That is what he was doing now.

'Bucephalus?' he began. Bucephalus, or Bruce as he was known more often than not, snorted. He was listening. 'This is a dangerous game I've got myself into,' said Tom.

'You didn't get yourself into it,' replied Bruce with a snort and a toss of his head. 'You've been trapped by those wretched Visconti people. Why you bother with . . .'

'You're right,' Tom interrupted him. It was never a good idea to let Bruce ramble on too long. 'If I could

177

just get Squire John out of that prison, we could leave Lombardy and forget about the whole damned lot of them.'

'How are we going to get him out?' asked Bruce.

'We'll find a way,' said Tom without conviction.

'Anyway, Tom,' snorted Bruce, 'it's a lovely day!' And the horse was right. It was a lovely day.

Out of sheer *joie de vivre* Tom gave three short, sharp whistles, and Bruce started bucking and kicking. 'Whoa there!' laughed Tom, patting the horse's neck. 'Just checking you still remembered! There, boy! It's all right!'

It was a little trick he had taught the horse in the early days, but it had been many years since they had last tried it out. Although – now he came to think of it – it was somebody whistling that had set Bucephalus off rearing and kicking during that boar hunt some weeks before.

'You almost got me killed on that hunt!' exclaimed Tom, remembering how he'd been unseated and then the boar had chased him off a cliff.

Bucephalus snorted something about not being responsible for the outcome when he was only obeying orders, and Tom laughed and patted his mane. The fact was, despite the problems all around him, Tom had not been able to stop his usual optimism welling up within him as he and Bruce wound their way across the plain of Lombardy. There were skylarks in the air above, so high up they were invisible, and yet their one long continuous song accompanied him from Pavia to Milan – as if it were one bird keeping him company the whole way. 'It'll be fine! It'll be fine! Get a move on down there! Get a move on down there!' they sang, and Bruce had picked up his gait as they travelled north.

The summer heat had become intense, and the distance had begun to shimmer and ripple as if it were gum arabic melting in an alchemist's retort. The road was dusty and Bruce's hooves sent up clouds of fine dry powder – the calcination of some worldwide alchemical experiment – as they clopped along under the broad blue sky.

Lombardy stretched out around them, its soul bared towards that implacable sky, as exposed as its people were to their all-powerful lord. And Tom, too, felt equally exposed and alone, riding as he was into the mouth of the serpent.

By the end of the journey, however, any sense of solitude had slunk away into the maze of narrow streets that clustered outside the southern walls of the city of Milan. These southern suburbs had become a city in their own right, and the streets were as crowded as the streets within the walls. Actually there were more donkeys on the street than people, but then that was not particularly unusual.

Nor was it unusual to see country folk approaching the great gates of Milan carrying vegetables in baskets on their heads, or beating donkeys that were almost invisible under their burdens – bundles of wood, sacks of flour, strings of onions, sacks of cabbages, and sometimes the odd chicken hanging from the saddle, mute and helpless. Nor was it unusual for a knight like Tom to have to wait for a moment while a herdsman guided his flock of sheep between the houses.

It was strange, Tom reflected, how most human beings would give way to an armed knight on horseback, but not sheep. In the sheep's world there was little difference between ruled and ruler. All human beings were just that to them – simply human beings – and their otherness, in the eye of a sheep, gave them anonymity and equality.

No, thought Tom, there was nothing unusual about today. Tradesmen joked to each other after a customer left. The cobbler reached up to lift a pair of boots from the rail above his head. A spice merchant shook the hand of a good customer who had just arrived to buy a little dried saffron and some cinnamon but not too much.

As Tom turned a corner, there in the middle of the

street, a tailor was holding up a man's arm as he fitted him with a half-made doublet. A little further on, at a low counter, a woman was bent over, examining a necklace, while the jeweller eyed her with undisguised contempt. He knew she was not going to buy it. He always knew which of his customers would and which of his customers wouldn't. And even when they did contrariwise to what he expected, they were simply the exception that proved the rule. The jeweller's wife knew better than to argue with him. She also knew better than to tell him about all she did when he was away buying precious stones. It was all perfectly usual.

There was not even anything unusual about the way the day was drawing to a close, nor about the way Tom could see the first lamps being lit in shops and homes, for his elevated position on horseback allowed him to see into windows that were too high for the ordinary pedestrian-on-the-street.

Nor was there anything in the least bit unusual about the smell of freshly baked bread that was now drifting across from a side street. It was delicious, but not unusual.

And yet there was something very different about the whole place. Something peculiar. For a while Tom couldn't quite put his finger on it, then he suddenly realised that it was staring him in the face . . . it was obvious . . . it was all around him . . . wherever his eye came to rest.

The entire town seemed to have been afflicted by a black plague – no, not the Black Death, although that was still around and claiming its arbitrary victims. But that was invisible and stealthy. This was a visible plague of blackness that was thrust in front of your eyes wherever you looked.

Out of every window hung a black cloth or shawl or blanket. The counters of shops were draped in black. The statues of the Virgin that stood at almost every corner were shrouded with black. Black was everywhere: on men's arms and in women's headdresses. Even the gatehouse of the city had caught the disease, with long folds of black fustian hanging from the loopholes on either side.

Strangely enough, however, nobody looked particularly dismal or gloomy. They just seemed to be going about their business as people usually do, which was, perhaps, why Tom had not at first noticed the outbreak of blackness. Now he had noticed it, however, the black epidemic was generating a gloom in Tom's spirits. He couldn't explain why, but he felt a chill rising up from his kidneys, and he was gripped by an illogical – but nonetheless powerful – foreboding as ominous as the Visconti emblem of the serpent swallowing a man which now loomed above him, painted over the entrance to the city.

Bruce too shivered under his girth. And that decided it! As far as Tom was concerned, if his horse felt something was wrong, then something was definitely wrong. Tom would need to be on the alert.

Which is more than can be said for the guard at the gate. Tom could see him through the open door of the guardroom; he was sitting on a broken chair rocking backwards and forwards with laughter.

The guard glanced up at Tom, but went on laughing and talking to someone else whom Tom couldn't see. Eventually, the man stood up and sauntered over. He looked at Tom curiously. In fact he looked at Tom so curiously that Tom's hand instinctively dropped to his sword hilt.

He held out his papers, and something about the way the guard took them made the skin on the back of his neck prickle. Was he imagining it? Or had the normal boredom of guard duty been replaced by something else . . . something keener . . . something sharper?

Tom glanced around nervously as the guard took the papers into the guardroom, saying: 'I just have to get this signed. New regulation.' He said it so casually that Tom didn't believe him.

Tom's hand closed around the grip of his sword. Whispering came from inside the guardroom. Why would he be whispering if he were simply asking for a signature?

Tom's nerves began to stretch like a bow string left out in the rain . . . instinctively he turned Bruce round 180 degrees, ready to make a fast exit, but the guards must have heard the manoeuvre, for before Bruce had completed it, two of them dashed out from the guardroom and seized the bridle.

Tom pulled out his sword and raised it over the two men. 'Let go!' he said.

'No!' shouted another voice. 'You! Drop the sword!'

Tom turned and saw the first guard standing in the doorway aiming a crossbow at him. Without a second thought, Tom struck at the soldier to his right, slashing his arm, and at the same time he flattened himself over Bruce's neck. Almost instantaneously, the bolt from the crossbow grazed the back of Tom's jerkin and hit the far wall. The maimed soldier screamed, but managed to cling on to the horse's bridle, and nothing Tom did could shake him off.

In desperation Tom suddenly gave three loud whistles, and Bucephalus obligingly reared in the air, tossing both guards to one side. But the horse's nerves were clearly stretched as taut as his master's, and he seemed to overreact. Before Tom could regain control, he found himself being flung through the air, and he landed sprawled across the injured guard.

The guard with the crossbow ran out of the guard-room, yelling to some others who had appeared from the auxiliaries' quarters, but Bucephalus's front hooves struck him in the face as the horse pirouetted, dragging another guard with him. The guard dropped his cross-bow, clutched his face and screamed before falling backwards, while the new guards bellowed incoher-ently. The men already on the ground were still cursing and sobbing in equal proportions, while Bruce snorted and pounded his hooves on the wood of the door.

Tom didn't stop to introduce himself to the new set of guards. He just leapt over the injured man, threw himself out of the gatehouse and ran down the street the way he'd come.

Such was the confusion that it was some moments before the guards realised that Tom had escaped, and, by the time they were in a position to give chase, he had disappeared into the side streets of the southern suburb.

Tom wasn't even sure whether they'd actually fol-lowed him. He flung himself first down one side street and then another, until he finally found himself outside a dismal inn of the sort no self-respecting knight who cared for his reputation would wish to be seen dead in – let alone alive. It suited him down to the ground. He ducked under the low doorway and entered.

If there had been a conversation going on, it stopped the moment Tom stepped over the threshold. Two men were sitting on stools in the dark interior. A woman was just lighting what was meant to be an oil lamp, but which gave so little light that it might just as well have been a slightly mouldy salad.

One of the men was emaciated and had very few teeth. The other wore his hair unfashionably long. Both looked as worn and ragged as their clothes.

The woman, by contrast, had all the appearance of someone scrubbed and bright and fresh. A cheerful red cord fell gracefully from her shoulder. As she coaxed the wretched lamp into giving a little more light, her presence seemed to make the room brighter than it really was.

Tom ordered a little wine and some water, and then turned to the two men. He was slightly disconcerted to find they were both staring at him.

'It's been a fine day,' he nodded.

The thin man grunted in a way that gave Tom absolutely no idea whether he was agreeing or disagreeing. The man with the unfashionably long hair bared his teeth for several moments. Tom wasn't certain whether he was snarling at him, smiling at him or merely exercising his facial muscles in some arcane religious ritual related to the worship of teeth.

'You'll get nothing out of him,' said the thin man, nodding towards his companion. 'He can see you. He can hear what you say. But he don't know what you are. I can see you. I can hear what you say. And I know what you are.'

Tom had no idea how the conversation had arrived at this point, or what was meant by it, but it certainly wasn't the sort of discussion any self-respecting spy would want to find himself plunged into from the word 'Go!'

'How interesting,' he said, in a tone of voice that he hoped would vividly communicate his urgent desire not to hear another word. He turned away from the two men and looked out of the window. No sign of a hue and cry so far. Maybe he was going to be lucky.

On the other hand he had already had more than his share of ill luck for one day. He had lost his papers and – what was worse – he had lost his horse. How he was going to retrieve either he had no idea. And on top of that he wasn't even in the city of Milan. He was still outside, with very little prospect of being able to get in.

And then what had actually happened in the gatehouse? Had the guard really been acting suspiciously towards him or had it all been in his own mind? The more he thought about it the more he realised that the guard had only acted aggressively when he turned Bruce around . . . maybe it was simply Tom's nervousness that had made them suspicious.

But if he had just committed an act of monumental folly, it was too late now. He couldn't just walk back to the gatehouse, apologise for maiming not one but two – maybe more – of the duke's guards and ask politely for his papers and horse to be returned.

'You mustn't take any notice of them two,' said a voice in his ear. It was the cheerful woman with the red cord hanging from her shoulder, and for an instant Tom thought she was referring to the injured guards. But as she bent to place the wine on the bench beside him, her low-cut bodice displayed an amplitude of bosom that momentarily wiped all other thoughts from Tom's mind.

'They're both mad as cuckoos,' said the cheerful woman, nodding towards her other two customers.

'Thank you,' said Tom, and he fumbled for a way to inquire why the town was in mourning, without sounding like he was a total stranger who had no idea what was going on in the city. All he could come up with was: 'Who died?'

The cheerful woman, however, looked mystified. 'Neither of them has died yet!' she explained rather carefully, as if to someone who couldn't spot a rock if it were thrust under his nose. 'Although you could be forgiven for thinking they had.'

'No, I didn't mean them . . .' Tom suddenly became aware that the cheerful woman was now rubbing his shoulders rather vigorously.

'I could put a bit of life into you, sir, if you'd care for me to?' she was saying rather quietly.

'What I meant was . . .' But before he could say any more, he became aware that the cheerful woman had stopped rubbing his shoulders and was now staring at him.

'But we know each other . . . don't we?' she was saying.

'I don't think we do,' said Tom.

'You've been here before, haven't you?' said the cheerful woman.

'No, I haven't,' said Tom.

'But I know you . . . I know I do . . .' said the woman.

Tom glanced out of the window. In the fading light the streets looked suitably sinister, but there was no sign of any pursuit, and Tom began to think that perhaps it would be better to take his chances out there on the streets, rather than stay any longer in this particular inn.

Not that he didn't think the cheerful woman wouldn't be a perfectly charming companion who could probably put a considerable amount of life into him, if it came to that, but right then Tom had other things to think about.

For a start, once it was really dark, he had to find some way of getting back into the city. He then had to find his way into Regina della Scala's presence. He had to find his squire, John, and release him. He also had to find Bucephalus and rescue *him*. Given a perfect world, he probably even ought to try and get his papers back.

It was going to be a busy night as it was, and 'having a bit of life put into him' wasn't really on the agenda.

But the cheerful woman now had his arm in a firm lock.

'Where was it we met? It was here . . . wasn't it?'

'I don't think so,' Tom tried to sound really definite about this, as he tried to extricate his arm.

'No . . . let me think . . . I'll get it in a moment . . .'

'Would you let me go, please?' said Tom. He tried to say it as politely as possible, but really it isn't one of those things that's got a polite way of being said.

'We *have* met . . .'

Tom felt he simply couldn't bear another round of this particular quiz.

'I have an important appointment with the duke. So I'd better be off.'

Now these words, spoken with so little thought, had a remarkable effect on the cheerful woman with the red cord. She sprang back from Tom as if he'd just announced that he had the plague. The cheerful expression that had seemed so habitual to her was instantly replaced by a look of fear that made her appear considerably older.

'Of course, we're in mourning here!' she stammered. 'We don't go round enjoying ourselves at a time like this!'

'Mourning for *who*?' Tom would have liked to have asked, but he didn't want to prolong the conversation, so he just muttered: 'Fine . . .', put a coin on the bench and extricated himself forthwith from the inn and the charms of the lady with the red cord on her shoulder.

Once in the street, Tom stood and listened. Not only were there no signs of a pursuit, there were no signs of anything threatening whatsoever. On the contrary, everything seemed remarkably amicable. It was the time of that Italian ritual, the *passagiata*, when people stroll up and down, nodding to each other, tipping their hats, stopping to talk, smiling and generally doing all the things that people do when they are enjoying the cool of the evening air. Even the barking of a nearby dog sounded more like *joie de vivre* than a warning.

And just above the hum of street conversation and the dumb chorus of footsteps, the soft evening breezes carried the bells of the six monasteries and eight nunneries of Milan to every quarter of the city and its suburbs.

Tom was sitting on a low stone wall opposite one of the grander buildings in the southern suburb. He wasn't quite sure what went on in there, but it was sufficiently important to have its side wall decorated with paintings. And one of these paintings now began to engage his attention.

It was a curious picture of a man hanging by his left foot from a gallows. A devil was pulling out his tongue while a bearded figure – who could have been Bernabò Visconti himself – was pointing the man out to an executioner.

Tom shook his head and smiled. He'd seen these *pittura infamante* – or 'paintings of shame' – in many Italian cities. They were a way of holding the enemies of the city up for public abuse and ridicule – or, rather, the enemies of the powerful oligarchs and merchants who controlled the city.

Tom turned his head on one side to get a better

impression of the victim of this particular *pittura infamante,* and the moment he saw who it was the explanation for everything that had happened since he had arrived in the south suburb of Milan hit him at once – like Ann cutting the Gordian knot.

He was staring at a picture of himself.

Chapter 21

Milan 1385

The moment he recognised who it was hanging upside down on the gallows, he became aware of all the other people who were also staring at it. Many of them were laughing. Some were shaking their heads. Some stopped to point at it, others simply walked by nodding at it.

Presumably the guard at the gatehouse had seen this picture and so had the cheerful woman in the inn, and – as far as Tom could see – it would be only a matter of minutes before one of these passers-by would recognise the object of their ridicule sitting there admiring his own portrait.

Trying to recreate his celebrated impression of an invisible carrot, Tom pulled his hood over that incriminating red hair and covered his mouth with his hand, as he muttered: 'Time to get moving, legs.'

And his legs did.

*

Some time later, night had fallen – pretty heavily. As a matter of fact, it had crashed down around Tom while he was fast asleep.

Tom had found a hiding place in a small lean-to shed up against a house in a narrow alley. There he'd curled himself up, safe from the gaze of passers-by, and he had occupied himself until it was past curfew by trying to stay awake. But somehow or other he had failed.

He only realised this when he was rudely awoken by the night falling on top of him. At least that's what he assumed it was. In fact it was a man who had stumbled against the shed with such force that part of the roof had collapsed. The door also gave way and the man tumbled inside, adding his own weight to the number of inanimate objects that simultaneously hit the recumbent Tom.

Tom leapt to his feet.

'Ssh!' said the man. 'The nightwatch'll hear you!'

Tom was about to give the fellow a piece of his mind, when he realised that, intoxicated though the man may have been, his advice was nevertheless perfectly sound. There was certainly no point in attracting the attention of the nightwatchman.

In any case, by the time these thoughts had flashed

through Tom's mind, it was hardly worth saying anything since the fellow appeared to be fast asleep. It was
almost as if he had handed his sleep on to this stranger,
like the baton in a relay race.

Tom eased himself out of the alley, and looked about.
All was still. What is more, it was both moonless and
starless, which meant that as far as Tom was concerned
it was a beautiful night.

Now the trouble with city walls is that they're generally constructed so as to keep out besieging armies. It's
an aspect of their design which makes them even more
tricky to negotiate for the occasional civilian who
wishes to gain unofficial entry.

Tom gazed up at the height of that massive construction. There was a time when he might have thought of
climbing it – in fact he remembered doing exactly that
the first day he met Ann . . . or Alan, as he then took
her to be. These walls, however, were quite a different
matter. They were too high to even contemplate scaling
without the requisite siege equipment.

But there must be a way in, he told himself, and he
started to walk around the perimeter of the city looking
for the single chink in its armour that would be all he'd
need.

Now, as it happens, the Milanese in those days were
particularly proud of their water. The city was set

equally between two rivers, the Ticino and the Adda, and the good people of Milan were forever boasting about their endless supply of healthy, natural fresh water. They didn't need cisterns or conduits, they said, they simply brought in the fresh water that surrounded them in such abundance. Almost every house could proudly point to its well, and even in times of drought the supply never failed.

What is more, the city was entirely encircled by a deep wide ditch, and this ditch, as the Milanese never tired of pointing out to foreigners, contained not fetid, stagnant water, such as you might expect to find in any run-of-the-mill moat, but beautiful fresh spring water full of fish and crabs.

Tom had been walking along the banks of this remarkable ditch for some time, before it suddenly occurred to him that here might be the very chink in the armour of the city that he was seeking. He knew that the miraculously fresh and healthy water of the ditch had to flow into the city itself at some point. Perhaps if he could find that point, he could squeeze himself in along with the water.

As it happened, Tom had just reached one of the southern postern gates. It was of course firmly closed and bolted, but as he stood there listening to the echoes of the door he'd just rattled, he heard another sound. It was the sound of water flowing underground.

A quick inspection of the flow in the ditch confirmed that this was, indeed, the point at which the superior quality ditch-water was allowed entry into the city: it was flowing in directly under his feet and then under the postern gate.

Without stopping to think any longer, Tom stripped off his clothes. He tied them up into a tight bundle and then did what you might consider to be a very odd thing. He started to throw the bundle against the city wall. He did this several times, and you could have been forgiven for thinking that he had taken leave of his senses, until he finally managed to do what he'd been intending to do in the first place: he succeeded in tossing it high enough to go clean over the city wall, just next to the postern gate.

The next moment Tom had plunged into the beautifully clean and healthy water of the Milan ditch and discovered that the Milanese had a tendency to exaggerate about these things.

For a start, despite the day's heat, the water was freezing cold. It didn't feel at all healthy to Tom. And secondly, the visibility under the water was less than nil. Of course this is not strictly speaking possible, but that's how Tom thought about it. The night itself was black as pitch – that's why he'd had such trouble throwing his clothes over the wall – but underwater the blackness seemed to be trebled . . . or worse than that. Underwater the blackness took on a supernatural quality that allowed it to leak in through his eyes and fill his soul with feelings and thoughts too horrible to bear a name.

Tom broke to the surface again, gasping for air. He held on to the bank for some time trying to calm himself. 'Stop being a complete rabbit!' he told himself severely. 'It's just water, and it's dark. There's nothing special about that.' But all the same he found his spirits crushed out of him by the thought of having to plunge back down into that ghastly blackness.

'Come on, Tom! You've just thrown your clothes over the wall,' he reminded himself. 'You've got to go . . . you've no choice.'

And that was it. He had no papers, he had no horse, he had no clothes, and now he had no choice. He took a deep, deep breath and dived back into the inky stream. Down he swam, and forward . . . feeling with his hands in front of him . . . trying to keep the fear down in his chest . . . trying not to imagine something unholy . . . something unspeakable . . . suddenly flying at him from the invisible nearness . . . and at that moment his hands suddenly touched something . . .

Panic seized Tom again and he struggled back up to

the surface, only to find he was now under the postern bridge and there was no surface . . . the water came up right to the roof of the channel. His lungs were by this time at bursting point. He struggled round in the water and swam back desperately, feeling the rough stone of the underside of the bridge . . . it seemed to go on and on . . . he couldn't carry on another second . . . his lungs craved the air . . . he had to breathe! He didn't care whether it was air or water – he just had to take a breath . . . even if it was water it would be better than this . . . but at that second the roof of the channel rose a few inches and Tom thrust his head out of the water gasping and retching for air.

His head whirled and it took him some moments to gather his wits. When he did, he realised that what his hands had come up against, back down there in the inky depths, was a metal grille. Of course! The good people of Milan wouldn't have left this as a secret way into their city. There must be an underwater barrier of some sort across the channel.

He was a fool for thinking he'd be able to get in here. And he cursed himself for throwing away his clothes before he'd found out whether he could or not.

'Right!' he told himself. 'Situation, Alternatives, Action . . . well, the situation is obvious. The alternatives are to go back to Pavia without my clothes or . . .

or what? To try and see if the portcullis is totally impenetrable?'

Once again Tom's heart sank like a millstone in a mill-pond. How could he go back down there, knowing there was no way up to the air? He stared through the black night at the black water and shuddered, both with the cold and with the fear of what he must under-take.

'You have no choice,' he reminded himself, took a deep breath and plunged back in. This time he swam faster, and before he could even think of turning back again he'd reached the portcullis. Feverishly he started to explore it with his hands. It quickly became apparent that he didn't have a chance of getting through the gaps in the ironwork, but then he went down . . . his lungs already starting to ache . . . and suddenly . . . wonderfully . . . he discovered the bottom of the port-cullis was a few inches off the bottom of the ditch.

He was almost sure he could squeeze under it, but now he was running out of breath again, and he real-ised that he had no idea how far would he have to swim on the other side before he could come up for air. So he swiftly turned around and swam back to his breathing place on the bank.

His teeth were now chattering like a hundred death-watch beetles at an undertakers' picnic, and he was shivering uncontrollably. But the next second he was diving back down into the blackness, and then he was squeezing under the portcullis, and next moment he was through and swimming up, and suddenly he broke the surface and was gratefully pulling in great gulps of air. He was frozen, he was shaking, he was half dead, but he was inside the city.

Well . . . sort of . . .

The water ran along a channel in between the city wall and another wall that rose four or five feet above the level of the water. It was impossible to haul himself out.

A little further along, however, Tom could see an iron ring fixed into the wall. He managed to pull himself up onto this, and, prising his fingers into a crack in the stonework above, he was able to pull his feet up into the ring. From there, he was able to stand on the ring and could just reach the top of the wall.

Normally it would have been a simple matter to pull himself up, but he felt as if the water and the blackness between them had washed all the strength out of him. Eventually, however, he got his leg over the wall and then dropped into the street outside the southern postern gate.

All he had to do was find his clothes . . . but what clothes? Surely they weren't that dark object that had somehow become lodged up on the roof of that house next to the gate?

'Here we go again,' said Tom, and he dragged himself onto the lowest window ledge. Then he hauled himself up to the upper window and, balancing on tiptoe on the window ledge, managed to reach the bundle on the roof. At which point the adjacent shutter of the window was flung open and a woman's hand reached out and yanked him into a room.

'Rudolpho!' whispered the woman. 'You're naked!'

The interior was as dark as the night outside, and Tom could see the woman no more than she could see him, but that didn't seem to inhibit her in the slightest, for she was now running her hands over his back and kissing him before he could think of what to say.

'And you're wet!' she cried. 'Oh! You're so impetuous!' And she kissed him again and again, once more preventing Tom from speaking.

To tell the truth, Tom couldn't think what to say. The moment he opened his mouth, this unseen woman would realise he was not her Rudolpho, and she'd presumably scream blue murder and bring the nightwatch down on him.

Then again, her hands were now straying to parts of his anatomy that made it imperative that he say something. So he pinned her arms to her side.

'Oh Rudolpho!' she managed to say, 'I love it when you're rough!'

Tom clapped his hand over her mouth and whispered into her ear: 'Don't scream. I'm not Rudolpho, I was just getting my clothes from your roof.'

The moment the woman heard Tom's voice, she went absolutely rigid, and the next minute she was kicking and biting and it was all Tom could do to restrain her.

Eventually, however, she stopped and Tom was able to whisper: 'I'm not going to do you any harm. I'm simply going to get dressed and leave, and I apologise for the intrusion. It was all a mistake.'

When he felt certain she had calmed down sufficiently, he removed his hand from her mouth. She didn't scream and so he released her altogether and felt around for his bundle of clothes, which had fallen on the floor.

'Who are you?' she hissed.

'I am Sir Thomas English,' said Tom. 'I'm frightfully sorry for waking you up.'

By this time Tom had located his bundle of clothing and had started to pull on his hose, at which point the woman suddenly started to scream.

'I could understand it if you'd started screaming when I took my clothes off – but why now when I'm putting them on?' he growled at her under his breath. 'It's so irrational!'

The next second, however, Tom thought it was perfectly rational. There seemed every reason to scream, for a figure had just appeared at the window and was currently whispering:

'Filippa!'

'Oh! Rudolpho!' she cried, running to the window.

'Sh!' whispered the figure at the window. 'You'll wake your husband!'

'Thank goodness you're here!' hissed Filippa.

'What is it?' whispered Rudolpho, jumping into the room.

Filippa was apparently too overcome to explain anything to her lover, and was now happily sobbing in his arms. And Rudolpho, for his part, was only too happy to console her. Tom grabbed his doublet and shoes and made a dash for the window.

'Ah!' yelled Rudolpho in alarm. 'Your husband!'

'No!' was all Filippa could get out.

'No?' exclaimed Rudolpho.

'I'm just leaving,' said Tom, but before he could reach the window, he felt his arm grabbed.

'Cheerio!' said Tom.

'Filippa!' cried Rudolpho. 'There's a half-naked man in your room!'

'It's not what you think!' said Tom, groaning inwardly at the thought of having to explain the situation all over again. Mercifully he was spared the bother, as Rudolpho, at that precise moment, punched him in the stomach.

Tom doubled up as Rudolpho span round and glared at Filippa – as well as it is possible to glare in darkness.

'What's going on?' he hissed.

'It's not what you think!' exclaimed Filippa.

'It's not her fault!' Even in this extremity, Tom felt he ought to put the record straight. 'She thought I was you . . .' But he might as well have saved his breath, for Rudolpho was not, apparently, in the right mood for listening. Kicking someone or punching them, yes, but certainly not listening to them. What Rudolpho really wanted to do was to hit Tom over the head with the first thing that came to hand. It happened to be the chamber pot.

'Not the pot!' cried Filippa, who was nothing if not house-proud, though inclined to postpone emptying out the night soil for days on end. But it was too late – the contents of the pot had already been generously distributed around the room.

'Ow!' exclaimed Tom, momentarily forgetting the need for silence.

'Sh!' cried Filippa, following suit.

'Fiend!' screamed Rudolpho, throwing all caution to the wind, as well as the chamber pot, and at the same time getting a stranglehold on Tom's neck.

Now Tom had nothing personally against Rudolpho, apart from his knee, but during their short acquaintance he'd not been over-impressed with the fellow's ability to see the best in human nature. And, indeed, if you could have looked into Rudolpho's brain at that precise moment, it's doubtful whether you could have told whether he thought he was wringing Tom's neck or his lover's . . . to be honest, either would have done.

Tom, for the third or even fourth time that night, suddenly found himself struggling to breathe, and he felt a darkness coming down behind his eyes, as he desperately struggled to free his windpipe from the demonic grip of the enraged Rudolpho.

But it was no use . . . Rudolpho's hands tightened, and although Filippa cried and tried to pull Rudolpho away, the man seemed possessed with an almost supernatural energy, until suddenly it all changed. Tom realised he could breathe again.

He opened his eyes to discover that an even more enraged figure had just hurtled through the door. The newcomer was holding a candle and by its light Tom could see his assailant for the first time. He was a handsome enough fellow, even though his face was contorted in rage. Tom could also see Filippa for the first time, and he was surprised to see how plain she was, considering she had two men fighting over her affections, for the bringer of the light, Tom had no doubt, was Filippa's husband.

The good gentleman had been harbouring suspicions about his wife's behaviour for some time, and it was not exactly a surprise to now enter her room and find that his suspicions were fully justified. What he had not bargained for, however, was to find her entertaining not one but two lovers. The effect on his already disturbed mind was terrifying.

He leapt onto the nearest lover, who happened to be Rudolpho, and proceeded to vent the pain and anger that had built up through the years on the skull of that unhappy man.

Filippa screamed, Rudolpho roared, and Tom leapt out of the window.

Plain as she was, he would have liked to have said goodbye to the lady and to apologise once again for intruding, but he decided that this was not the best moment.

And so it was that Tom landed in the street, struggled into his doublet and shoes and ran as fast as he could, just a second before the nightwatch appeared around the corner.

Chapter 22

Saint-Flour 1361

As Tom, Ann and Emily made their laborious way towards Sir Robert Knolles' army, Tom found himself struggling with a confusion of feelings.

On the one hand he was feeling optimistic about the future. Emily had promised to have a word with her brother, Guillaume de Valois, as soon as they'd rescued him from his prison in England.

'He'll make you his squire – no doubt about it!' said Emily. 'If we rescue him, he'll probably knight you into the bargain – just like that!'

And yet there was something else that acted as an undertow to this promise of a future tidal wave of happiness. But whatever that undertow was, Tom didn't want to examine it too closely just now. For the moment it was enough that Emily was happy and being unusually gracious in her dealings with him.

Terry Jones

What's more the pair of them had found a joint pro-ject, which seemed to bring them closer with every mile they travelled . . . and it was all the doing of the good folk of Marvejols . . .

The townsfolk had been so grateful for their release from the Beast of Gévaudan that they had given Tom, Emily and Ann a present each. Emily was given a new dress, which she said made her look like a peasant and refused to wear. Ann – or rather Alan – was given the very crossbow with which she had shot down the Beast. And Tom was given a *citole*.

'Well, it's very nice of them,' said Tom to Ann as they were making their way out of Marvejols, with the cheering citizens seeing them off, 'but I haven't a clue what to do with it.'

'Well, it's no good looking at me,' replied Ann. 'I'm tone-deaf.'

'I'll show you,' said Emily. And she took the musical instrument out of Tom's hands and started tuning it as they walked along.

Some time later, Ann and Tom were intrigued to hear genuinely melodious sounds coming from their companion. They turned to see Emily playing the *citole* as she strolled along, looking for all the world like an angel who had just dropped down from heaven. Well, at least that's what Tom thought.

'I never knew you could play!' exclaimed Tom, when she'd caught them up.

'Every young lady plays a *citole* nowadays,' said Emily. It was, apparently, a well-known fact.

'Is that what this is?' asked Tom, taking the instrument back from Emily. It was the shape of a fiddle only smaller, and instead of being played with a bow, Emily had been strumming the strings with a quill that had been tucked through the strings.

'It's considered the most suitable thing for young ladies,' said Emily. 'I'll teach you to play, if you like.'

'Except I'm not a young lady,' pointed out Tom.

'It's not *only* young ladies who play it,' she replied. 'Anyone can play it. I'll show you as we walk along.'

And that was how they covered many miles of France, with Ann hurrying on ahead and Emily and Tom dawdling behind, as Emily taught Tom the notes and chords of the *citole*.

Tom had always been a quick learner, and pretty soon, Emily was teaching him tunes and songs that she had learned. And by the time they reached the town of Saint-Flour, Tom was able to play and sing: 'Lady Do Not Look at Me', and 'So Sweetly My Senses Are Imprisoned'.

'They are both composed by Guillaume de Machaut,' said Emily. 'He is our greatest songwriter in France.'

As far as Tom was concerned Guillaume de Machaut was the greatest songwriter in the world. His songs so closely expressed what Tom was feeling. Or was it the other way round? Perhaps it was the songs that were suggesting Tom's current emotional state? Maybe the love-longing of the songs was like a contagious illness and Tom had contracted it.

Certainly, whenever Emily touched his fingers to show him the right string or help him to the right fret, he felt as hot as if he had a fever.

Ann was waiting for them on the bridge.

The town of Saint-Flour was perched above the river Ander on a steep promontory. It was surrounded by a fine city wall and had a look of impregnability that was only partly diminished by the fact that the town had spilled over the wall and down onto the banks of the river.

These suburbs were draped around the hillside like the necklace around Emily's neck, thought Tom, who was still feeling poetic as a result of the his exposure to Guillaume de Machaut. This suburb was ringed by its own wall, which ran along the edge of the river, and yet there were more buildings on the other side of the water which remained unprotected, and most curiously of all, there was an odd little house on the bridge itself.

Ann was sitting on the parapet of the bridge with her back against the little house.

'What have you two been up to?' she asked.

'Emily has been teaching me some songs,' said Tom guiltily – although why he should feel guilty he had no idea.

'He learns quickly,' said Emily the Great Teacher. 'Play "So Sweetly My Senses", Tom.'

'I'm not sure I can remember it all.'

'Just play what you can,' said Emily.

'I'd like to hear it,' said Ann.

So Tom lifted the *citole* into the playing position, fumbled for the right chords for a moment, and then sang:

'So sweetly my senses are imprisoned
When love holds me in such a sweet prison.
I never want to be released
So sweetly my senses are imprisoned.'

There was a short silence after he finished, and then an almost inaudible voice murmured: 'That was beautiful.'

For a moment, Emily and Ann each imagined they had simply heard their own thoughts, so soft and intangible was the voice – indeed it was hardly a voice, more the shadow of a voice.

'Did you say something?' whispered Ann, but Emily shook her head.

'Hello?' said Tom. 'Is someone there?'

But there was no one to be seen and there was no reply.

'That's weird,' said Ann. 'I could swear I heard someone say, "that was beautiful" – which, by the way, it was, Tom. How did you learn that so quickly?'

'He's naturally very musical,' said Emily, as if it were all her doing.

'Sh!' said Tom. 'Listen.'

The three of them held their breaths and listened . . . and then they could hear it . . . so faint it might not really exist . . . but there it was . . . the ghost of a sound of someone sobbing.

'It's coming from inside,' whispered Ann, who had her ear up against the wall of the little house on the bridge.

'It can't be!' whispered Emily.

'Listen,' said Ann. And they all put their ears to the wall of the little house in the middle of the bridge, and they too heard, coming from within, the faint sound of a girl sobbing.

'How could there be anyone in there?' whispered Tom, for the little house in the middle of the bridge of Saint-Flour over the river Ander was no more than a couple of metres square. Moreover, it had neither door nor window.

'Hello?' Ann called into a small slit that was the only opening in the wall. But the only reply was silence. The sobbing had stopped.

'Is there anyone there?'

The silence hung there for some moments until eventually the shadow of a voice said: 'I am sorry. I should not cry.'

'Who are you?' asked Ann.

There was a slight pause . . . as if whoever it was was a little taken aback by the question.

Then came the reply: 'I am the Maid of the Bridge, of course.'

'We are strangers,' said Tom. 'We have only just arrived.'

'What are you doing in there?' this was Emily joining in.

'I am the Maid of the Bridge,' was the only reply.

'But how do you get in and out?' asked Tom.

'I don't.'

Tom began to feel he wasn't really following this conversation at all.

'You don't go in and out?' asked Ann. 'What do you mean?'

There was silence, in which they could hear the girl

inside the little house shifting. 'What are you talking about?' repeated Ann.

'I am supposed to stay here,' said the invisible girl.

'Have you done something wrong?' asked Emily.

'No.'

'Then why are you in there?'

Again there was a silence, as if the girl were trying to decide whether to answer such an obvious question.

'I am the guardian of the bridge.'

'The guardian of the bridge!' Tom couldn't help exclaiming. He wanted to go on to say: 'You're stuck in that box! How can you guard anything!' But somehow he felt it was not quite the right thing to say under the circumstances.

So it was Emily who said it: 'But you're stuck in that box!' she exclaimed. 'How can you guard anything?'

'I pray,' said the Maid of the Bridge.

'You pray?' asked Ann.

'That is my job,' said the Maid of the Bridge. 'They say that as long as I am here, praying, the bridge will be safe. The English will never destroy it or sack the town of Saint-Flour.'

'But when do they let you out?' asked Tom.

There was yet another silence. Then the voice came again only even quieter, so that it was hardly there at all: 'I volunteered with the rest. They chose me to be the Maid of the Bridge out of all the other girls in the town,' said the Maid of the Bridge. 'I have endured four months since they walled me in . . .'

'They walled you in?' Tom's voice was almost hoarse.

'Yes. Of course. It is a sacrifice.'

'You mean they'll never let you out?'

'I am near the church of St Christine. I can hear the services.'

The three friends went quiet – partly because none of them could think what to say, and partly because a little old man was shuffling across the bridge towards them. He looked at them hostilely – as if they were intruding on his private bridge.

'Good day to you,' said Tom.

The old man glared and mumbled 'good day' back at them before shuffling up towards the little house. He put his mouth to the slit in the wall and whispered:

'Giovanna!'

At the same time he produced a slice of bread from under his cloak. He poked it through the slit, and the friends watched as it was taken in by the anchoress.

'Thank you, Iacobus,' said the Maid of the Bridge.

'I wish I had more to give,' said the old man.

'May heaven bless your kindness.'

The old man looked round at Tom, Ann and Emily,

and Tom once again felt they should not be there, especially as the old man kept on looking at them.

Tom glanced at Ann and Ann glanced at Emily and Emily glanced at Tom, and then, as if on a prearranged signal, the three of them turned and started walking away from the little house on the bridge into the faubourg of the town of Saint-Flour.

But before they got out of earshot they just heard the old man whispering: 'Giovanna! Will you bless my knee – it has been hurting again . . .'

They could not really hear her reply, but each would have sworn that the words that drifted over the bridge in the evening air were: 'Iacobus! Tell my mother I dreamed of her . . .'

Chapter 23

Saint-Flour 1361

'We sacked Auxerre last year,' said the soldier. Tom and Ann were sitting under the vines drinking wine and eating pieces of preserved duck. The soldier was an Englishman who looked as if he had been created specifically to make barrels out of. His head alone was the size of a firkin and seemed to come straight out of his shoulders without a neck. His chest was a good hogshead and his thighs were kilderkins.

He also seemed to have personally taken over the function of a barrel, and had spent the best part of the evening filling himself up with gallon after gallon of wine and beer.

'The main army's still there, but some of us have come further south. Rich pickings down here they say.'

Ann had found the previous conversation a trifle tedious. It had mainly concerned the various ways in which an Englishman of a certain barrelage could mistreat Frenchmen. But her ears pricked up at this last observation.

Tom, meanwhile, was dreading having to eat while listening to yet more accounts of what you can do with livers, spleens, bowels and kidneys once they've been surgically removed on the battlefield. But he was absolved from such punishment by Ann interrupting in her best Squire Alan voice:

'Who led the English into Auxerre?'

'That rogue Bob Knolles!' grinned the human butt. 'God save him! He's downed more Frenchies than I've downed cups of wine!'

It seemed such an unlikely claim to Tom that he was about to question it, when the Englishman went on:

'Here's to the rogue!'

The Englishman raised his tumbler to his lips just to show how well he did his sort of downing.

But Ann was frowning. 'Sir Robert Knolles has not returned to Brittany then?' she asked.

The Englishman shook his head. 'I should think not! He's doing all right where he is for now,' he grinned. 'But some of us have come further south. You'll meet Bob Knolles' Englishmen all the way from here to Auxerre. Good luck to 'em!'

Ann's face seemed to light up with this news. 'There

are members of his army even as far south as here?'
she asked.

'Look at me! I'm one of 'em – though it's only a few
of us come this far.' He nodded over to the other table,
where a ragged group of Englishmen were currently
slumped over their cups of wine in a state of possibly
terminal intoxication.

Tom watched Ann look the men over eagerly, and
then turn away. The barrel-man dropped his voice:
'We're just scouting this place now, you see. Should
make a pretty penny out of Saint-Flour.'

'What'll you do?' asked Tom. The Englishman looked
at Tom as if he had just fallen out of heaven. Then he
threw back his head and – well, I suppose he laughed,
but it sounded more like the bubbling of lava in a vol-
cano.

'What'll we do? Why! We don't attack the town!
That's what we'll do!'

Tom kicked himself. Of course, that's how most free-
booters made their money. A big enough army could
charge whatever it liked in return for the favour of not
burning somewhere to the ground.

At that moment, however, Tom forgot all about the
economics of mercenary armies, for Emily had
appeared, looking like the sun in splendour.

'How does she do it?' wondered Tom. 'We walk for

mile after mile along the dusty roads and she disappears for a couple of hours and reappears looking as if she were hosting a banquet for the king!'

The English barrel-man gave a low whistle.

'Now there's some pretty plumage and no mistake,' he muttered. 'She'd be worth a penny or two for the plucking.'

He was suddenly looking around the other tables, craning what would have been his neck if he'd had one, in order to see better.

'A princess like that must have a fair-sized escort with her, but I don't see none.' There was a rising excitement in his voice. 'Now listen, here, my fine friends, we can line our pockets tonight if you stick with me . . . let's see who this elegant lady is with . . .'

It was at that moment that Emily reached their table and sat down.

'You started without me!' she pointed out.

She looked so beautiful that Tom could neither speak nor think for a few moments. But Ann could.

'Emily!' she snorted. 'You can't expect us to wait around forever while you dress up in that fancy costume as if you were a lady!'

'Where is my food?' asked Emily, going straight to the point.

The English soldier, meanwhile, was looking from

Emily to Tom to Ann. Tom knew exactly what was going through the man's mind. Perhaps if the fellow had poured slightly less wine into his barrel chest, his thoughts would have been slightly less transparent. As it was Tom could almost hear the gold coins already jingling in the man's head.

'You're too late to eat!' It was Squire Alan speaking. 'We've got to report at the guardhouse, remember? Sir William and his men are expecting us before sunset.'

'What are you talki—' began Emily, but Tom cut her off.

'You're right!' he exclaimed, having suddenly realised that Ann was reading the English soldier's mind in exactly the same way as he was. 'There are thirty men-at-arms waiting for us – and we're sitting here stuffing our faces!'

'You may have been stuffing *your* faces, but mine has not been stuffed for some time,' replied Emily. 'And I intend to stuff it now.' Whenever Emily was hungry she had no time for the subtleties of conversation.

'I'm having the goose,' she announced.

'No . . . you're not! You're coming with us to find your escort!'

Tom and Squire Alan both had a hand under Emily's arms and were trying to lift her off her seat.

'Wait up there!' The English soldier had leaned

across and grabbed Emily's wrist. 'It seems to me like this fine lady don't want to go nowhere,' he said.

'Take your filthy hand off me! You oaf!'

Emily was finally beginning to come round into the conversational frame.

'That's why we've got to go,' hissed Ann in Emily's ear. 'He means trouble!'

'Now seems to me you wouldn't be so unfriendly as to leave before we've taken a drink or two together,' leered the vat-like Englishman. 'Ow!'

This last remark was addressed to Emily, who had just freed her wrist from his grip and slapped him across the face.

'How dare you lay hands on me! You scum!' she said, and suddenly and unexpectedly she punched the man extremely hard on the end of his nose.

'Owwwwwww!' he yelled. Tom sympathised. He knew what Emily's punches were like.

'Let's get out of here!' whispered Ann, and she and Tom started to make for the door.

But Emily was sitting down again on the bench, and was signalling to the serving girl with the tray of food.

The barrel-like Englishman was too astonished to move. He was just sitting there holding his nose and – oddly enough – crying.

'Well! Don't sit there snivelling,' Emily said. 'I have

no intention of eating my meal at the same table as pigs' droppings like you. Make yourself scarce!'

She waved him away with her delicate white hand, and without another word the tun of English soldiery grabbed his wine jug and obediently staggered over to join his soporific companions, where he too slumped over the table with his head in his hands.

Ann and Tom looked at each other.

'Damn! They've already given her some goose,' muttered Tom. 'We'll never get her away until she's eaten it.'

'Why does she have to come down looking like that?' growled Ann. 'Has she no idea how to look inconspicuous?'

'No. She hasn't,' said Tom. It was a matter of fact.

But then how could Emily – the beautiful Emily – ever look 'inconspicuous', thought Tom. Even if she dressed in rags from head to foot, she'd still be as lovely as the sun coming up out of the sea, as beautiful as . . .

'That drunken slob of an Englishman,' it was Ann puncturing Tom's romantic reverie, 'is not going to give over just because she punched him. We can't stay here.'

'But we can't walk around the streets with Emily dressed like that!' said Tom. 'She'll attract all the robbers in town.'

'And not just the robbers,' retorted Ann.

'What d'you mean?' asked Tom, but Ann was looking at him with such a mocking smile that he thought
maybe he wouldn't bother to find out.

'I've got an idea,' said Ann, and she suddenly became
Squire Alan again, and was striding over to the bench
where the English barrel-man was still sitting and snivelling.

Squire Alan sat down beside him and put a hand on
his shoulder. 'Listen!' he whispered. 'If you want to
make some real money tonight, I know where they
keep the town treasure.'

The English soldier stopped snivelling and looked at
Squire Alan. 'What are you saying?'

'We need some strong hands. There's gold and plenty
of silver florins involved. We just need someone big like
you. But for goodness sake don't tell your mates. We
can just divide it up between ourselves.'

The man narrowed his eyes. 'Where's this treasure?'

Ann glanced round the other tables, conspiratorially.
'I can't tell you here . . . but meet us outside the inn
when night falls and if you come with us, you'll find
out.'

'I can't trust you,' said the Englishman. It was probably the only accurate thought he'd had all evening.

'That's up to you,' whispered Alan. 'If you don't
want to join us, don't. One thing is for sure – there's

more than enough treasure for each of us. But we need some brute force.'

The English soldier turned this over in his mind. Brute force was the sort of thing he was good at.

'All right. Maybe. I'll see,' he said and downed his wine.

'But we can't do that!' exclaimed Tom 'It's totally and completely and utterly crazy to even consider it!'

'It makes my blood boil,' said Ann, 'to think of these fine, upstanding burghers all buying into that superstitious rubbish!'

'How d'you know it isn't true?' asked Emily.

'It's worse than stupid! It's barbaric!' snapped Ann. 'How is walling up that poor girl in that dreadful place going to keep their precious bridge safe?'

'But should we be interfering in the town's business?' began Tom.

'Should *they* be making a human sacrifice? Because that's what it is!' Ann was more passionate than Tom had ever seen her.

'We've got to get to Auxerre . . . it's only a few days north of here . . .' said Tom.

'We'll get there,' replied Ann. 'But I'd never forgive myself if I didn't try to help that poor girl.'

'Don't you want to see Peter de Bury?'

'I'll see him soon enough,' said Ann, and at that point Tom realised there was no arguing with her.

Emily had been persuaded to change into something less eye-catching, and the three of them were now waiting for the English barrel-man to appear.

'Why is *he* coming?' Emily was scowling.

'The best way of neutralising an enemy is to get them on your side,' explained Ann. 'It's an old technique. Besides we're going to need him. It's not easy to demolish a wall, you know.'

'But what happens when he finds out there isn't any treasure on the bridge?' Tom thought it was such an obvious question he couldn't believe Ann hadn't thought of it.

'How d'you know there isn't?' asked Ann.

'Er . . .' said Tom. It was an equally obvious point.

'Sh!' said Emily. 'He's coming.'

The English soldier-cum-barrel was rolling down the street towards them, and came to a rest beside the trio.

'Right!' he whispered – clearly relishing the cloak-and-dagger scenario. 'Let's go and open this treasure chest up!' He was carrying a couple of iron bars.

'Look out for the nightwatch,' whispered Tom.

And the little party crept down the hill from the sleeping town of Saint-Flour, to release the Maid of the Bridge.

Chapter 24

Milan 1385

Sir Thomas couldn't think of a single decent disguise shop in the whole of Milan.

'Typical, isn't it?' he said to himself. 'Just when you need one, you can't find one.' Actually he couldn't think of a single decent disguise shop in the whole of Italy. In fact, come to think of it, he couldn't think of a single decent disguise shop in the whole world. Such things just didn't exist back in the fourteenth century, any more than they do today.

'But wouldn't it be great?' thought Tom. 'If I could just walk in off the street and say: give me a beard and a new set of clothes. Oh! And some new papers please?'

However, in view of the dearth of disguise shops, he would have to fend for himself. One thing he was quite certain about was that he couldn't walk around Milan as he was. He'd seen yet another *pittura infamante* featuring himself and a gallows. This one had been in the square outside the Basilica Nova.

It was all very well to walk around with his hood up, but as the day began to get hotter that in itself would start to look suspicious.

He decided there was only one thing he could do.

The girl who brought up the water looked at him curiously. He was sitting in an upstairs room of an inn, looking out of the window. He still had his hood over his head.

'It's warm,' she said, nodding to the jug she'd just put beside him.

'Thanks,' said Tom, and then waited for her to go, but the girl stood by the doorway, leaning up against the wall with her arms folded.

'Thank you,' said Tom again.

'It must be cold,' she said.

'What must be?'

'Where you come from . . . Norway . . .'

'I come from England,' said Tom.

'Is that further than Norway?' she asked.

'Well . . . no . . . it's not . . .'

'But it's cold,' she insisted.

'Not always,' replied Tom. 'Sometimes it's almost as warm as it is here.'

'Huh! This place . . .' she snorted.

'Aren't you proud of your city?' asked Tom, for most Milanese were.

'We have the best water in the world,' she replied.

'So I've been told,' said Tom.

'Would you like to take me to England?' asked the girl suddenly.

Tom narrowed his eyes and looked at her. 'I haven't been there for some years,' he said.

The girl merely sighed and said: 'You can take me there if you want.'

Tom began to feel that this was not at all the conversation that he needed right now.

'I would very much enjoy showing you my country and my home . . . but I'm not sure I have either any more . . .' and it was Tom's turn to sigh as he remembered a little cottage amongst the bindweed and dandelions, where old Molly Christmas looked after him and his sister, Katie, after their parents had died in the great plague.

Ah! Katie . . . what had become of her? He wondered. She would be a wife and mother now, and even her children might well be grown up . . . but it was all another life . . . someone else's life . . . not Tom's . . . he had run away when the abbot wanted to put him in his school . . . he had run away to find the

231

Terry Jones

deserts of Arabia, the court of Prester John, the land of Saladin, the plains of Asia, the glittering streets of Constantinople and the frozen wastes of Russia . . .

'Aren't you going to wash then?' The serving girl's voice suddenly brought him back to the present.

'Yes,' he said. 'But I would rather do it alone, if you don't mind.'

The girl gave him another queer look and said: 'I wouldn't mind going to England . . . anywhere . . .'

'Well, if I decide to go back to my country, I'll let you know,' said Tom.

'I'll be here,' she said, and for the first time she smiled and then was gone.

But her questions hung around him like interfering flies around a compost heap – buzzing in his ears and provoking into life old memories that he thought he had long ago discarded. And the thoughts that now leaked from that mulch of old feelings and desires made him restive and oddly dissatisfied with the present.

Tom poured the water into the bowl and threw off his hood and doublet. He wet his hair, took up his razor and without more ado began to scrape at his scalp.

Tom had never been bald before. He felt the smooth surface of his skull and looked at his distorted reflection in the pewter jug. The whole operation was an unqualified success, for he found himself looking at the bright pink scalp of someone he'd never seen before.

A surprising relief swept over him, and for the first time since he'd discovered the *pittura infamante*, he was able to think straight about the situation.

Regina della Scala had warned him that Bernabò suspected him of treason. It seemed most likely that the Lord of Milan would have ordered the pictures when Tom had disappeared. Or, there again, could it perhaps be the work of Donnina de' Porri? Could she have accused him of making advances to her after all? And would that mean that Squire John was in grave danger . . . or worse?

Whatever the explanation, his mission was going to be even harder than he had anticipated.

The next day, Tom presented himself at the kitchen gates of the palace of Bernabò Visconti, wearing a bright red tunic, only slightly frayed at the cuffs, and brandishing a *citole* – both of which he'd picked up for a bargain price in the market.

'I can do "The Squire of Low Degree",' he told the steward. '"Sir Orfeo" and a novelty number called "King Edward and the Shepherd". They are all English tales but, of course, I can render them into Italian for your guests.'

Terry Jones

'Can't you do any good plain Italian tales?' replied the steward. 'My lord is out of sorts with the English, since one of those sons of perdition not only plotted against him but even tried to make love to the Lady Donnina.'

Ah! So he was guilty on both counts, but on the other hand the steward didn't seem to recognise him as the son of perdition in question.

'It is painful to hear of the evil deeds of one's own countrymen,' said Tom, bowing his head in collective shame. 'But yes, I have by heart several tales of Signor Bocaccio and several other notable songs of Lombardy and Tuscany.'

The steward nodded Tom into the servants' quarters.

'You will be required to play at supper with the other musicians. You may sing something while the dishes are being cleared.'

Tom had counted on the steward needing some new blood amongst the musicians, and had rightly guessed that even Bernabò Visconti's steward wouldn't let the lack of identity papers get in the way of employing fresh entertainment.

He was back in the court of Bernabò Visconti, and the only identification he needed was his *citole*. The snag was that instead of being an honoured guest, he was now a minstrel, and that meant he was a menial –

hardly someone who would be allowed to mix with the likes of Regina della Scala.

'Oh, and you . . . what's your name?'

Tom turned – the steward was calling after him.

'Robin of Arundel,' said Tom.

'Robin. Right,' nodded the steward. 'My lord will expect you to sing a tribute to the memory of Regina della Scala.'

Tom's jaw hit his *citole*. 'Is the Lady Regina della Scala dead?'

'Why do you think there's so much black around town?' asked the steward.

'The townsfolk must have been very fond of her,' said Tom.

'The townsfolk are very fond of their money.' The steward had lowered his voice. 'Anyone not wearing mourning is fined. I hope you've got a suitable elegy you can adapt.'

'How did she die?' asked Tom innocently.

The steward looked around carefully. Nobody seemed to be taking any notice of them. He narrowed his eyes, looking shrewdly at Tom, and then in an almost inaudible voice, he whispered carefully and slowly: 'She died of . . . natural . . . causes.'

'Oh!' said Tom.

The steward kept looking at Tom, as if he were trying

to work out how Tom's head stayed on his shoulders.

'Don't believe them as says she was poisoned . . .' whispered the steward.

'Of course not,' said Tom.

'The Lady Donnina loved Regina della Scala well enough,' breathed the steward.

'I know that to be true,' said Tom, 'from my own experience.' He bowed to the steward and made his way inside.

So that was it! The Lady Donnina had seemed to get on well enough with Regina della Scala, but clearly not well enough to prevent her from poisoning her.

Tom found a place in the servant's loft with a sinking heart. If Regina della Scala was dead, so too was any hope he had of extracting information about Bernabò's plans. What's more, if he had feared the Lady Donnina before, now he was petrified of her . . . how could he ever hope to extract information out of such a woman? He knew it was simply beyond his powers.

He might just as well pack up and go home . . . except that he had to find Squire John.

The town of Milan may have been in mourning for the wife of its lord, Bernabò Visconti, but Bernabò Visconti himself didn't appear to be. It's true he was wearing black from head to foot, but then he'd always thought he looked rather good in black. And it's true that all the lords and ladies of the court and all the servants even down to the least menials were suitably fitted out in black. But the overall effect was one of elegant chic rather than mourning.

There was certainly nothing mournful about the quails and the sauced pigeons that they ate for the evening meal, nor about the sweetbreads and the sliced boar's head. Nor was there anything the least melancholic about the wine that flowed – white and red – out of the copious gilded jugs.

And although Tom had been given a black tunic to wear in his function as a minstrel, the music that he found himself joining in during the feast fitted well with the un-grief-stricken atmosphere of laughter and gaiety that filled the hall.

Eventually the dishes of the first course were cleared away, and Tom saw the steward whispering to the great Lord and pointing in his direction.

This was it, then. Would Bernabò recognise the erstwhile treacherous Englishman? Tom suddenly realised that the tests so far had been quite modest . . . he'd been talking to people in ill-lit rooms and doorways. Now he was to step forward as the centre of attention . . . an attention which it was his duty to hold for some time . . . while people ran their eyes over every inch of his body and every pore of his skin. It was hardly a comfortable position for a would-be spy in disguise to find himself in.

However, there was no going back now.

Tom took a deep breath as the Lord of Milan raised his finger towards him, and stepped forward. All eyes in the room turned on Tom.

Chapter 25

Saint-Flour 1361

The moon was peering over the city of Saint-Flour as if it were trying to get a better look at what was going on down below on the bridge over the river Ander.

Tom, Ann, Emily and the huge barrel-shaped Englishman, whose name unsurprisingly turned out to be 'Barrel', had arrived on the bridge without being spotted by the nightwatch. They crept up to the little house in the centre of the bridge and Ann whispered through the slit in the wall.

'Giovanna!'

There was a pause, and when the reply came, it was from someone who was already wide awake:

'Who's there?'

'It's us,' whispered Ann, still in her Squire Alan mode. 'The strangers who talked to you earlier.'

'The one who sang? Is he there?'

239

'Yes, I'm here,' said Tom.

'We've come to get you out,' whispered Ann.

'No . . .' came the response.

'Yes!' cried Tom. 'We really have!'

'What's all this about?' The rough voice of Barrel the Englishman cut over the sound of the river running below them. 'Who's in there?'

'She's the guardian of the treasure,' whispered Ann.

'Well, look out, lassie!' cried the Englishman in English. 'That's all mine now!' And before anyone could stop him, he had started attacking the wall with one of the iron bars.

'No! Stop! Please!' cried the Maid of the Bridge.

'Mind out in there!' yelled the Englishman.

'Careful!' said Tom. But Barrel seemed to have been seized by some powerful demon that doubled his strength and halved his powers of comprehension. He had loosened one stone already and was in the process of smashing it in without the slightest regard for anyone who might happen to be on the other side.

'Watch out for the girl!' cried Ann.

'Please stop!' cried the Maid of the Bridge.

'Where's the gold!' yelled Barrel, smashing the iron bar into the next stone and prising it loose with surprising ease.

'You mustn't do this!'

A face had appeared in the opening that had been created. It was a thin white face – the face of a ghost or of someone who was not quite alive and not quite dead.

But the Englishman didn't even see it . . . he was far too preoccupied smashing at the stone like a man possessed. Bits of rock flew in all directions, and the next moment a second stone had been dislodged.

'Please!' cried the ghost from inside.

'Stop that!' cried another voice.

'It's the nightwatch!' yelled Emily, taking to her heels across to the far side of the bridge in search of a hiding spot.

'Stop them!' cried another member of the watch.

'It's going to a good cause!' cried Barrel, who was totally unaware of the new arrivals. 'Ah!'

This last exclamation was occasioned by an arrow which had grazed one of his arms before bouncing off the wall of the little house. Another arrow shot past Tom's ears and disappeared through the hole in the wall.

'Aaaargh!' This arrangement of letters is a rather unsatisfactory attempt to represent the noise that the Englishman made as he turned on the nightwatch. It was the sort of noise a performing bear might make when it turns on its tormentors or that an ogre might make as it tears the wings off a fairy.

You see, all his working life Barrel the Englishman had felt he'd missed out. Everything had pretty much gone wrong for him ever since he first left England, which was some seven years ago now. He had signed up in the Black Prince's army with the usual hope of getting rich quick. But despite the staggering victory at Poitiers in which the king of France himself was captured and held for a king's ransom, none of that staggering amount of money (three million golden ecus, they said) had trickled down his way. Barrel had always found himself either on the wrong side of the ditch when a nobleman was captured, or stuck in the tavern, when the most profitable looting took place.

Perhaps it was his dedication to filling up his barrel shape with the appropriate alcoholic liquids that made him less alert than his companions when it came to pillaging and plundering, but somehow he had always just missed the rich pickings that he had understood would await any soldier in the employ of the English Crown.

Even when Sir Robert Knolles had sacked the town of Auxerre, he'd been under the table in an inn somewhere and had missed the party of a lifetime – or so his mates told him.

But despite all the disappointments and missed opportunities, he'd clung to the one dream of getting rich quick. So when Ann had told him of the treasure that was kept in the little house on the bridge of Saint-Flour, he suddenly saw an end to his years of humiliation. Here was treasure to be divided up and – miracle of miracles! – no one to divide it up with! You see, I am afraid that Barrel had not only no intention of sharing the treasure with his mates, whom he'd left back at the inn, he also had absolutely no intention of sharing it with Tom, Squire Alan and Emily.

No! For the first time in his professional career, Barrel thought he was about to acquire the riches that he had always deserved. And, befuddled though his brain may have been, he had no intention of letting anyone – especially the nightwatch – get in the way.

He therefore charged at the three nightwatchmen, quite oblivious to yet another arrow that sped past his shoulder.

How the three nightwatchmen could miss such a bulky target is a mystery, although it should be freely admitted that none of them were experts with the bow, being craftsman and traders in their normal lives. What is more, all of them were of a nervous disposition. This nervousness was not at all diminished by the sight and sound of a roaring, maddened bear made out of barrels windmilling down the bridge towards them.

Terry Jones

To tell the truth, at that moment the three night-watchmen shared an identical thought, although none of them were to ever discover this, for reasons which will soon become apparent. Each one of them, unbeknownst to the others, found the idea flashing through his brain that somehow the Maid of the Bridge had been miraculously turned into a huge bear. And now it had broken out of the little house on the bridge and was intent on wreaking revenge on the good townsfolk of Saint-Flour for her incarceration.

It was an absurd idea, of course, but perhaps not so absurd for people who were prepared to wall up a girl to protect a bridge.

Jacoppo, the eldest of the nightwatch (and a cabinet maker during the day), turned and ran. Ernesto, the youngest (a spice-seller), simply jumped off the bridge into the shallow waters of the Ander, where he splashed and stumbled before reaching the other bank some way downstream. Frederico, the third member of the nightwatch (and a tailor), stood there in horror as the miraculous Avenging Bear descended on him. His mind whirred, but failed to tell his body what to do. The result was that he remained rooted to the spot, as he thought: 'The Avenging Bear has a sword!'

And that was the last thought he had upon this earth, as Barrel brought the sword slicing down upon him.

However, Frederico had been holding a crossbow. He had been given it by a German *condottiere* in lieu of payment for a handsome gown he had made for him. Frederico was the only member of the nightwatch to own such a weapon, and he always carried it fully wound up and loaded whenever he was on duty. He never actually used it, of course, but it gave him a nice comfortable feeling of power as he patrolled the darkened streets of Saint-Flour, for it was beautifully made.

Barrel, in his headlong charge, however, had failed to notice what a splendid weapon Frederico was pointing at him. The result was that the same moment he sliced through the nightwatchman, Frederico's finger slipped the catch and the bolt shot out of the crossbow and straight into the barrel-like chest of the Englishman.

Now being shot at point-blank range by a crossbow is not something that you can walk away from with a shrug of the shoulders. In fact it's something you simply don't walk away from.

Barrel was no exception. He sort of grunted and sank to his knees. He didn't protest against his fate. In a way he knew he had it coming. He knew, really, in his heart of hearts, that he would never get his hands on a vast chest of treasure. He knew really, deep down inside, that he had led a dissolute life of drinking and killing and drinking and torture and drinking and . . . well, just drinking, and that he would meet a sticky end one day when he was least expecting it, and it just happened to be today.

He knelt there for some moments, on the bridge of Saint-Flour, taking in the sound of the rushing water below him, and then he keeled over and his spirit departed to wherever spirits go.

Tom and Ann, all this time, had been cowering behind the little house on the bridge, and watching the events take place with a horrified fascination.

Ann's first reaction was a curious one considering the circumstances – well, that's what she thought anyway. She immediately felt responsible for the death of the Englishman.

'But it wasn't your fault,' said Tom later, as they were strolling along the road towards Massiac.

'But if I hadn't persuaded him to come with us, he would still be alive.'

Ann was determined to keep her guilt intact. It was most unlike her, thought Tom. Why did she care a fig about the dreadful English soldier? But then there was a lot about her that seemed to be different and he didn't really understand.

That was later, however. For now, they were still on

the bridge. The destruction of the nightwatch meant that at least they could complete the rescue.

Tom and Ann raced round to the other side of the tiny house on the bridge, where the Englishman had partially torn down the wall.

'Giovanna!' shouted Ann. 'Where are you? Can you get through this hole?'

There was no answer.

'Hurry, Giovanna!' Ann was now whispering again, although she couldn't have told you why. 'Before the rest arrive!'

But Giovanna's voice came out of the blackness.

'I can't leave. I have chosen to die here.'

'But why?'

'To protect the city!'

'But it's all stuff and nonsense!' whispered Ann. 'Your sitting here and praying isn't going to keep the bridge safe. The only thing that'll do that is a proper troop of armed men. It's just the town's too mean to pay for them!'

'I can't leave.'

'Yes! You can! You can get through this hole! Come on! I can hear people coming!' cried Ann.

'No . . .' said the ghost voice. 'I shall never leave . . .'

'Someone's coming!' whispered Tom.

'Quick!' cried Ann.

But there was no answer.

'Look!' shouted Ann, 'you can get through!' And she pushed herself into the hole that the Englishman had made. 'Giovanna! Don't be pathetic!'

Tom watched Ann disappear though the hole in the wall at the same time as he saw the rest of the towns-folk appear in the street that led up to the bridge. One moment they weren't there, the next moment they were. One moment Ann was there, the next moment she had been swallowed up by the gaping hole. Tom found himself thinking: 'Perhaps this little house on the bridge swallows up young women and never lets them out again.'

He yelled: 'Ann!' as her legs disappeared through the hole in the stonework.

Ann didn't reply.

'Ann!' hissed Tom. 'They're coming!'

The townsfolk had gathered in a small uncertain group, but now a leader appeared to have joined them and they had begun advancing cautiously up the street.

Ann's face appeared in the hole in the wall. She looked for all the world like the Maid of the Bridge: she had gone deadly white, and she seemed suddenly to be more like a ghost. 'I knew it!' said the irrational voice inside Tom's head. 'The little house on the bridge has swapped one girl for the other ... or else it makes them all the same!'

But his rational voice said aloud: 'Let's get out of here, Ann!!'

'She was right!' said Ann. 'She'll never leave this dreadful place.'

'Make her!' said Tom. 'Push her out!'

But Ann was already hauling an inert body through the hole. The Maid of the Bridge fell at Tom's feet. Her simple shift was soaked with blood, and the shaft of one of the nightwatchmen's arrows protruded from her chest.

'She's dead! And it's my fault!' said Ann.

'Look out!' yelled Tom. Another arrow had just parted his hair and slammed into the wall above Ann's head. It seemed that the nightwatchmen weren't the only armed folk in the town. Tom grabbed Ann's hand and yanked her out of the hole, and before another arrow could be fitted to another bowstring, the pair of them were running for their lives over the bridge of Saint-Flour, and across the river Ander.

And before the good (though unfortunately superstitious) townsfolk of Saint-Flour had reached the little house on the bridge, Tom and Ann had disappeared into the darkness beyond.

Chapter 26

Les Gorges de l'Alagnon 1361

'You were right, Tom, I shouldn't have meddled in other people's affairs.'

They had been walking along a well-travelled road which ran beside a river which was in the process of rushing back to where they had come from, as if keen to investigate what had happened there. On either side, well-ordered hills of farmland had accompanied them, but now the country grew wilder. The hills had turned into steep cliffs that crowded in on both the road and the river – pushing them ever closer together until they were both squeezed into the dismal constraint of a gorge.

Tom and Ann were striding on ahead, whilst Emily was dawdling behind, strumming on Tom's *citole*. Ann kept on shooting exasperated glances behind, as Emily tried to remember the words of 'Come Hither, Love, and Lie by Me' or some other ditty.

Eventually Ann shouted back: 'Oh! Shut up!' and Emily stopped strumming and looked up rather hurt.

Tom had never seen Ann like this.

'But you didn't know they were going to shoot her,' said Tom.

'If I hadn't interfered, they wouldn't have. She'd still be alive.'

'But what kind of a life was *that*?' asked Tom.

'That's not the point,' snapped Ann. 'We don't "put people out of their misery" like dogs or cats!'

'I didn't mean that,' Tom was stumbling for words. 'But it was right to try and rescue her. It's barbaric walling her in like that!'

'Yes, we had no choice . . .' agreed Ann, but it sounded like an accusation.

What had happened to the old Ann? Tom wondered. The old Ann was so full of confidence. The old Ann always knew the answers. The old Ann was so free from doubt.

'I'll never forgive myself,' said the new Ann. 'Never.'

Tom looked across at his best friend. He felt confused and foolish. It was as if he had lost someone dear to him, and yet this was Ann walking alongside him in the same way that Ann always walked alongside him. True, she was dressed as Squire Alan, but there was nothing un-Ann-like about that. In fact he found it reassuring that she was still able to carry off her disguise as a boy. And yet for some reason he couldn't shake off the feeling that the old Ann had been shot in the night by a stray arrow and he hadn't noticed . . .

But no . . . that was wrong too . . . hadn't Ann seemed different ever since they'd rescued her from the Pope's prison in Avignon? The more he thought about it the more it seemed that *that* was where they'd left the old Ann: incarcerated somewhere in that ghastly fortress of paranoia.

And it wasn't as if he didn't like the new Ann. In some ways, the new Ann was more sympathetic, more . . . he couldn't say *likeable* because there was nothing about the old Ann he didn't like, but he felt he could put his arm round the new Ann and tell her that everything would be all right and that, whatever she thought she had done, he believed in her and always would believe in her – none of which would have occurred to him to do to the old Ann.

'Stop where you are!'

The words were French, but there was no mistaking the accent. It was best Cheshire.

'We're English!' cried Tom. 'Don't shoot!'

Four armed men had ridden out from behind a large rock and were now blocking their path. Two were pointing crossbows at them and the other two had drawn swords.

'I don't care if you're *Ethiopians*!' said the man from Cheshire. 'Grab 'em!'

And before they knew what was happening, four more had emerged from the rocks and Tom, Ann and Emily found themselves pinioned with their arms behind them. What happened next was, in truth, a demonstration of sheer professionalism and expertise. Tom's bundle was unceremoniously snatched from him by a soldier who was, unaccountably, wearing a turban, and the next minute, hands were all over him searching for the possessions on his person.

Emily was screaming blue murder as the men made coarse jokes and ran their hands over her rich clothing. Ann, or rather Squire Alan, was fighting and kicking with all her strength and with such effect that not a single soldier had been able to lay a finger on her.

'All right!' said the man-at-arms from Cheshire. 'That's enough. Tie those two up and let the young lad follow if he wants.'

With that Tom and Emily were unceremoniously hog-tied and thrown across a couple of the horses. The party then wheeled about and rode off deeper into the wilderness of the gorge. And Ann, who had retreated to a safe distance, had no option but to run after them, if she wished to keep her companions in sight.

A mile down the road, they passed under the supervision of an impossibly high-sided castle perched on an equally impossibly high-sided crag. But if the owners of that magnificent place had once intended to enforce their law upon the land, they must have given up long ago. Now the castle no longer deigned to look down on the goings on of mere mortals living out their lives on the earth below. It had been abandoned.

The path and the river, however, seemed to have developed a symbiotic relationship and were getting along together just fine: as the one grew wider, the other grew narrower. They had just reached a point where it was the river's turn to spread itself and indulge in idle chatter as it bubbled over a shallow bed.

Here the riders wheeled their horses into the water and started to wade across to the dismal bank on the other side. Tom had the feeling that they were crossing the river Lethe into the underworld, which, in a sense, was to prove to be not far off the mark.

Once across, they scrambled onto the bank between some trees and found themselves in a camp, hidden from view under a shelf of rock. Like toads under a stone, Tom thought, but of course he didn't say that.

About fourteen armed men had gathered in this

particular troop of *routiers,* as they were called by the locals. They were mostly English, but one or two were German and there seemed to be a couple of Frenchmen too. The arrival of the captives was greeted with whooping and catcalling.

Tom and Emily were bundled off the horses and thrown in front of the man who seemed to be their leader. His face was weathered, and he had a scar right across his forehead that reached down across his eye and onto his cheek. It seemed a miracle that his eye could have survived such a sword stroke as must have produced that gash.

'So? What have we got here?' he asked.

'We picked them up on the road to Lempdes,' said the man from Cheshire. 'She looks like she might be worth a fair ransom,' he added, nodding at Emily.

'Quite a lady!' agreed the leader of the troop, looking her up and down. 'What's in there?'

'Don't you dare touch those!' exclaimed Emily.

One of the others had produced the bundle of Emily's clothing.

'Open it up!' ordered the leader.

'Don't you . . .' began Emily, but then she stopped, as the leader turned to look at her. He had blue eyes that seemed to light up as he smiled at her, and for a moment Emily simply stared at him. But then she turned away with such disdain that his smile turned into a chuckle, and Emily's gesture was spoiled.

Meanwhile the bundle was thrown onto the floor and the men quickly opened it up, whistling with appreciation at the rich clothes that were revealed.

'Yes . . . yes . . . those are the Valois *fleur-de-lys*, if I'm not mistaken,' murmured the leader. 'It seems to me, gentlemen, we may have struck richer than we could have possibly imagined!' And once again he looked Emily up and down appreciatively, but this time she returned his gaze without flinching.

'I'm English!' interrupted Tom. He had finally managed to get rid of the gag that they had tied round his mouth. 'And she's a good friend of mine!'

He nodded at Emily.

The leader turned on Tom, and smiled an icy smile. 'I couldn't care less if you were *Ethiopian*.'

'That's exactly what that fellow from Cheshire said,' Tom wanted to say, but instead he simply muttered: 'Well . . . we're on the same side, aren't we?'

Tom hadn't realised he was making a particularly funny remark, but once it had escaped his lips, he knew he had. It was – apparently – hilarious.

'I don't know whose "side" you're on,' remarked the scar-faced leader, doing an alarmingly good job of controlling his amusement. 'But we're on *our* side.'

'*Il a raison!*' said a Frenchman in a mail coat.

'*Ja,*' said a German. '*Wir sind auf unserer seite!*'

And once again, Tom found himself the centre of a hilarious round of laughter, which would have satisfied a court jester's wildest dreams.

During the general uproar, Tom noticed that the Frenchman had sidled up to him.

'*Je vous connais,*' he said. 'I know you.'

'I don't think you do,' replied Tom.

'Yes . . . yes . . . I do . . .' insisted the Frenchman, but before he could say any more the leader was rapping out commands.

'Untie the girl. Give her some food. But get rid of the boy. We'll get nothing for him.'

'Oh! And there was another lad hanging around . . .' said the man from Cheshire. 'Looks like he's caught up with us.'

He nodded towards the trees down by the river, where Ann had just appeared. She was warily keeping her distance, but peering intently across at the encampment.

'Good old Ann!' thought Tom. 'She'll think of a way of getting us out of this! That's what she's doing now . . . she's studying the layout of this place and working out how to rescue us . . . situation . . . alternatives . . . action . . .! That's it! She'll know what to . . .'

But the thought petered out in his mind, because Ann had suddenly started behaving in a very odd way indeed.

'She's gone mad!' was Tom's first thought. For, instead of waiting for night or until there was no one around to attempt a rescue, Ann was now walking – quite deliberately and slowly – into the very centre of the *routiers'* encampment.

It must be a trick, thought Tom. Ann must have some plan . . . at least the old Ann would have had a plan, and maybe walking into the middle of the danger could have been part of it . . . but this wasn't the old Ann . . . this was the new Ann, and the new Ann walked as if in a dream right into the midst of those bandits and robbers.

Once there, she turned to the scar-faced leader with the blue eyes and the flashing smile, and said something that was to change Tom's life forever.

'Peter,' she said. 'Peter de Bury!'

Chapter 27

Milan 1385

Minstrels normally performed behind a screen, or up in a gallery . . . somewhere separated from the important people in the hall. That way they did not interfere with the conversation and, more crucially, they couldn't eavesdrop on any secret matters of state that might be being discussed. Minstrels, you see, were frequently employed as spies.

Bernabò Visconti, however, showed contempt for most things. He showed contempt for most people, and he showed contempt for most customs – including the positioning of minstrels. Which is how Sir Thomas English, currently in the guise of the minstrel Robin of Arundel, found himself being brought forward into the centre of the hall to sing an elegy in memory of the late Regina della Scala, the deceased wife of the Lord of Milan.

And there, sitting next to the great Lord of Milan, sat

the woman who had – in all probability – poisoned his wife. How could he sing something which would console the one without antagonising the other?

Tom's nerves were wound up as tight as the strings of his *citole*. He had only had a few hours to cobble together a musical tribute. Even a professional musician would have found it taxing, and Sir Thomas was not a professional musician. Of course not! A professional musician was a paid entertainer – the lowest of the low. Mere riff-raff. Sir Thomas could, of course, play and sing – after all, he was an accomplished knight – but he would never have demeaned himself by receiving money for his artistic endeavours. His playing and singing was strictly for the boudoir or the private chamber. Public performance on the scale on which he was about to embark was not in his remit.

Besides, it also didn't help knowing that he was a wanted man. The Lord of Milan had had his picture put up all over town, alongside a text accusing him of treason and of attempting to seduce his favourite mistress. Perhaps singing to the court was not the best method of keeping out of the tyrant's way. Even though he'd shaved off his red hair, he could still be recognisable, and every eye was now turned on him as he stood there before the ruthless and unpredictable Lord of Milan.

'You've got a song about my wife?' barked Bernabò.

'I have an elegy, my liege,' said Sir Thomas, and he bowed deeply.

'Then let's have it! If it's good, I'll give you this!' Bernabò pulled a brooch off his coat and flung it down on the table. 'If it stinks, you'll spend the night in the kennels!'

And then he barked again with that humourless laugh of his, and, of course, the whole court joined in.

Tom knew only too well what spending a night in the kennels might mean. If he were to be locked up with the Great Danes, he would not see the light of another day. Tom suddenly knew what a jelly felt like sitting on a hot plate.

And, talking of heat, Tom had just noticed that the temperature in the stuffy hall had pulled one of the strings on his *citole* out of tune.

'My lord,' said Tom, quickly fiddling with the way-ward string, 'the Lady Regina della Scala shines in all our minds like the evening star – beautiful amidst the darkness of her loss.'

There was an automatic smattering of applause. There always was nowadays whenever anyone said anything about the Lady Regina della Scala. Tom bowed, still retuning his string. Bernabò, however, was getting impatient. He signalled to him to start, muttering at the same time: 'And don't make it too long!'

Tom finally got the string to the right pitch and launched into his elegy, which began, roughly speaking, on the following lines:

> 'When I see her empty place
> I remember how her grace
> Lit the room and filled the hall.
> Now the clothes I wear are black,
> Could I have my lady back
> I'd count myself the Count of All.'

He went on like this for a dozen more verses, each one ending with the refrain 'I'd count myself the Count of All'. The tune was an English one, which he knew would be fresh to Italian ears. A lot of the content was borrowed, but he hoped no one would recognise it. Looking round the faces of the court, it was hard to tell how anybody was reacting.

It was even harder to tell how the great Bernabò was reacting. He was just sitting there with his eyes shut, nodding in time to the music. Tom was rather pleased with the refrain 'I'd count myself the Count of All', which worked just as well, he thought, in Italian as in English. And paying a compliment to the Count of

Milan was probably more important, Tom calculated, than paying one to his deceased wife.

At last, Tom reached the end of his elegy. He played the final flourish and bowed low. There was total silence.

'Well, that's it,' said Tom to himself. 'My career as a minstrel lasted precisely one number. Pity, really. I actually rather enjoyed the performance.'

Tom kept his head down in the bow. He could already hear the Great Danes snarling and snapping around his ankles.

He finally felt he couldn't stay bowing any longer, and straightened up. Glancing round the faces of the court, he instantly realised that whether they liked it or not was totally irrelevant. Every courtier's eyes were fixed on the great Bernabò. Of course! Nobody could possibly have an opinion until the great man had expressed his.

Bernabò, however, was at that moment particularly inscrutable. He was sitting there, eyes shut, head nodding, just as if he were still listening to the song. The Lady Donnina was equally inscrutable. She sat there beside her lord simply staring at Tom. Before her gaze, Tom felt quite naked ... exposed ... as if every secret in him was written all over his body for all to read.

'That is it, my lord,' said Tom, making another elaborate bow. 'There is no more.'

His heart was beating like a drum as he waited to hear his fate. A dog sniffed his crotch. Actually it was a real dog that had been prowling around the hall, but Tom couldn't help reacting as if it had been the first of the Great Danes come to tear him to pieces. He gave a great yell. A ripple of amusement went round the hall.

But still the Lord of Milan simply sat there, eyes closed, nodding. Every eye in the place swivelled back from Tom to the lord, waiting for the word.

Eventually the chief steward, who was standing just behind the count, jogged him discretely, and the great man woke up. Bernabò looked around in some surprise, saw Tom still holding his *citole*, and – perhaps to cover up the fact that he had fallen into an alcohol-induced stupor, or else out of relief that yet another tedious elegy was already over – immediately clapped and shouted: 'Bravo! Robin of Arundel! Well done!'

And with that the entire hall burst into polite applause and Tom bowed again, and felt the sweat trickling down under his armpits. At the same time he brushed away the dog that had been sniffing around him.

The steward bent down again and whispered something to Bernabò, who obediently picked up the brooch and flung it at Tom.

'Here! Buy yourself a new horse with that!'

The thought flashed through Tom's mind: 'He knows I've lost my horse! He must know who I am! The game's up!' and the returning image of the kennels made him miss the brooch. It fell with a clatter onto the tiled floor.

'You minstrels always let your money slip through your fingers!' roared the Lord of Milan. The entire court naturally joined in roaring with laughter and this made Bernabò roar again with mirth – at which point Tom realised that the great Lord of Milan had far better things to do than remember the face of an Englishman who'd left his court some weeks before.

He gratefully snatched up the brooch and retreated back into the safety of the musicians' enclosure, where the others had already struck up a pleasing dance melody that was setting everyone's feet tapping.

There would soon be dancing and flirting and merry-making in the black-draped court of the Lord of Milan. Bernabò himself was already caressing the Lady Donnina de' Porri's cheek with his hand. Soon, no doubt, he would be leading her off to bed, and leaving the court to its unbounded pleasures.

Yet it would be wrong to think that Bernabò himself

Terry Jones

did not regret his wife's death. He had always valued her highly for her common sense and her good advice. Indeed she was the one person in the whole state who ever dared oppose his whims or moderated his behaviour. Moreover her financial advice was always impeccable.

Bernabò already missed her guiding hand and – who knows? – perhaps her death had left him feeling just that little bit vulnerable, despite his power and arrogance. He may even have had an inkling of the disaster that was soon to engulf him, and which would be entirely the result of his overweening pride. For a wretched fate was soon to overtake the Lord of Milan, and it is possible that Regina della Scala would have prevented it.

But all that was in the future.

For now, Bernabò Visconti was drunk. His head was turning slightly and he rose, leaning on his mistress's shoulder. He did not see the look that the Lady Donnina de' Porri shot towards the musicians' enclosure. Nor did he hear her whisper to the steward to fetch the minstrel who had just sung of Regina della Scala and bring him to her chamber.

266

Chapter 28

Les Gorges de l'Alagnon 1361

Peter de Bury stared at the youth who stood in front of him, and who claimed to know him so well. He was certain he had never seen this young man before . . . his mind ran through several encounters he had had over the last two years, but he could not place him. And yet there was something familiar about his eyes.

'Don't you recognise me?' asked the youth.

'I have never seen you before in my life,' replied Peter de Bury. It was always safer to start with a denial.

The youth seemed to collapse inside, like a lantern extinguished.

'Curious . . .' thought Peter de Bury, 'he can't be after money.'

Then an even more curious thing happened. The youth spoke in a softer – an almost feminine – voice that Peter somehow recognised, one that penetrated through the many thicknesses of skin that he had been forced to acquire over the past years.

'Peter! Don't you know me?' asked the youth.

And then he took off his cap and gazed into Peter's blue, blue eyes and said: 'I have been living and dreaming of this moment for so long . . . I'm Ann.'

As she said these words, Ann saw a most extraordinary change take place in the longed-for and much-worshipped face of Peter de Bury.

For a second he looked as if he were seventeen again. His face was suddenly wiped clean of the scar and the lines that had gathered in the intervening time. The weathered features suddenly no longer seemed to belong to the same person . . . they were outward artefacts that were not attached to the inner man . . . and that inner man was the beautiful youth she had last seen in the garden of her father's house back in Woodstock, near the great city of Oxford.

They had kissed the summer before. Peter had then spent the best part of the year in the service of the Earl of Exeter, and she had not seen him. But there had not been a day when she had not thought about him, nor seen his face in her mind's eye.

Then he had returned. They had walked for a short while (although it may have been a couple of hours) in her mother's orchard, hidden by low branches of apple and pear, and he had told her he was going away. He did not know for how long. But he was going far away. He was going to join the Black Prince's army in France. He would get rich. He would send word. But he did not know when he would ever see her again.

And then he was gone.

At first she did not think it was possible. She woke up every morning and thought she had dreamed that Peter had gone, but that in fact he was still there . . . perhaps sleeping in the room next door. But then she would wake up properly and realise that that was the dream. The reality was that Peter de Bury had gone out of her life.

It was on one of those mornings that she had formed the plan of running away and going to find Peter, wherever he might be. Perhaps she would have waited for the spring to turn to summer, if something had not happened to make her decide to leave then and there.

Her father had ordered her into the *solar* – an upper room in which there were actually glazed windows, which were a matter of great pride to the whole family. When she entered, her father was standing with an elderly man whose face she could not place.

'Girl,' said her father. 'This man is to be your husband. He has asked for your hand and I have agreed.'

The elderly man bowed to Ann, and his eyes ran eagerly all over her. She felt as if she had been assaulted by that look. And she knew that, whatever happened, whatever it took, whatever would transpire, she would never . . . never . . . let that man – whoever he was – touch her.

And that was it, really. She ran away the next day with all the money she could lay her hands on. She regretted that. She did not want to steal from her father. She was also sorry that her father would lose the not inconsiderable dowry that the elderly man had promised to hand over on their wedding day. He was, it turned out, a wealthy merchant from Oxford, whose wife had died the previous year, and who enjoyed the thought of buying his way into a family with some claim to nobility.

In Oxford, Ann had taken on the identity of the Squire Alan. She had bought some boy's clothes, pretending she was taking them to her twin brother who was living with a noble family some miles away. She had then borrowed some scissors, and cut short her hair. In the town of Wycombe, she had encountered the thoroughly disreputable Sir John Hawkley, who, mistaking her for a boy, had taken her on as his squire. Some time later, on the way to Sandwich, she had met Tom, and the two of them had journeyed together with Sir John to France to join Edward III's *chevauchée*.

But all the time, every step of the journey, Ann was keeping her ears open, hoping to glean some information about Peter de Bury and his whereabouts.

It was not until they were in the Duke of Lancaster's retinue, encamped outside Reims, however, that she first had any real news of him. A young man who had been in the Earl of Exeter's retinue and who had known Peter well told her that the youth she sought had become a squire to Sir Richard Markham and that Sir Richard had left the Black Prince's army and joined up with Sir Robert Knolles.

Now Sir Robert Knolles was a man of considerable abilities, but one who preferred to fight the French without having to share the spoils of war with the English Crown. Naturally Sir Robert swore allegiance to the king of England, and naturally the king of England often found Sir Robert's depredations against the French useful in the campaign of terror by which he hoped to seize the French throne. Anything that weakened and demoralised the country over which he hoped to one day rule was fine by Edward III. But the fact remained that Sir Robert was a mercenary and a freebooter, fighting for no cause other than to make himself richer.

But then perhaps that was all any of them were

doing – those knights and lords, those dukes and earls – perhaps they were all in it for what they could make out of it? That's what Ann thought, anyway.

In any case, if Peter de Bury was fighting with Sir Robert Knolles, that was where Ann wanted to be. Even if Sir Robert Knolles was burning and devastating towns and villages throughout France, killing and maiming wherever he went.

And now here she was face-to-face with Peter de Bury after three years, or was it more? She had hardly recognised him when she had seen him from a distance. But there was something about the way he walked, something about the way he carried himself, that told her instantly that it was him.

And now she was closer to him, neither the sun-browned skin nor the scar across the eye could disguise who he was. He was her Peter . . . only there was something else about him that she did not recognise. There was something in those blue eyes of his, something in the way he looked at her, that was unfathomably different from the Peter de Bury who had become the familiar companion of her mind.

All this went through Ann's thoughts as she saw his expression change when she told him who she was.

'Ann?' said Peter de Bury. 'You mean you're not a boy?'

'I'm Ann!' Ann blurted out. 'I love you! I've come all this way to find you!'

Tom was still lying hog-tied on the ground where he'd been thrown. From there he saw Peter de Bury's eyes glance around at his companions, who were all trying to hide their smirks with varying degrees of lack of success.

'Ann?' repeated Peter de Bury. 'Ann from Woodstock? . . . ha!' He looked round at his men, and pointed to Ann. 'We played together as children,' he explained.

Emily, who had been untied, was busy snatching her clothes back from the various ruffians who had picked them up, but she now stopped and turned to look from Ann to Peter de Bury.

'That's right!' said Ann. 'We were childhood sweethearts.'

'Well! This calls for a celebration!' called out Peter de Bury to those around him. 'Let's open up that cask of good Burgundy!'

He clearly knew how to win the hearts and minds of his men, for a cheer went up at this suggestion.

'Oh, Peter!' cried Ann, and the next second she had run across to him and thrown her arms around his neck and was kissing him all over his face.

Tom, once again, noticed Peter de Bury's eyes flicking around the faces of his men. They were all now watching him, waiting for his order. Even the imperious Emily was standing there watching Peter de Bury as if waiting for him to announce the next move. It was clear why he was the leader.

After a while he prised Ann off his shoulder and said in a kindly voice: 'Well, I wouldn't have recognised you!'

'I almost didn't recognise you!' laughed Ann, holding on to him as if he might disappear again. She looked round – radiant with happiness – and suddenly noticed Tom on the floor.

'Oh! And these are my friends!' she said to Peter de Bury. 'That's my best friend Tom . . . we've had such adventures together you won't believe it . . . and that's Emily.'

'Fine,' said Peter de Bury. 'You'd better untie him,' he told the man from Cheshire. Then he held Ann and looked into her eyes.

For Ann, that was the moment she'd been waiting for . . . the moment when her eyes met those cool blue eyes of Peter de Bury, and even though they were so cool something inside her melted as it had done all those years ago in her mother's orchard back in Woodstock.

'Oh, Peter!' was all she could say.

'I can't wait to hear about everything that's happened to you,' he said.

That evening, the companions sat around the fire, drinking the good Burgundy wine and eating pieces of the lamb that was roasting on the improvised spit. Tom kept watching Ann. He had never seen her so happy or so unlike the Ann he had known. She seemed neither like the old Ann nor like the new Ann: it was as if a totally alien being that had been lurking inside her all this time had now taken her over.

Ann told the stories of their adventures: of Sir John Hawkley and the shipwreck, of the siege of Laon, of how she and Emily escaped from the unwelcome hospitality of the Abbot Gregory in the great city of Troyes by climbing down through the lavatory, and of how she was imprisoned in the Pope's palace at Avignon and finally escaped with Tom and Emily by jumping from the roof.

But it was not Ann telling it, it was a young woman whom Tom had never met before, describing adventures that had happened to somebody else.

And all the time Ann's eyes never seemed to leave Peter de Bury's face. It was as if his features (that she remembered so well and yet that seemed so different) contained some special eye-adhesive that only affected her. Perhaps she was examining him to make sure that this was indeed the Peter that she had been seeking all this time and not some imposter that had occupied his body.

Terry Jones

Sometimes, when he was looking round his men, or sharing a joke with them, a dreadful fear clamped itself around her heart, and she was convinced that her search had not ended, and that she was still looking for the Peter de Bury she had loved all this time.

But then he would turn to her and smile and it was all right.

Tom, meanwhile, was doing his best to defend the beautiful Lady Emilia de Valois from the rude advances of the soldiery amongst whom they now found themselves.

'Well, I wouldn't mind making my bed next to 'ee!' Tom caught one of them leering at her, and he had been just about to tell the man to mind his manners, when Emily felled the fellow herself, with one of her most lethal and withering looks. It was hard to act the part of the chivalrous knight defending your lady when the lady in question was quite capable of defending herself, thank you very much.

A moment later, Tom noticed the bandit with the turban slipping his arm around the beautiful Emily's waist. In no time, Tom had drawn the sword that Emily had bought him in Marvejols, and leapt to her defence. The result was not dissimilar to when he had last attempted to use the thing. Only this time, the bandit

276

with turban shook his head, and simply walked straight up to Tom and said:

'You're too young to be playing with a dangerous weapon.'

Upon which the man wrested the sword out of Tom's grip and, much to the amusement of the others, threw it off into the brambles that crept down to the river-bank.

Tom was so humiliated he couldn't face retrieving the sword for the time being. But he noted where it had disappeared and determined he'd get it back when no one was looking. At least the man in the turban had given up interfering with Emily, thought Tom, so per-haps he'd scored a partial victory after all.

And in a way he couldn't blame these rough soldiers for the way they milled around Emily like moths around a flame. In that bandits' lair, under the over-hanging rock, surrounded by the harness of warfare, Emily looked lovelier than Tom had ever seen her.

At the same time, Tom couldn't help stealing occa-sional glances at Ann and Peter de Bury. Of course, he'd known for a long time that this had been her goal, and he had been happy to accept it as *his* goal too. Yet now they had reached it, he was overtaken by a feeling of loss. And the more he tried to focus on the miracu-lous presence of the beautiful Emily, the more he kept remembering little moments between Ann and himself, when they had seemed to be an inseparable team, each one essential to the other.

'Tom, I'm tired. Come and lie down beside me!'

It was the beautiful Emily speaking. Tom's train of thought came back to the present: what was this? Emily – the lovely Emily – was inviting him to make his bed beside her? He knew, of course, that she was just protecting herself from the soldiers who were now getting ready for the night, but even so it was an invitation that made his heart beat out of all reason.

Emily had wrapped herself in her thick black cloak, so that she was encased as tight as a chrysalis. Tom lay down beside her, with his head resting on a small roll of clothes. And he lay there full of wonder – to think that he was spending the night beside the lovely Emily, under the stars . . . how could life get any better?

At the same time, he noticed Ann going with Peter de Bury to find their bed away from the others on the other side of some rocks. But at that moment he felt Emily's dainty arm come to rest on his shoulder, as she snuggled up against his back. He hardly dared to breathe lest he should disturb her, or lest she took that magical hand away from his arm.

And he lay there all night, not daring to move.

*

The next morning Tom could have sworn he had not slept a wink, but Emily was up and about already without his noticing. She had already dressed and done her hair, and had tied her clothes up into their bundle ready for Tom to carry. She had even taken the small roll from under Tom's head to include in her pack.

'Come on, sleepyhead!' said Emily. 'Let's get away from this lot.'

Tom struggled to get himself up onto his feet. The *routiers* were stirring too, packing their horses and making preparations to break camp.

'Surely you're not going to miss breakfast?' he muttered.

'I couldn't stomach anything after watching Ann fawning over that villain . . .'

It was so unlike Emily to willingly forgo breakfast that Tom knew there was no point arguing, but at that moment he felt an iron grip on his arm. He span round only to find the Frenchman looking intently into his eyes.

'I come from Compertrix,' said the man.

'Compertrix?' repeated Tom blankly.

'In Champagne,' said the man.

And suddenly Tom's mind was racing back to a little village outside Chalons-sur-Marne in the region of

Champagne, where the poor villagers were so hard-pressed by both the ravaging English marauders and the avaricious French nobility that they had taken to living underground. There he had been befriended by the giant Anton. Together they had journeyed to Avignon, to plead with the head of the Catholic Church to alleviate the suffering of the villagers by cancelling the taxes they were due to pay him.

'You took a message from my poor village to the Pope!' whispered the Frenchman. 'You must be returning with His Holiness' reply?'

Tom was about to say: 'The only reply I got from the Pope was arrows!', when Peter de Bury suddenly appeared from behind the rocks, and the Frenchman instantly melted into the busy *mêlée* of the waking camp.

Ann was hanging on Peter de Bury's arm. She had become a spendthrift with smiles, bestowing them on whomever her glance happened to fall. It seemed as if she were trying to use up a lifetime's supply of smiles all in one morning.

'Hi!' said Peter. 'Where are you two off to?'

'England,' said Emily, who had clearly decided not to waste more words than was absolutely necessary on these ruffians.

'Are you going too, Tom?' asked Ann, throwing him one of her most valuable and radiant smiles.

'Yes,' said Tom. 'I'm glad you found Peter.'

'Oh, Tom, I'd never have done it without you,' said Ann. By some miracle of willpower, Ann had detached herself from the side of Peter de Bury and now stood opposite Tom. She put her hands on his shoulders and kissed him on the forehead – as a mother might kiss a small child whom she is sending out to play.

'I expect you would have done just fine,' said Tom. 'I'm really glad it's turned out right for you.' He smiled and Ann turned to Emily.

'And Emily, thank you too,' she said. 'It's been good knowing you.'

'Yes . . .' said Emily. And then it was Emily who suddenly had her arms around Ann. She kissed her briefly and held her just for a moment. Then she picked up her pack of clothes and handed it to Tom.

'Come on,' she said.

Ann turned back to Peter, still looking as if she were walking on clouds of good fortune and happiness. And Peter was smiling too. All the world seemed to be smiling this morning. Except that Peter's voice was not smiling.

'You're not going anywhere, my fine Lady de Valois,' he said. 'You're staying with us.'

Chapter 29

Milan 1385

When Tom received the summons to attend the Lady Donnina de' Porri in her chamber, he thought: 'I suppose I could save time and trouble by handing myself over to the executioner straight away!' Whatever the Lady Donnina had in store for him, he was convinced it was not compatible with his staying alive. Had she seen through his disguise? If not, why had she sent for him? To scold him for singing the praises of the woman she had murdered?

If she knew who he was, would she be suspicious that he had returned to the court in disguise? Or could he bluff her into thinking that he was playing safe? After all, Regina della Scala had warned him that the Lord of Milan suspected him of treachery.

Tom had little expectation that he could outwit the Lady Donnina. And even if she did not suspect him of anything, there was another reason to fear the Lady

Donnina. Just suppose the reason for summoning him to her chamber was perfectly harmless . . . perfectly benign . . . that might be even worse . . . Tom could hardly bring himself to think of it . . . just suppose she squeezed his hand again . . . Tom broke out in a cold sweat.

Donnina de' Porri was having her golden hair brushed when he was shown into her room. Sir Thomas English was quite shocked for a moment. He was used to seeing great ladies only once they had been groomed and dressed – prepared and packaged for presentation to the world.

But great ladies were not so concerned about how their servants saw them, and Tom had to remind himself that he was now a mere minstrel . . . a menial at the beck and call of the great lords and ladies of the Visconti court of Milan.

And yet the Lady Donnina looked perfectly lovely whatever her state of dress or undress. She also seemed to be perfectly well aware that Tom was not a servant.

'I saw through your disguise the moment you stepped into the hall,' she said. So he might not have escaped the kennels after all.

'I did not dare return any other way, my lady, seeing my Lord Bernabò suspects me of treachery.' Tom was relieved to hear how convincing it sounded.

'Indeed,' said Donnina de' Porri. 'I didn't think you'd be so committed to our little business.'

'And, my lady, you forget I have come for my squire, John!'

The Lady Donnina arched her graceful eyebrows: 'So? You have news of Gian Galeazzo?'

She indicated a stool near the foot of her bed. Tom perched on it and took a deep breath. He was suddenly acutely aware that perhaps no more than fifty feet from where he sat, amidst the tapestried luxury of this lady's boudoir, his squire was lying in darkness on the stone floor of a filthy dungeon. And John was lying there at the behest of this fine lady, who now sat so comfortably in front of Tom.

Whatever he was to say next might well determine John's fate.

'My lady. I have spent some considerable time with Gian Galeazzo, and I have been able to observe him on many occasions – sometimes on quite intimate terms.'

'And you have formed an opinion as to his character and intentions towards Milan?'

'I have indeed, your ladyship.'

'This pretended religiosity of his,' said Donnina de' Porri, turning to look at Tom. 'It *is* a fraud, is it not?'

The Lady Donnina's maid began to twist the lady's

284

hair into a braid, because that was how she preferred to sleep.

'My lady, I had heard much about Gian Galeazzo devoutness and religious zeal. It is common knowledge . . .'

'It causes my Lord Bernabò to despise his nephew, and therein lies the danger. That is why Regina della Scala was convinced it is a stratagem.'

'But I have seen it for myself!' exclaimed Tom. 'When I first met him, he kept me on my knees in prayer for two hours!' Tom's complaint was so heartfelt, the Lady Donnina laughed.

'You are not used to devotion, Sir Thomas Englishman!' she smiled.

'My devotion is to you, my lady,' said Thomas.

'Just tell me the truth,' she said.

'From everything I have seen of your nephew, I am convinced that the stories of his piety are not exaggerated,' Tom continued. 'Nor are the tales of his timidity.'

'Ah! And how have you tested this timidity? Perhaps you have threatened to beat him with a broom?' There was the ghost of a smile around the lady's lips.

Tom smiled too. 'My lady, to threaten your nephew even with a broom would be more than one's life is worth. Gian Galeazzo takes care to surround himself at all times with men-at-arms. Even when he prays. And he never leaves his palace without a guard of at least three hundred soldiers. I have heard him say that he lives in such constant fear that he cannot sleep or eat.'

'What or who does he fear?' asked Donnina de' Porri.

Tom looked hard at the lady. It was always difficult to guess how to present unpalatable information to a great person. Punishing the messenger was a notoriously popular sport amongst the tyrants of Lombardy.

'Misguided as he is, Gian Galeazzo lives in mortal fear of his uncle, Bernabò, my lady. He is convinced that your lord wishes him ill. Of course such an idea is preposterous, as we both well know . . .'

The smile around the mouth of the Lady Donnina de' Porri seemed to become a little more intense.

'My Lord Bernabò loves his nephew as an uncle should. Rather it is myself and the late and lamented Lady Regina della Scala who have entertained suspicions of Gian Galeazzo. My lord's late wife was convinced that his pretended holiness was a deception designed to lull my lord into a false sense of security. Perhaps we are too worldly here in Milan. We think every act of piety is a charade. We take every man of God for a hypocrite.'

Tom raised his eyes to those of Donnina de' Porri's. She was smiling, but she did not seem to be joking.

'Your piety is famous throughout Lombardy, my lady. You have endowed many houses for nuns as well as hospitals for the poor.' He chose his words carefully.

'Bravo! Sir Thomas!' smiled the Lady Donnina de' Porri. 'We shall make an Italian of you yet!'

Tom bowed. 'I forgot to offer my condolences on the death of Regina della Scala. It is a tragic event.'

'Indeed. You see how the whole court mourns.'

It was impossible to say whether the Lady Donnina was being ironic or not.

'I hope she would have felt that I had adequately fulfilled the commission that you both entrusted me with.'

'I am sure the Lady Regina della Scala would have been overjoyed to hear that her suspicions of her nephew were unfounded,' replied Donnina de' Porri, though the way she said it, it could have meant the reverse.

Tom continued: 'Then perhaps I may ask your ladyship if it is possible to fulfil your side of the bargain?'

Donnina de' Porri stopped her maid and dismissed her with a flick of the hand. The maid was gone instantly. No servant ever questioned an order in the court of Bernabò Visconti.

'And what was my side of the bargain?' she turned

towards Tom, and the collar of her robe fell to one side, exposing her shoulder.

'My squire . . . John . . . your ladyship remembers? You promised to release him when I had finished my commission.' Tom did not dare look away from her.

'But you have not finished, Sir Thomas.'

'You wish me to go back to Pavia?' Tom's heart wasn't in his mouth but it was certainly a good few inches up his gullet. He knew something bad was coming, but he had no idea how bad.

'No,' said the Lady Donnina de' Porri, favourite mistress of Bernabò Visconti, the ruthless Lord of Milan. 'I do not wish you to leave Milan.'

She stood up and walked across to Tom. 'I wish you to stay here.'

And with that she ran her hand over his shaved head.

Blind panic seized Tom. 'My lady!' he whispered, as he struggled to his feet. 'I know you are devoted to my lord, Bernabò. I feel my presence here may compromise you in some way.' He nodded towards the door that led into the duke's chamber, while at the same time he made for the opposite doorway that led to the stairway.

The Lady Donnina was too quick for him, however. She slipped effortlessly in between him and the exit, and at the same time her hand cupped the back of his neck.

'Oh no, Sir Thomas. Do not go before you have collected at least part of your reward . . .' and she pulled his face towards her own.

'The only reward I seek is the release of my squire John.' Tom's throat had gone dry as a bone in the sun. 'That will be more than adequate.'

Tom felt the slight pressure on the back of his neck and his face was brought another inch towards that of the Lady Donnina de' Porri.

Even at such close quarters, the Lady Donnina's beauty was enough to bring a ghost to the table. Her skin shone in the candlelight and, this close up, her eyes became dark lamps, urging the gazer to slip off his robes of common sense and take a dip in those pools of forgetfulness.

'I intend to be as generous to you as I possibly can be, Sir Thomas,' murmured the Lady Donnina.

Tom tried to focus on the thought of his squire John – shivering in the black dungeon below at this lady's command.

'My lady, I fear I am placing you in great danger, to be here in your chamber, when your lord is next door,' he said.

'My lord is drunk as a pig,' she whispered. 'You have

no need to fear him.' And her lips brushed against Tom's.

He concentrated every bit of his mind on the image of Squire John, lying amidst the filth and detritus of a cell floor.

'Your ladyship's generosity is beyond anything I deserve . . .' he began, but she stopped his mouth with her hand.

'I do not want to hear any more excuses, Sir Thomas. I want you . . .'

'But your ladyship!' he protested. The lady smiled.

'I want you . . . to tell me what you really found out at my nephew's court.' And with that the Lady Donnina clapped her hands and the door of her chamber was flung open, and there stood the last person Tom was expecting to see: his squire John.

Chapter 30

Les Gorges de l'Alagnon 1361

At least Peter de Bury's band of *routiers* hadn't killed him. That was the one bright spot as far as Tom could see. It's true he was trussed up like a hog for slaughter, and he'd been thrown upside down on a pile of rubbish behind some rocks, but he was still alive. He was in pain where the cords were cutting into his wrists and ankles, but – as far as he could tell – he was definitely alive. Otherwise how could he have felt the bruise on his back where he'd been kicked by the man in the turban? And if he wasn't alive, surely they wouldn't have bothered to gag him again. No, he was definitely alive, and that was a plus.

On the other hand, the outlook in almost every other way wasn't too bright. As far as Tom could see, he had about as much chance of getting away from this dreadful place as the rubbish onto which he'd been thrown.

The mercenaries had broken camp and were now milling about in readiness to leave for richer pickings elsewhere. Emily was strangely quiet, and sat there glowering at Peter de Bury and Ann.

And Ann? What could have happened to her? Why was she going along with all this?

Had Ann – the real Ann – the old Ann – the true Ann that Tom knew and loved – had she run away to Tartary or the deserts of Arabia? Who was this new person who now twisted her hand into Peter de Bury's arm, until he brushed her away?

As Tom lay on his rubbish heap, he could hear Peter de Bury issuing orders and laughing with his men above the noise of the horses' hooves clattering on the stones and the clanking of arms and armour. Then he heard footsteps.

At last! Ann had come back! She'd come to release him! Of course she wasn't going to let him be abandoned to die alone at the bottom of a gorge.

Her footsteps came round the rock and the next minute Tom felt himself being jerked up and turned round, so that he now lay face up, jackknifed over a rock adjacent to the rubbish heap. To make matters worse he found himself gazing up into the eyes not of Ann but of the scarred but handsome Peter de Bury.

'I suddenly felt sorry for you,' smiled Peter de Bury.

It should have been good news to Tom, but somehow his heart sank to hear it. 'It's not very pleasant to be left to die of cold and hunger, so I'll take pity on you,' and with that Peter de Bury pulled out his knife.

Tom struggled and wriggled, trying to speak through his gag.

'What's that you say?' said Peter de Bury. 'Well! Nobody's going to hear you anyway!' And he cut the gag away from Tom's mouth.

'What harm have I ever done to you?' gasped Tom.

'It's not what you *have* done; it's what you *might* do,' smiled Peter de Bury, and he grabbed Tom's hair, pulling his head round towards him.

'Don't you care what Ann thinks?' asked Tom. It was his last card.

'I don't care what anybody thinks,' said Peter de Bury. 'I only care what people *do*, and if they can do anything to harm me or my men, then I have no choice.'

Those clear blue eyes pierced Tom's as keenly as the knife in Peter's hand would soon be piercing his throat. Tom squirmed, his heart and mind racing each other as if they were both trying to escape in different directions. Then suddenly a familiar voice came from the other side of the rocks.

'Peter!' shouted Ann. 'What are you doing?'

The knife was hovering an inch away from Tom's throat. Peter quickly moved it down to Tom's wrists.

'I was just going to cut your friend free,' Peter de Bury told Ann. 'But you're right. It's probably better not to.' He put the knife away in its sheath, and strolled across to Ann.

'But you're not going to leave Tom here?' said Ann.

'Yes he is!' yelled Tom.

'Of course not!' laughed Peter. 'I'll tell the guard captain at Lempdes that Tom's here, and they'll release him once we're safely away.'

'Don't believe him!' Tom called.

'I just don't want him following us around and causing trouble. That's all.' Peter had put his hands on Ann's shoulders and was looking into her eyes with such openness and affection that even Doubting Thomas would have had no alternative but to believe him.

'He was going to kill me!'

That's what Tom was about to shout, but something stopped him. Perhaps it was the way he saw Ann looking at Peter – he simply couldn't destroy whatever it was that made her look at him like that, even if his life was at stake. It was absurd. But there it was. Tom said nothing, and Peter de Bury and Ann walked back around the rocks and disappeared from Tom's view.

But then Ann reappeared and whispered: 'Don't worry, Tom. It'll be all right!'

'I'll be fine, Ann!' Tom called back, as casually as if she were off to the shops. He tried not to let her hear the fear in his voice or see the pain that his current position was causing him, as he struggled to turn himself over so that at least his back wasn't breaking, but it was harder to do than he imagined.

At the same time he could now hear Peter de Bury shouting to his men, and the sound of horses impatient to be off. A few moments later he heard the splashing of waters as the troop crossed the river and set off down the gorge.

Then all was still. Tom was left alone in that desolate spot with the certain knowledge that no one was going to help him. No matter what Peter de Bury told Ann, Tom knew he had been left there to die of cold, dehydration or starvation – whichever got to him first. Or perhaps it would be the wolves.

Tom wriggled and struggled and with a great effort managed to turn himself round. But the moment he did he almost regretted it, for in the new position he found that his nose was buried in the rubbish.

'Urgh!' he exclaimed. 'What on earth have these characters been eating?!'

With a bit more struggling he managed to get his

nose out of the foul-smelling garbage, and the next minute he was rolling away from the heap and onto the stony riverbank.

Once again, he wasn't sure that this new situation was any better than the last, since the riverbank had been thoughtfully furnished with a lot of sharp stones that cut into his back and side. Nevertheless he set about trying to loose himself from his bonds. He was reasonably certain he could, and yet every time he tried, he found the cords cutting deeper into his flesh. It was almost as if they had been designed to do so.

After several hours, Tom found every little movement had become a cross of fiery agony. His wrists were bleeding and whenever he tried to twist into a new position the pain got the better of him. Eventually he just lay there, stymied and exhausted. It was then that he was hit by a tidal wave of despair and (he was surprised to discover) humiliation.

The sun had begun to set, and Tom was just resigning himself to a cold night in the open with only the company of wolves to keep his mind off being eaten alive, when he heard horse's hooves coming up the road and then crossing the shallow river.

Had Peter come back to secretly finish him off? He tried to twist round, shouted out with the pain of moving and collapsed back into the position he started in. He heard someone dismount, and the next moment he was seized by the shoulders. With the strength of sudden panic, he wrenched himself round and, for the second time that day, found himself looking into the eyes of the Frenchman in the mail coat.

'You must not die,' said the Frenchman, and he cut the cords that bound Tom.

'Thank you,' said Tom, hardly daring to believe his luck. In fact he half thought that he must have slumped into an exhausted sleep, and this rescue was simply a dream. 'Thank you,' he said again.

'You have to get the Pope's message back to my people in Compertrix in Champagne,' said the Frenchman. 'They are waiting for you.'

Tom wanted to say: 'The Pope cares nothing for your people. All he cares about is the money in his coffers and the power in his hands. Don't hope for any mercy from that man, even if he were to deign to give an answer to you . . .'

But Tom bit his lip. What use would it do to tell the man the truth? Let him believe this little bit of hope in this seemingly hopeless world.

'Here,' said the man. 'I found you this.' They were standing in the remains of the bandits' camp, and the Frenchman was thrusting the reins of a horse into Tom's hands. 'The owner had no more use for it,' he said, and he passed his hand over his throat. Then, without another word, he jumped onto his own horse and rode off into the gathering dusk.

Tom turned to look at the horse. It was the first time he had actually owned one of his own . . . if you could call it 'owning' something when it had come to you via an act of murder. Nevertheless he instantly loved this horse. It was young and fiery but it had an intelligence in its eyes that made Tom feel that he would be able to communicate with it, and a wave of optimism surged through him.

'I'll call you Bucephalus,' Tom told the horse, and patted its neck.

The next moment he vaulted into the saddle and turned his new mount to face the way the *routiers* had gone.

'Well!' he explained to his horse. 'You don't think I'd leave Emily and Ann in the clutches of a bunch of villains like them!'

And with that he kicked Bucephalus's sides gently and the horse obediently broke into a trot, as Tom set off in pursuit of his erstwhile tormentors.

Chapter 31

The Wolf's Leap 1361

Tom spent that night in a hay-barn outside the town of Lempdes. He gathered the hay around him and was so warm and exhausted that he didn't wake up until the sun was high in the sky. He could hear people moving around outside the barn; they had discovered Bucephalus, and were discussing what a fully-fitted war horse was doing tethered to a post outside their barn.

Some said that with another couple of neighbours they would be able to seize the man-at-arms was who must be hiding in the barn. Others said it would be safer to bolt the doors and burn the place down. It was at this point that Tom stuck his head out of the door and steered the conversation round to less belligerent tactics.

By the time he left, he and the farmers had become bosom friends, and both he and Bucephalus had eaten enough breakfast to last them to the end of the month.

But Tom was anxious to be off. He had no idea how far ahead Peter de Bury and his men had got, but they now had over a day and a half's start on him, and he reckoned that even if he rode flat out for the rest of the day and tomorrow, he probably wouldn't catch up with them until the day after. And goodness knows what might have happened to Emily and Ann in that time.

But as it turned out, he didn't have to wait that long nor ride that far before he caught them up . . . or at least before he caught up with one of Peter de Bury's party. It was the Frenchman in the mail coat.

The man had dismounted on a small promontory, surmounted by a ruin, which looked across to the sudden rocks that rise up where the river Allier joins the Alagnon – a place known as Le Saut du Loup, or Wolf's Leap. The Frenchman was staring down at the confluence of the rivers when Tom drew up alongside him.

He glanced at Tom for the briefest of moments and then returned to scrutinising the riverbanks beneath them.

Following his gaze, Tom saw some tiny figures down below, whom he took to be Peter de Bury's men. They had stopped by some cottages, huddled up under the cliffs, and he could see figures running this way and that, with the soldiers giving chase on horseback.

Smoke was rising from the thatch, and as Tom and the Frenchman watched, one of the cottages suddenly burst into flames.

'He is a cruel man, Peter de Bury.' It was the Frenchman who spoke, but he was voicing exactly what Tom was thinking.

'Why do you follow him?' asked Tom.

'He is no worse than most.' The Frenchman shrugged. 'And I have to live. Father Michael always said God would provide for us. But he did not. My wife died. My child died. I could stay in Compertrix and starve and join the already dead – or else join one of the companies. It is eat or be eaten in this world.'

His eyes returned to the scene of distant carnage below them. Were those the screams of crows or humans? It was hard to tell from up here.

Tom stared down and as he did a subtle horror began to circulate around his veins. Was that Ann he could see – that slight figure in a blue jerkin and brown hose running after the villagers? Of course not! That was impossible. Ann could not have changed that much! Even her infatuation for Peter de Bury could not have turned her into a marauder . . . surely? Tom's head seemed to explode with the impossibility of it all.

But if that was Ann, Tom decided, it was even more

urgent that he save her – he had to save her from herself.

And that was the moment he remembered his sword. Or rather he remembered he'd forgotten it. It was somewhere in the brambles down by the river. As he remembered the circumstances of its loss, how the man in the turban had taken it from him and tossed it into the brambles, Tom turned bright red. No wonder he had blotted the memory out – nobody wants to remember moments of humiliation.

'I have to rescue my friends,' said Tom. 'Will you help me?'

The Frenchman turned and looked at him.

'I have helped you once,' he said, 'so that you can return to my village and tell them the Pope's message. Why should I do more?'

'There is no Pope's message,' said Tom.

The Frenchman stiffened. 'You did not deliver our message?'

'I delivered it to him in person,' said Tom. 'But the Pope did not want to listen to it. His only care is himself.'

'Then he is no different from anyone else in this terrible world.'

'But that's not so! The Pope may not care, but there are people who do!'

'Who? Who cares about anyone but themselves?'

'Well . . .' Tom thought for a moment. 'You do! You care about your village, what is it? Compertrix . . . up in Champagne! That's why you helped me escape and stole a horse for me! And I care about people too – I cared about the people of your village, even though I had never met them before! I was prepared to carry Father Michael's message to the Pope on their behalf.

'And I care about my friends,' Tom went on. 'There are many, many of us who care about other people . . . and I don't believe we're the small minority of mankind! I bet we're the majority! There are some people who want to make us believe that all men are selfish and greedy, and that there is no other way, and that man has always lived through violence and conquest. Well, I don't. And I suppose it's up to those of us who don't believe that to oppose – with every breath in our body – those who do.'

The Frenchman screwed up his eyes and sucked his cheeks in, as if he were tasting a sour plum.

'What can we do?' he said. 'Take the present situation – let's talk about the here and now. There are a dozen of them and only two of us.'

'You will help me then?'

'Like you said, we have to stand up against those

who believe that greed and violence are the only human currency,' said the Frenchman.

Tom stared at this man who had helped him once before and was now prepared to put his life on the line to help him again, and yet whose name he did not even know.

'My name is Tom,' Tom extended his hand. The Frenchman took it.

'Jean,' he said. 'My name is Jean.'

'But first, Jean, I must go and fetch my sword – I left it at the encampment.'

The Frenchman smiled. 'It didn't seem to be much use to you when you had it,' he said gently. And once again Tom blushed. 'Besides, who knows what will have happened to your friends before you get back?'

Tom looked down at the mayhem going on below. He could see his point.

'In any case, one sword or two swords – it won't make much difference against a dozen. We shall have to rescue your friends by other means.'

There was enough noise coming out of one of the unburned cottages to wake the dead. And there were certainly plenty of dead to wake. The bodies had been thrown in a heap round the back of the barn.

In the meantime, Peter de Bury and his men had obviously found a heartwarming supply of food and wine, and since early afternoon they had been busy warming their hearts, which, it must be admitted, needed quite a bit of warming.

Now a raucous conviviality made the humble dwellings shake, and the thatch was rustling with disturbed creatures, as drunken voices rang out threateningly about their undying love for a girl with golden hair.

Darkness had fallen over the confluence of the rivers Alagnon and Allier, and Tom and his new friend, the Frenchman Jean, had found it easy enough to approach what remained of the hamlet unobserved. The *routiers* seemed to have become uncharacteristically nonchalant in their safety precautions, for no one appeared to be on guard, and Tom was able to creep right up to the shutters of the nearest cottage and peer through a crack.

The merrymaking had reached that stage when it is compulsory for at least one member of the group to be lying on the floor at any given moment. To achieve this they either fell off their stools of their own accord or tripped over a dog that seemed to have happily shifted its loyalties to its new masters, and was now defiantly curled up in their midst pretending to be asleep.

'I can't see Ann or Emily,' Tom whispered.

The Frenchman nodded towards the other cottage, which stood in darkness.

'Perhaps they're in there,' he said.

Tom hoped Jean was right. He couldn't imagine how either Emily or Ann could fit into these drunken celebrations . . . and if he could imagine it, he didn't want to.

And then he came up against the same thought: why was Ann going along with all this? Peter de Bury might be handsome, he might be extremely dashing for all Tom cared, but surely whatever fantasies she'd been entertaining about him all this time, she could now see him for what he was?

Or was the new Ann blind to all that? Did that shining that Tom had seen in her eyes when she looked at Peter de Bury blot out everything else? Is that what 'love' did to people? Could it reduce the most rational, most independent, most resourceful person Tom had ever known to this? What was it? Thraldom? A kind of enchanted slavery?

And as he thought about all this, Tom discovered something strange. No matter how much he tried to focus on the idea of rescuing Emily, he found it was Ann for whom he was really risking his life.

'All right!' Tom whispered to Jean. 'Let's do it!'

*

The two of them silently slipped away from the cottages and approached the barn, where the horses had been tethered. There was something sinister about it now they knew about the corpses piled behind it, but neither of them said a word to the other.

Jean threw a stone across the path, and it skittered across the rough ground, hitting the door with a dull *thunk*. Tom shrank himself back into the shadow of a bush. Jean stood behind a water butt. The barn door remained shut. No one came to see what the noise was.

The pair crept up and opened the door a crack. They could hear the horses stirring within. Again, Jean tossed a stone across the barn floor, letting it rattle across the earth until it hit a wooden post. Still no one moved.

'They haven't even posted a guard for the horses!' He sounded rather shocked.

'Lucky for us!' said Tom.

The drunken singing was now ringing across the farmyard to reveal that the girl's hair was in fact *real* gold and that the singers were going to sell it in the market next day, and by the time the singers had got round to enumerating the things they were going to buy with the money, Tom and Jean had the horses untied and stampeding out of the barn and across the yard.

Tom and Jean ran as fast as they could into the darkness that huddled up close to the buildings. There they crouched behind a bush to watch what happened next.

As luck would have it, one of the *routiers*, whose name happened to be Martin, had wandered out to relieve himself. For a few befuddled moments, the sound of yelling coming from the barn didn't strike him as at all odd, but then his brain suggested that since all the companions were inside yelling about all the ways a girl's hair was going to make them rich, there shouldn't be anyone else in the barn to be yelling about anything else.

At this point a couple of brain cells that had not received the battering that Martin had intended for them, suggested that something might be amiss with the horses. But by the time the surrounding brain cells had pulled themselves together enough to respond to this outstanding suggestion, the sound of thundering hooves threw them back into confusion.

Martin turned to see a dozen horses stampeding across the yard towards him. For a second he thought that he too would enjoy joining in the stampede with the horses.

'I am a horse too!' he found himself thinking. But then the two still-active brain cells managed to impress on the others that this might not be a good idea.

Furthermore these still-active brain cells succeeded in suggesting that their owner – as a non-horse – really ought to try and stop the real horses before they disappeared into the night.

Martin tried to grab the reins of the first horse, only to find that the majority of his brain cells had now totally abandoned their normal duties and had either retired for a well-earned rest or were asleep on the job. With only two active brain cells to guide his limbs, he misjudged his grab at the reins, fell forward into the horse's flank, tripped and found himself rolling on the ground, trampled under the hooves of the following horses. His yells of pain and panic called his plight to the attention of the Big Spenders indoors (who had by this time sold all the girl's hair).

Several figures staggered to the door and proceeded to cheer the horses on. However, one of the more perspicacious of the brigands pointed out that the horses were theirs, but if the creatures continued on their present course they soon wouldn't be.

This remarkable insight had an equally remarkable effect upon the men. With the kind of enthusiasm that can only come from total inebriation, they gave chase – falling over each other and bumping into posts and pigsties as they did so. The man from Cheshire fell over a leather bucket and lay on the floor giggling hysterically, before he managed to stagger to his feet and blindly follow the rest.

Tom and Jean watched until all the men had vanished into the darkness, and their yells and laughter had become a distant disturbance along with the cicadas and bullfrogs. The two rescuers then raced across to the darkened cottage, where an unsteady glow of candlelight was now leaking through the shutters. Tom put his eye to a crack and saw the beautiful Emily coming downstairs with a candle in her hand.

He ran round to the front and reached the door of the cottage at the same time as Emily.

'Emily!' he whispered. 'Quick! Now's our chance! They're all chasing their horses!'

'Tom!' said Emily.

'Where's Ann?' and he pushed past Emily and ran to the stairs and shouted up: 'Ann! Quick! We've come to get you!'

'Ann isn't here,' said Emily.

'She's with Peter!' exclaimed Tom.

'No she isn't!' said Emily.

'Well, where is she then?' Tom felt surprisingly cross that Ann wasn't where he thought she'd be. Then he added: 'Peter de Bury was going to kill me!'

'I don't know where she is,' replied Emily. A coolness seemed to have crept into her voice.

'She's not upstairs?'

'No.'

'Then she must be in the other house!' Tom hurried back to the doorway. Jean was already running across to the other building. 'Come on!' Tom yelled to Emily.

But Emily didn't move.

'They'll be back soon!' called Tom. But Emily still did not move. 'Emily?' Tom stopped and turned.

'I'm not coming,' said Emily.

'What?!' exclaimed Tom.

'I'm staying here,' said the beautiful and imperious Emily.

'What are you talking about?' Tom raced back to her. 'What do you mean "you're staying here"?'

'Exactly that,' replied Emily, and Tom could now hear the same coldness in her voice that she used when addressing doorkeepers and servants.

'But this morning you were desperate to get away from these bandits!' exclaimed Tom. 'Are you crazy or something?'

'I don't think the lady wants to go,' said another voice. Tom turned and by the flicker of Emily's candle he could just make out a dim figure descending the rickety stairs. It was Peter de Bury.

'Where's Ann?' shouted Tom.

'How should I know?' retorted Peter.

'She's with you!' exclaimed Tom.

'No she isn't,' came the cool reply. It matched his cool blue eyes and the coolness of Emily's voice.

Tom turned to Emily in frustration.

'What's happened to Ann?' he demanded. 'And what about your brother? Have you forgotten we're going to rescue him?'

'Of course I haven't forgotten,' replied Emily. 'Peter is going to help me find him. I've got a real knight now, Tom. I shan't be needing you any more.'

In the confusion of feelings that overwhelmed Tom at that moment, perhaps the one that overrode all the rest was an indignation on the part of Ann. Peter de Bury – worthless though he might be – was Ann's lover. Undeserving and ungrateful as he was, Peter had been the focus of Ann's thoughts and hopes for the last two or three years. How could he betray her like this? Come to that – how could Emily just take him over like this? But above all – where *was* Ann? What on earth had happened to her?

And then a sudden terrible thought entered Tom's mind, and the moment it did, it became a certainty. He saw it all in a flash of insight. This Peter de Bury had realised just who Emily was . . . and that the Lady Emilia de Valois was not only a rich prize as a hostage

. . . she was an even richer prize as a wife . . .

Tom stared from one to the other. It was so obvious. Instead of slaughtering these poor villagers for their sides of pork and their casks of wine, Peter de Bury could escort the Lady Emily to England, and if he could engineer her brother Guillaume's escape from his English prison, he would be richly rewarded. And if, in the meantime, he could make the lovely Lady Emily want him for her husband, he could become wealthy beyond his wildest dreams and become a fine French lord into the bargain.

Tom suddenly remembered with a painful clarity the look that he had seen in Ann's face when she gazed at Peter de Bury. What was the trust he saw in that look worth now? He suddenly realised how inconvenient her love must have appeared to Peter de Bury. Instead of being a wonderful gift, it was the only thing standing between him and the rich pickings to be made out of the Lady Emilia de Valois!

Tom's stomach, which was already inside out, now turned itself upside down, back-to-front, topsy-turvy and vice versa all in one spasm. He knew what had happened to Ann.

Chapter 32

Milan 1385

'Ah! Il Medecina!' said the Lady Donnina de' Porri, favourite mistress of Bernabò Visconti, the Lord of Milan.

A man in his forties, with a grizzled beard, strode into the room followed by two burly men who held between them the emaciated figure of John, Sir Thomas English's squire.

'My lady,' said Il Medecina. 'We shall soon get to the truth of this.' And the two burly men threw Squire John onto the floor, where he lay motionless.

The Lady Donnina turned to Sir Thomas and smiled: 'Surely you don't imagine I would believe your uncorroborated word, Sir Thomas? You want your squire back alive? You'll have to sing for him, minstrel!'

'Give us a full and truthful account of what you *really* saw in Gian Galeazzo's court at Pavia,' said Il Medecina, and one of the burly men quickly and

314

precisely snapped a length of cord around Squire John's neck as if he did it many times a day – which may well have been the case. He then began to twist it with a piece of wood. Squire John gasped as the garrotte began to choke him, but he didn't cry out. The fact was he couldn't.

'I have told you everything exactly as I saw and heard it,' said Sir Thomas English. 'No amount of torture you can inflict on my wretched squire can change that.'

'He has forty seconds more breath in his body,' said Il Medecina quietly. 'It would be best if you told us the truth.'

'Everything I have reported to the Lady Donnina de' Porri is as I observed it. It is the truth,' said Tom.

By this time Squire John had gone pale and his tongue was sticking out. Il Medecina nodded to the torturer and the man released the garrotte and threw the squire back onto the floor.

Strange how little noise torture makes, Tom thought. It's so casual, so ordinary, so painless for those who watch. His eyes ran over his squire, where he lay slumped on the floor, checking for signs of distress. There were plenty . . . but suddenly the youth glanced up at Tom, and for a split second their eyes met. Tom recognised that look in his squire's eyes: it was a look of defiance. It was a look that said: 'Ready when you are!' And in that instant Tom realised that John was not in quite as bad a state as he was pretending to be.

But the man with the grizzled beard was speaking.

'Sir Thomas Englishman,' said Il Medecina. 'To put it quite bluntly, we do not believe you. I shall now apply a little pressure to your squire. You would do well to take pity on him, for what we are about to do next will be extremely unpleasant for him.'

One of the torturers had grabbed Squire John's hands and was holding them while the second produced a pack of iron pins.

'There are twenty pins,' explained Il Medecina. 'They may not look much, but I can assure you the pain when they are inserted under the fingernail is excruciating.'

Then a most extraordinary thing happened. Tom suddenly felt the Lady Donnina de' Porri's fingers caressing the back of his neck. He turned and looked at her. She looked somehow excited, and the awful thought struck him that perhaps all this was just a late-night entertainment as far as she was concerned.

Il Medecina waved a jewel-encrusted finger at the torturer and the man pulled out the first pin. At the same time, Squire John locked eyes with Tom again, and Tom gave an almost imperceptible nod.

And that was it, really.

Tom suddenly span round, and caught the beautiful Lady Donnina in an armlock round her beautiful throat. The next moment he grabbed the hilt of Il Medecina's short sword, and yanked it out of its scabbard with surprising ease. The Lord of Milan's chief councillor reacted too slowly and caught the sword by the blade, cutting his hand as he did so. He gave a sort of howl and clutched the wound as blood spurted onto the floor.

Now Squire John had seemed – to everyone who had paid any attention to him recently – to be at death's door. He had hardly had the strength in his limbs to move. Whenever anyone hit him, it was like hitting a rag doll – there was really no spirit or response in him. In fact hitting him was no longer any fun at all, and they had rather given it up. Indeed his captors had thought so little of whatever life remained in him that they hadn't even bothered to manacle him when they brought him up to the grand lady's private chamber.

It therefore came as a considerable surprise when the near-dead John suddenly sprang into life.

He flung himself at the legs of one of his captors, bringing him down to the floor with a crash. At the same time he pulled the man's dagger from its sheath and span round as the other guard rushed towards him, and the knife slid into his ribs without him even being aware of it.

The guard had grabbed John by the neck and was trying to choke him again, but the force suddenly left him and a look of incomprehension overwhelmed the man's face. A second later he swayed and tottered forwards with the knife in his ribs. Tom leapt out of his way as he went crashing face forward to the floor – right on top of the other guard, who was trying to scramble to his feet. They both went down again, but the uninjured man rolled out from under his stricken comrade and started to rise to his feet again. Before he had straightened up, however, John had smashed a stool over the man's head and he sank back to the floor for the third time. And, oddly enough, his past life flashed up before his eyes just as if he were drowning . . . but of course no one was aware of this little miracle and the man had forgotten about it by the time he recovered his senses.

Meanwhile Tom had applied Il Medecina's short sword to the beautiful golden throat of the Lady Donnina.

'Do not for a moment imagine I wouldn't use this!' he informed Il Medecina, who was standing frozen to the spot looking at the bleeding palm of his hand. The Lady Donnina was gasping for breath as badly as Squire

John had been minutes before, and Tom made the mistake of loosening his hold on her neck to allow her to breathe. Whereupon, instead of thanking him politely, the lady immediately started to scream, and Tom was forced to put his hand over her mouth. To show her gratitude the Lady Donnina bit him, and he joined in the screaming.

'Stop that!' he cried, and thrust the sword under her nose where she could see it.

And all the time, the grizzle-bearded man stood there as if he had been turned to stone.

The fact is that Il Medecina's professional life was full of long-term stratagems and the careful assessment of tricky situations, secret information imparted in hushed whispers, short-term policies and good advice. He excelled in espionage and counter-espionage, in covering his tracks, in creating false impressions and in diversionary tactics.

He was a man with a deep understanding of human behaviour and of the political implications of any particular action. He knew the characters of many of the great rulers of Europe with whom his master, Bernabò, would have to deal, and if he did not already know of them, he knew how to find out about them – all about them. His opinions were sound, well thought out and generally impenetrable.

But Il Medecina's world was that of the observer –
the disengaged adviser – the politician – the counsellor.
It is true that he wore the latest kind of sword (short
and pointed for thrusting rather than slashing), but he
wore it merely because it was a badge of status. He
would no more think of drawing it than he would of
taking his clothes off in public.

Perhaps it was because he was used to such unlim-
ited power that he now seemed unable to comprehend
the raw physical challenge that confronted him. It was
almost as if it were all too simple for him to understand. It was too crude to be worthy of his attention,
and his mind seemed to simply switch off as he stepped
back and became once again the observer – watching it
all as in the abstract. Violence, although a political tool
he had used relentlessly and without pity, was, for Il
Medecina, entirely theoretical.

Tom and John, meanwhile, were doing as little theor-
ising as possible. They were just concerned with the
immediate problem of getting out of the nearest exit.

Tom dragged the Lady Donnina to the doorway,
while John slipped the key out of the lock. Tom then
pushed the lady back into the chamber and he and
John slid through the door and locked it from the outside.

The moment the key turned all hell seemed to break

loose in the room. There was screaming and yelling and the Lady Donnina was hammering on the door like a fury from the netherworld.

As Tom and John reached the stairs, a small gaggle of servants appeared. There was a kitchen maid, a couple of menservants, the butler and a cook, who was wielding a meat cleaver. Tom ran straight up to them.

'Quick!' he exclaimed. 'There's a grey-haired man attacking the Lady Donnina! The door's locked! Get the steward's key!' And one of the menservants ran off to find the steward. The others ran to the chamber door and started banging on it and yelling to the Lady Donnina inside.

'Are you all right, my lady?' yelled the butler.

'Stop those two men!' yelled Il Medecina, whose senses had returned to him now the immediate danger was passed.

'Leave the Lady Donnina alone!' shouted the cook, who was secretly enamoured of the Lady Donnina.

'What?' yelled Il Medecina.

'You'll pay for it if you harm her – you villain!' yelled the cook, raising his meat cleaver in anticipation.

'Did you hear what I said?' shouted Il Medecina.

'You monster!'

'Did you hear what I said? Stop them!'

'Who?'

Terry Jones

But by this time the steward had appeared, and the key was quickly turned in the lock – whereupon Il Medecina burst out of the door yelling:

'Where did they . . .' but before he could say 'go?', his grey locks had disappeared under a scrum of household servants, who in a flash had him pinned to the floor. It was only by a miracle that the cook did not finish the old man off with his meat cleaver.

'What the devil!' screamed the Lord of Milan's closest adviser.

'Oh! Your lordship! I do beg your pardon!' cried the butler, who was the first to realise the mistake.

'Where are they?' yelled the Lady Donnina.

'Who?' repeated the butler.

'The minstrel and the boy!' screamed Il Medecina. Whereupon the kitchen maid, the cook, the butler and the manservant all span round.

But by then Tom and John had long disappeared.

Chapter 33

Milan 1385

S ir Thomas English and his squire were walking across the main hall of Bernabò Visconti's palace towards the servants' quarters.

'Never run,' said Sir Thomas. 'It calls attention to yourself.'

'Right!' said Squire John. One of the things he admired so much about his master was the way he knew what to do in any given situation.

'If you run, you might just as well put up a large sign above your head reading: "This is who you're looking for!"' said Tom.

'There he is!' cried a guard who had just appeared at the other end of the hall, and Tom and John burst into a run without even giving Squire John time to say: 'Thanks for the tip, Sir Thomas!'

They crashed through the door that linked the servants' quarters with the hall and found themselves in the kitchen, where a party was in full swing. A musician was standing on one of the working tables, creating an admirable racket with the bagpipes. Some servants were already drunk enough to be able to make out the tune and were busy attempting to dance to it. Others were still in the process of achieving that enviable state. Still others were playing that well-known game: How Long Does It Take to Eat a Whole Ham in One Go?

Not a single person looked like they were in mourning for the Lady Regina della Scala, even though they were all still wearing black.

'It's the cook's birthday,' explained one of the serving maids. 'He doesn't know how old he is, but he says it's his birthday.'

'He says it every week!' grunted an old 'necessary woman', whose duty it was to make sure all the chamber pots were empty and clean.

At this point the pursuing guard burst into the kitchen.

'Where's that minstrel?' he yelled at Tom, who hadn't been able to elbow his way through the merry throng. 'Oh! It's you!'

Tom gave John a nod. It was time for a little more teamwork. John dived for the guard's legs and had started to topple him over when Tom noticed the man was carrying something.

'John! Hang on!' he called out.

As it happened, John was having some difficulty trying to topple the guard in the tightly packed kitchen: there simply wasn't anywhere to topple. More to the point the guard had grabbed a ladle from the table and was hitting John over the head with it.

Tom grabbed the guard's wrist to stop him, and pointed to the object in his other hand.

'Where'd you get that?' he asked.

'You left it in the hall,' said the guard. 'You won't get far without your instrument, minstrel,' and he held up Tom's *citole*. At the same time he dropped the ladle and cuffed John round the ear. 'What's the matter with you?' asked the guard.

'Sorry,' said John, scrambling to his feet. 'I thought you were someone else.' It wasn't much of an excuse, but it was the best he could think of at the time.

'Anyway, thanks, for bringing the *citole*,' interrupted Tom.

'By the way, I liked the song,' said the guard, and he grabbed Tom's sleeve.

'Thanks,' returned Tom, trying to free his sleeve from the guard's grasp.

Terry Jones

'I thought you hit just the right balance,' said the guard, holding on to Tom's sleeve.

'Oh good,' he said.

'You know, it's so easy to get all mawkish and sentimental in elegies, but you kept it light and fun. I thought.'

Now all this was doubtless good news for an aspiring minstrel, but at that moment, Sir Thomas English had more pressing things on his mind. So he thanked the guard yet again and turned to go, while trying to disengage his sleeve from the man's grip.

'I particularly liked the line about "I'd count myself the Count of All" – very witty. I thought.'

'Thanks,' said Tom, who had never been less interested in hearing a favourable critique of his songwriting abilities.

'And the way you sang it was spot on. I thought,' continued the guard – his hand still gripping Tom's sleeve.

'Sir Thomas!' exclaimed Squire John. 'Don't forget we have to be at my Lord Lodovico's lodgings before he retires!'

'Thanks for reminding me, John!' said Tom, and turning back to the guard, he managed to extract his sleeve from the man's grip. 'I really do appreciate your remarks – but I must go!'

'I thought perhaps you and I could share a flask of wine,' said the guard, reapplying his hand to Tom's sleeve. 'I'll buy it.'

'You're very kind,' said Tom, and yet again he pulled his sleeve away from the man's grasp. 'But my Lord Lodovico is waiting for me.'

'Well, tomorrow evening then?' said the guard.

'Yes! Yes! Good idea!'

'Right, tomorrow it is then.'

'Right!' Tom managed to get his sleeve free once again. But yet again the man clutched at it, and leaned forward and whispered:

'And maybe you could lose your squire? Eh?'

'Right!' said Tom, and finally he was free, and elbowing his way through the crowd in pursuit of Squire John.

The guard watched him go for some moments, and then muttered under his breath: 'A real musician doesn't leave his instrument behind.'

He was still holding the *citole*.

Tom and Squire John ran across the vast courtyard of Bernabò's palace. It was large enough to parade the troops in, and the vast loggias to the side were so big that the great lord often held jousting tournaments there in the shade.

'What's happened to the "no running" policy, Sir Thomas?' asked Squire John. He wasn't being the least ironic; he really wanted to know.

'There comes a moment,' replied Tom in between breaths, 'when all theories get superseded by events.'

In fact, they didn't seem to be attracting anyone's attention; night had fallen some time ago, and their progress through the unlit emptiness of the courtyard went unremarked except by some bats that were startled into wheeling and diving in and out of the loggias. As it happened, the guard at the main entrance also heard their footsteps coming rapidly across the gravel, but as he was expecting some drinking companions, he merely assumed it was them and that they were in a hurry to see him.

Before they reached him, however, Tom and Squire John stopped running. They ducked into a doorway, and began to stroll through a service area and then down a narrow passage that led to a side entrance in the walls that was used only by servants of Bernabò Visconti's household.

The guard on duty was an affable sort of fellow, who grinned when he saw Tom and said: 'I'd count myself the Count of All!'

Tom began to wish he'd never thought of the wretched line.

'Very clever!' said the guard, nudging Tom in the ribs.

'We're just going out for a short time,' said Tom, trying to steer the conversation to more pressing matters.

'As a matter of fact, I write a little myself,' said the guard. 'Perhaps you'd like to hear some of my verses?'

'How about when we come back?' suggested Tom.

'Really?' said the guard. It was the first time anyone had showed the slightest bit of interest in his poetry. His companions-in-arms all regarded him as a timid soldier and a man without a single streak of aggression, and therefore the last person to write poetry – at least the sort of poetry that they would be interested in.

As for his mother – her first question whenever he arrived back at the little stone farmhouse in Umbria, where she kept her hens under the same roof as herself, was always: 'So who have you killed now?' To which he would reply: 'No one, Mama, but I have written a whole poem.' And his mama would turn away to milk the goat. She regarded poetry as a sinful waste of precious resources, especially at a time when what was really needed was for God to send more rain and for the cow to produce more milk.

And so it was that, partly owing to the frustrated literary ambitions of one of Bernabò Visconti's guards, Sir

Thomas English, currently disguised as a minstrel, and his squire John, found themselves at liberty once again in the night-enfolded city of Milan.

A short walk down the street towards the Porta Romana brought them to the corner of the Visconti Palace. Built up against the high walls was a series of low wooden structures that stretched back into the darkness.

'There's a shortcut to the stables down here,' said Sir Tom, who had already turned down the narrow lane between the sheds.

'The stables, Sir Thomas?'

'Of course! I've got to rescue Bucephalus.'

'Oh,' said Squire John, but what he really meant was: 'Isn't that a bit risky, sir? You know my Lord of Milan guards his horses closer than his children! And he guards *them* pretty closely!' But he felt it was not his place to question his master.

'Aren't you going to say: "Isn't that a bit risky, sir?"' asked Tom.

'Well . . . possibly . . .'

'"You know my Lord of Milan guards his horses closer than his children!"' continued Tom. '"And he guards *them* pretty closely!"'

'That's just what I was going to say!' exclaimed the squire.

'Good!' replied Tom. 'Never take what I say for granted. Always question everything!'

'Right!' said Squire John, who was always anxious to do his master's bidding. He glanced sideways at Sir Thomas, however, and then took a deep breath and began:

'Sir Thomas! Talking of Bernabò's children, there's something I must . . .' but he never got any further because that was the moment when the first dog started howling.

Why the dogs had been so quiet up to now is anybody's guess. Normally Bernabò Visconti's dogs kept a sizeable proportion of the population of Milan awake in their beds at night with their constant barking and howling.

You see the Lord of Milan kept a lot of dogs. Not just two or three to fawn on him as he strode around the palace, nor just a couple of dozen for hunting. Bernabò Visconti kept a *lot* of dogs. And Tom and John's short-cut to the stable led through the place that was known by the good citizens as the '*cà di can*' – the doghouse. It was here that the tyrant of Milan kept the majority of his dogs.

And when I say 'a lot' of dogs, I mean 'a lot'. He didn't keep fifty or even seventy dogs. He didn't keep just a couple of hundred dogs. He kept a *lot*. Five hundred dogs? Uh uh! The Lord of Milan never did such things by half. He kept more like a thousand dogs. At least that's what the good folk of Milan reckoned.

The truth was even more preposterous.

In all Bernabò Visconti the Lord of Milan kept around five thousand dogs. He couldn't resist buying more and more of the creatures. It was a mania.

He knew that the majority of his fellow rulers – the princes, kings and emperors of Europe – regarded him as a beast himself, and so he surrounded himself with even more beasts, as if to dilute his own beastliness. Outside his chamber he kept a menagerie, including an ostrich, and in the grounds of his palace you could find lions and leopards and even a sad gazelle that could hardly raise its head above its knees, so sick it was for the prickling heat of the veldt that it remembered in the pores of its skin.

What was the matter with the world? Didn't they know the Lord of Milan commissioned books? That he paid his minstrels more than any other prince in the world? That he built almshouses and churches to the glory of God and the worship of his own magnificence? And yet those snobs that sat on the lofty thrones of Europe still saw him as a monster! As a beast! Well, he was worth more than any of them. And that was why he kept so many dogs.

But five thousand dogs take a lot of feeding. So he housed many of them in the homes of his subjects and cut off the hands or heads (depending on the weather) of those who either underfed or overfed those precious animals.

It was, perhaps, the single most resented imposition that the good people of Milan suffered under their lord.

By the time Tom and John had taken another step, a second dog had taken up the howl. By the time they had reached the third kennel, forty other dogs had joined in. The next footstep caused the palace walls to echo with the howling and barking of two thousand dogs.

Perhaps Tom and his squire John should have turned and fled there and then, but they didn't. They kept on their way through the *cà di can*, heading towards the stables.

The uproar from the dogs, however, had not gone unremarked in the guardhouse, and, even though the barking of the dogs was a daily event, one or two guards appeared round the corner to investigate. They were in time to see Tom and Squire John disappear round the back of the doghouse.

In the meantime, more guards emerged from the stables, and were now blocking the narrow alleyway of the *cà di can* ahead of Tom and John.

'Should we keep walking to allay suspicion?' asked Squire John.

'No fear!' replied Tom. 'Run!'

To their right Tom had noticed another alleyway, and it was down this that he now plunged with John hard on his heels. It was a dead end. Tom came to a stop and so did John. And so, luckily, did the pursuing guards.

That was the good news. The bad news was that the guards had stopped in order to release several of the dogs, and these now came hurtling towards the fugitives.

It's pretty unnerving to be charged at by guard dogs at the best of times, but it was even more unnerving in this instance since these particular guard dogs were reputed to have developed a taste for human flesh, upon which the Lord of Milan was supposed to feed them from time to time.

'Uh oh!' said John, as the dogs fought each other for the honour of the first bite.

'There's only one way!' said Tom.

'Which is . . .?' John was always keen to hear his master's opinion.

'Up!' said Tom, and the next minute they had both vaulted up onto the low kennel at the end, and were running across the uneven roofs of the *cà di can*, and the dogs were left jumping up and sinking their teeth into nothing more satisfying than thin air.

'And then down!' yelled Tom, and before John had the chance to say: 'But down's just water!' Tom had leapt and landed in a shower of spray.

Squire John hesitated for no longer than it took a couple of the hysterical dogs to bark once before he too plunged into the dark water of the Milan canal and was following his master, swimming desperately towards the postern gate.

Some time later Tom's head bobbed up above the glinting surface of the canal outside the city of Milan. He was gasping for air and his lungs felt as if they had already burst. He clung to the bank of the canal while he coughed up a considerable portion of it back into the proper channel. Then he looked around for his squire, and was surprised to find him grinning cheerfully from the shore.

'You look like you've drunk half the canal, sir!' said Squire John.

'How the devil did you get up there so quickly?' panted Tom.

'I used to be village champion,' replied Squire John. 'I could swim right round the castle moat without coming up for breath more than twice! Grab my hand, sir!' And Squire John pulled Sir Thomas English up out of the Milan canal.

They stood there for some moments, catching their breath and dripping water into the puddle that had formed around them. They could hear the dogs of the *cà di can* still shattering the night with their howling and barking.

Eventually John broke what would have otherwise been the silence.

'Sir Thomas, I hate to say this, but there's something I haven't told you.'

Tom shook the water out of his ears and said: 'Well, it'll have to wait. We've got to do something first.'

'What's that?' asked John.

Tom looked at his squire and hesitated. He was not at all certain how the young man was going to receive what he was going to say next.

'Well . . .' ventured Tom. 'We still haven't rescued Bucephalus . . .'

'So we need to get back into the city to rescue him at once!' exclaimed Squire John.

'I thought you wouldn't be very keen on the idea.' Tom was slightly surprised at John's enthusiasm.

'No! No! It was exactly what I was going to suggest, sir!'

'Let me get this clear, John,' said Tom. 'You were going to suggest trying to get back into the city?'

'Well, that's what you're suggesting too, sir . . .' replied John.

'Yes, but . . .' Tom thought for a moment. 'This anxiety of yours to return to the city, John, it couldn't have anything to do with a certain young lady by the name of Beatrice?'

Squire John flushed.

'She visited me in prison!' he said. 'She swore to come with me to the ends of the earth!'

'John!' Tom sounded rather exasperated. 'I do *not* think that is a sufficient reason for undertaking an enterprise that is so risky . . . so fraught with danger . . .'

'But you want to do it too, sir!' pointed out John. Tom closed his mouth and stared at his squire.

'All right!' he said. 'How are we going to do it?'

John shrugged. 'Er . . .' was the best plan he could come up with.

'Er is not a plan of action,' Tom pointed out.

'No,' agreed John.

'Well, I suggest we start at the obvious place,' said Tom.

'Which is?' asked Squire John.

'The main gate,' said Tom. And with that they set off

around the path that followed the perimeter of the city wall. John was not quite sure that the main gate of the city of Milan was the most obvious place to effect an illegal entry, but he told himself that Tom would have worked out a plan and that in the fullness of time he would get to hear of it.

If the truth were to be told, however, Tom had absolutely no plan in his head whatsoever. He just hoped something would suggest itself by the time they reached the gate. That, however, was something they were not destined to do.

They had walked at least halfway round before the gate came into sight, and Tom still hadn't worked out much of a strategy. He thought that he might try and talk his way in, but what he was going to say still hadn't progressed beyond the 'good morning, how are you?' stage.

He had just moved the hypothetical conversation on to: 'My friend and I have business in the city but we were waylaid by bandits and all our papers were stolen . . .' when the two of them froze in their tracks. The main gates of the city of Milan were opening.

'Why are they opening the gates at this hour!' murmured Squire John.

'Maybe they're looking for someone . . .' muttered Tom. 'Like us.'

At which point they heard shouts and the clatter of horses' hooves on stone and a troop of mounted soldiers rode through the gates, with the distinct air of looking for someone.

'Uh oh!' said John.

'Uh oh!' agreed Tom, and before the last soldier had passed under the portcullis, the minstrel-knight and his squire had disappeared down one of the narrow lanes of the city beyond the gates. The heroic rescue of Beatrice and Bucephalus was going to have to wait.

They ran as fast as their wet shoes allowed them, and turned a corner.

'Sir Thomas!' exclaimed Squire John.

'What?'

'Look!'

'The guards?' gasped Tom.

'No!' whispered John, his voice almost quivering with excitement. 'There! D'you see?'

'No!' whispered Tom. 'Where?'

'It's you!' Squire John was pointing at the wall of the grand house that featured the *pittura infamante* of the red-haired man dangling upside down from the gallows. 'Look, that's your hair!'

'What's my hair got to . . .?' began Tom, but at that moment they heard hooves and shouts. 'Quick!' Tom pulled his squire away from the portrait on the wall, and into a courtyard.

It was a small enclosed court, with several doors leading off it. Tom and John shrank back into the shadows behind an old barrel that was standing outside one of the doors, as the clatter of hooves approached. The troop of guards rode past the wall that bore Tom's *pittura infamante*, without looking at either it or the courtyard in which Tom and John were hidden.

As luck would have it, however, a thin, mean-looking dog had taken it into its head to follow the horses, and this creature now strayed into the courtyard. It wandered past them and proceeded to sniff around the corners of the walls.

Tom slipped out of the shadows and stuck his head around the building to see that the troop had reached the further end of the street.

'Let's go!' hissed Tom, whereupon the dog assumed that he was included in the invitation and gave a bark of excitement!

'Sh!' hissed Squire John, but the dog was determined to show how much it appreciated its new friends and started alternately licking the back of John's legs and yapping cheerfully.

'Sh!' whispered Tom, but it was too late. The last soldier had turned in his saddle as the pair ran out of their hiding place and back down the road pursued by the extraordinarily elated dog.

'There they are!' cried the guard, and the troop reined in their horses and turned them round with some difficulty in the narrow street. By the time the entire troop had changed direction, Tom and John had disappeared round the next corner.

Tom and John ran and ran, desperately looking for an open doorway or side alley, but there was none. Meanwhile the increasingly rapid rhythm of hoof-beats behind them drove them forward like drums beating forward the vanguard on the field of battle.

Then suddenly there they were! The troop rounded the corner, the leader yelled, his horse snorted and whinnied, and they charged towards the fugitives.

Instead of running, however, Tom suddenly stopped in his tracks and span round. John was so preoccupied with escape that it was a dozen strides before he realised that his master was no longer by his side. When looked back, he saw Tom raising his fingers to his mouth, and as the horses bore down on him, he gave three shrill whistles.

At once the leading horse reared up in the air and bucked – taking the leader of the troop totally by surprise. The man was thrown off the saddle and into the path of the other horses, who had no room to manoeuvre. The hooves of the next horse struck the fallen guard and the horse stumbled and fell, bringing total confusion into the narrow street, as the following horses either shied away or followed suit, pitching their riders onto the roadway.

'Bucephalus!' shouted Tom, as the leading horse galloped towards him, and before a single guard had scrambled to his feet, Tom had leapt onto the saddle of his old horse. The next moment he had pulled his squire up behind him and they were both speeding off into the night and out of the southern suburb of the city of Milan.

Chapter 34

The Wolf's Leap 1361

Peter de Bury stood there smiling coolly, with the beautiful Emily's hand holding his. Tom found himself staring at Peter's hand. Had that hand taken Ann's life? Or would Peter de Bury have got one of his men to carry out so menial a task?

Tom's mind was about to explode in an excess of anger, resentment, sadness, hatred, loss, regret, envy, rage and several other emotions, when Jean the Frenchman came up behind him and asked:

'What's happened?'

'He's murdered Ann!' was all Tom was capable of saying.

The cool smile on Peter de Bury's face grew even cooler and wider, showing off his remarkably white teeth for a brief instant.

'Why do you think I would do that?' he asked in a voice pleasant enough to freeze a lobster in its tracks.

'What have you done with her?' yelled Tom, and before he knew what he was doing, he had leapt at Peter de Bury, with his fists flying in all directions . . . though mostly in the direction of Peter de Bury's extremely handsome nose.

What happened next was unclear to Tom, but instead of finding himself triumphantly standing with one foot on the defeated Peter de Bury's chest and the grateful Emily gazing admiringly up into his eyes, he found himself flying backwards across the room and landing with a crunch against the far wall. His head snapped back and hit the doorpost and the next minute Peter de Bury was on top of him. A knife jumped into Peter's hand as if by magic, and a second later Tom lost consciousness.

The sequence of events which Tom consequently missed was as follows:

The Lady Emilia de Valois shouted: 'Look out!' Whereupon Peter de Bury looked up from the unconscious Tom in time to see Jean the Frenchman draw his sword. Now Peter was well aware that size really does count when it comes to cold steel, so he leapt to his feet and in a single deft movement positioned himself behind the lovely Emily. He stood there with his nine-inch knife pointing at Jean's two-foot sword.

'If I were you I'd take your friend and get out of here!' he advised the Frenchman.

Jean looked down at the unconscious Tom and then across at Peter de Bury and the lady. Then he grunted, swung Tom up onto his shoulders and stumped out of the house. It was good advice, Jean decided, for no matter how much longer his sword might be than Peter's knife, there were other things to consider . . . like the return of the other bandits, whom he could already hear swearing and cursing as they stumbled back empty-handed.

Tom started to come to his senses as Jean staggered through the night.

'What happened?' he muttered.

'I'll tell you later,' mumbled the Frenchman, as he helped Tom up into Bucephalus's saddle. He then jumped onto his own horse, and led Tom away from Le Saut du Loup, towards the north.

Dawn was just putting a little colour into the red roof tiles of the village of Nonette, as Tom and Jean the Frenchman rode up through the thin morning mist that had gathered in the valley. A few women were already fetching water from the stream, and the occasional dog raised its head to watch the two men ride by, but decided it was too early to make the effort to bark.

345

Jean and Tom sat by the stream that ran by the side of the road and splashed the cold water on their faces.

Tom was silent, and Jean kept glancing at him sideways.

Eventually he said: 'There was nothing you could do.'

'I should have killed him,' said Tom. He'd never imagined those words would pass his lips.

'He said he hadn't murdered her,' said the Frenchman. 'He said he didn't know where she was.'

'Do you believe that?' asked Tom.

'Well . . .' said Jean, 'what reason would he have to kill her?'

'You saw him,' replied Tom. 'He was hand in hand with Emily. She says he's going to be her knight and she's going to England with him to rescue her brother.'

'That's still no reason to kill Ann,' observed Jean.

'Don't you see? He got rid of Ann because she was in the way! As long as she was around he couldn't make love to Emily!'

The pallor of Tom's face had now been replaced by a red flush. Perhaps it was the action of the cold water.

'He's the devil!' he muttered, and suddenly the image of Ann, dressed as Squire Alan and standing in front of the Duke of Lancaster, bold and fearless, leapt into his mind and he couldn't stop a howl of rage and sadness escaping from his lungs.

And with that howl, a dozen other images of Ann flashed through his head and lit up his clouded brain like lightning strokes: Ann, dressed as Alan, climbing the city wall when they first met, Ann riding alongside Sir John Hawkley as his squire, Ann dressed up in the armour of Sir Geoffrey de Bernay, Ann leaping from the roof of the Pope's palace in Avignon . . .

During this internal storm, Tom had become a crumpled heap on the ground, sobbing and crying and shaking – an inconsolable cornucopia of grief. The Frenchman watched him for some time, and then he reached out a hand and touched him gently.

'There,' he said. It was all he could say.

And then another image of Ann blew up over Tom's mental horizon, and obliterated everything else. It was the image of Ann looking up into the face of Peter de Bury. For an instant Tom thought the image would also wipe away his grief and allow him to return to the world of the living, but instead the grief instantly multiplied like a virus and, taking hold of Tom's body, shook him in such violent spasms that Jean the Frenchman could only put his arms around the youth and hold him – as if to keep his soul and body together.

*

Sometime later, the sun rose up above the surrounding hills, dispersing the clouds and mist, and found Tom and Jean the Frenchman breakfasting outside a small house that belonged to one of the women who had been fetching water.

'I can't just leave her,' Tom was saying. 'I have to find where he buried her.'

'If he did . . .' replied Jean the Frenchman.

'Surely he would've buried her!'

'There was a pile of unburied bodies round the back of the barn,' pointed out the Frenchman.

'Maybe that's where she is!' Tom was on his feet and would have been halfway to the door if Jean hadn't pulled him back.

'You can't go back there!' he said. 'They'll still be there – they've got no horses and they won't leave until they've drunk all the wine and eaten all the food . . .'

'But what if she's lying on that pile of bodies and she's still alive!' exclaimed Tom. A whole chain of impossibilities were now chasing through his mind disguised as plausibilities.

'A moment ago nothing I could say could persuade you that she wasn't dead,' Jean pointed out.

'But . . . I have to make sure!' Tom was trying to pull himself away from the Frenchman's grasp.

'Listen! If you go back there you're a dead man!' said Jean.

'I don't care!' replied Tom, and he wrenched himself free and was making for his horse Bruce.

'Well, I'm not staying around to save you,' said Jean.

'I'll be ok!' shouted Tom, and he wheeled Bucephalus around and headed back the way they'd just come.

All was quiet when Tom arrived back at Le Saut du Loup; the *routiers* must have been sleeping off their celebrations of the night before, thought Tom as he crept across to the back of the barn where he and Jean had seen the pile of bodies. He reached the far end and paused to draw a deep breath. Could he really go ahead with this? When he'd been speaking to Jean, he had hardly thought of the implications . . . but now that he was about to come face-to-face with real corpses of real people the whole thing felt very scary.

And what if Ann's body were amongst them? That, he told himself is precisely why he had to go through with this. He felt the blood pounding in his ears, as he cautiously peered around the corner.

There they were.

Tom could feel his stomach rising and his feet suddenly became too heavy to lift off the ground.

Terry Jones

'Now come on,' he told himself. 'It's just a pile of dead bodies . . .'

'What!' screamed another voice inside him. 'Dead bodies! Get me out of here! And in a *pile*? You must be joking! You'll never get me to walk over there!'

He shut his eyes for a moment and then forced his feet to move forwards . . . but after a few steps they came to a halt.

He opened his eyes and stared at the heap of corpses. It was strange how they didn't look how he had imagined . . . the limbs stuck out at odd angles, with here a leg protruding sideways and there an arm crooked into an impossibly painful posture.

And they were all quite, quite still. Tom knew it was obvious that they should be still, but at the same time the stillness surprised him . . . astonished him . . . it was inconceivable that creatures that had recently possessed the ability to move about in freedom and think whatever they liked could have become so rigid.

And that was the moment when he saw her.

'Ann . . .' his lips formed the word but his voice had no power to make itself heard. He closed his eyes again and waited. Perhaps the image would have changed when he next opened them. But, when he did, there was no mistaking it: her blue tunic was just visible at the bottom of the heap, and he could see her leg in

350

its brown hose, crooked at an unlikely angle to the body . . .

Tom had known all along that this was how it would be. He had seen it all in his mind's eye. And he knew what would happen next: his head would swim, and his knees would buckle, and he would collapse to the ground. But that isn't what happened at all.

Something else took hold of him . . . not despair or grief or even horror. Instead a cold, brutal anger welled up inside him. And, though it was cold and brutal, it didn't feel wrong – it felt like a clean, pure emotion . . . almost like joy . . . an anger that raised him above his fellow men. It was an anger that gave him a purpose in life: he had to kill Peter de Bury. It was as simple as that.

Moments later Tom was on his horse racing back towards the *routiers'* abandoned encampment in the Gorges de l'Alagnon.

The horse seemed to understand his urgency of purpose as the two of them charged back down the road they had travelled together for the first time only the day before. Bucephalus tossed his head neither to left nor right, as if he were focused solely on the journey ahead, and he seemed to need no prompting as he flew over the ground, kicking up a dust cloud behind them that, as far as Tom was concerned, blotted out the future.

It was not long before the country closed in around them and the walls of the gorge concentrated their minds on their ultimate goal. Somewhere, back there where the river broadened and the road became a narrow track, in a tangle of brambles, lay Tom's sword.

Or so he hoped.

And if he had seemed too puny or too irresolute to wield that blade in the past, now, he was certain, the anger in his soul would give him the cruelty to use that blade as he would have to use it – to kill another living human being.

He shook the thought from his mind, and tried to concentrate on Peter de Bury's dreadful crime. And the memory of Ann's pathetic corpse lying at the bottom of that pile of discarded bodies blew all other thoughts from his mind like a hurricane hitting a dandelion puff-ball.

The next moment, it seemed, they had reached the widest stretch of river, where the flat stone had sheltered the *routiers*, and Bucephalus seemed to know that this was their destination. The horse turned into the water and started to wade across almost, it seemed, without any guidance from Tom.

And before they had reached the other bank, Tom

had jumped off the horse's back and was running and stumbling through the water to the spot where the vegetation reached down to the shore. And as Bucephalus dragged himself up onto the bank, Tom was tearing at the brambles with his bare hands, almost unaware of the thorns that ripped his flesh.

But the sword had either sunk deep into the briar patch or else someone had removed it, for he couldn't see it, and the blood from his hands smeared across his face as he wiped his brow.

Where was it? He pulled again at a briar and thought for a moment he saw the glint of steel . . . but it was just some dew catching the sun as it fell from the thorns.

'Where is it?' he screamed aloud, in a fury of frustration. And the next minute he was kicking at the brambles and crazily stamping and cursing them until he had cleared a small hole and it was obvious that the sword was not there.

And then the world went mad indeed, for suddenly he heard himself being addressed by name and he turned and saw a figure in a blue jerkin with brown hose, standing on top of the flat stone, holding the sword. And the figure looked and sounded like Ann, and she was speaking words that seemed to make sense and yet didn't.

'Tom!' the apparition was saying. 'I thought you were dead!'

'I thought *you* were dead!' he replied to the apparition.

'I came back to free you but you weren't here. Then I found your sword in the bushes. You wouldn't leave it behind, I thought. So the wolves must have got you!'

The next minute Tom's head was swimming and his knees were buckling and he suddenly found himself on the ground, and Ann . . . the real live flesh-and-blood Ann . . . was kneeling over him stroking his hair and telling him it was all right.

'But I saw your body in the pile!' cried Tom.

'What pile?' asked Ann.

'At Le Saut du Loup! You were under the villagers Peter de Bury's men had killed!'

'I never went to Le Saut du Loup,' Ann replied.

'But I saw you there! You were running about after the villagers!' cried Tom.

'No,' replied Ann. 'I went with Peter as far as Lempdes, and then . . .'

She suddenly fell silent.

Tom waited for what she was going to say, but she seemed to have drifted off into some private chapel of thought.

'What happened in Lempdes?'

'Oh . . . it had happened before then . . .'

'What had?'

'The moment I saw him threatening you with his knife . . .'

'You saw?'

'Yes. He pretended he was going to cut you free, but I had already seen what was going on . . .'

'What happened?'

'I knew then that Peter de Bury was dead.'

'What?'

'I knew that the Peter that I had first met in Oxford and had been thinking about and longing for all these years no longer existed. It was like an eclipse of the sun. Something that I was so sure about and had taken for granted, like the sunlight, suddenly was no longer there.'

'I'm sorry,' said Tom.

'What happened to him?' asked Ann. 'Or did he never exist? Was the Peter de Bury I loved simply a construction in my own mind?'

Tom was at a loss to know.

'At first I tried to make excuses for him, but then when we got to Lempdes . . .' And here the words ceased to come. Ann collapsed onto the ground and great sobs escaped from her throat, like the gasps of a man drowning in sorrow. It was Tom's turn to put his arms round his friend and try if he could to comfort her.

'Was it Peter and Emily?' he asked nervously. Ann could not reply. But she nodded, and suddenly – whatever it was that had gone on – Tom did not want to know.

'Whatever happened,' said Tom. 'I love you, Ann.'

And he squeezed her hand, and Ann squeezed his back.

Chapter 35

Lombardy 1385

'What happened then?' asked Squire John. He and Sir Thomas were hiding in a convenient wood that stood beside the road from Milan to Lodi. They had decided to wait for daylight before they tried to re-enter the city to find the Lady Beatrice, natural daughter of the Lord of Milan. And as they sat there in the dawn of a May morning, with the unstoppable chatter of birds filling the branches and sky above them, Tom had found himself joining in the general hubbub by recounting the story of all those years ago, about Ann, Emily and himself.

'What happened then?' Tom repeated John's question as if it were the only memory he had. He turned over onto his back and placed his hands behind his head, and gazed up through the young leaves at the sky that was now transforming itself into a blue vault above them. 'Emily rescued her brother and would have married Peter de Bury too, but she never got the chance. I suppose you could say he met a fitting end.'

'You killed him!'

'No,' replied Tom. 'I didn't kill him. All that anger went out of me the moment I saw Ann alive. I couldn't have killed Peter de Bury once I knew she was unhurt.'

'So what happened to him? I suppose he got killed by the king's men?' asked Squire John.

'No, as a matter of fact, not. He was – ironically – murdered by bandits like himself. He got back to England with Emily all right, and she lodged in the king's palace at Eltham. He was on his way there to meet her, riding across the Black Heath that lies to the south of London, when he was attacked at a place called the Foul Oak. It was notorious for robbers. It's a mystery why he was riding alone and at night across such a place. You would have thought, as a bandit himself, he would have known better. Maybe he really was in love with Emily by then and thought it a risk worth taking. Who knows? Emily married some duke or other and I hear she bore him six children.'

'But what happened to Ann . . . and you?' asked Squire John. 'You'd told her you loved her . . .'

Tom picked up a stick and threw it across the glade.

'Ann . . . Ann . . .' he murmured, and stopped as if

his thoughts had come up against an impenetrable wall, higher than the city wall of Milan, stronger than the walls of Jericho. He glanced across at his squire and said: 'And the Lady Beatrice? Have you told her you love her?'

'Yes! Of course! I've told her a thousand times!' cried John, delighted to be talking about her.

'But she doesn't know that you are risking your life – and mine – to find her! I must be crazy to even talk about going back in there!' exclaimed Tom.

'I promised I would never leave her behind, and I swore that if I ever escaped I'd return for her.'

'But will she actually come with us?' asked Tom, suddenly serious. 'You know we might go to all this risk and she'll just say she doesn't want to leave her father!'

John shook his head.

'She loves me,' he said. 'She promised to follow me wherever I went.'

And he held out his hand for Sir Thomas to see. In the palm lay a ring that sparked with the intensifying light. Tom took it and held it up: a blue ring against a blue sky.

'All right!' he said. 'We'll need to get hold of another couple of horses and some documents, and . . . sh! Listen!'

Terry Jones

Beyond the now almost deafening chorus of bird-song something else could be heard some distance away. It was another kind of singing, not of birds but of humans.

Tom and Squire John broke the cover of the wood and looked down the road that led to the castle of Binasco and beyond that to Pavia. In the distance they could see a troop of pilgrims on horseback. There must have been a hundred of them, and as they drew nearer, Tom and John could see that the majority were carrying olive branches, which they were waving in time as they sang.

At their head rode a slight figure with a neat beard and a bob of dark hair cut short to just above his ears. He was dressed in a blue surcoat embroidered with gold and he wore his olive spray in his hat. He was surrounded by a dozen armed guards.

'Gian Galeazzo!' said Tom. 'What on earth is he doing here?'

'There was word in Bernabò's court that his nephew was going on pilgrimage to the Sacred Mountain at Varese,' whispered John.

'I didn't know that!' muttered Tom. 'Not much of a spy, am I? Sitting in prison in Milan, you knew more about what's happening in Pavia than I did! No wonder

360

the Lady Donnina wanted to get more information out of me.'

'Does he always travel with that many men?' asked John.

'Often three times as many,' said Tom. 'Let's get out of here! I don't want to have to start explaining what I'm doing.'

But it was too late. One of the guards had split away from the main group and was now riding hard towards them.

'Damn!' muttered Tom.

'He'll never catch us once we disappear in the wood,' said John.

'No, we'll hold tight. He won't know who we are anyway.'

'Sir Thomas Englishman!' shouted the guard as he drew nearer.

'Well, another theory bites the dust!' mumbled Tom.

'My Lord Gian Galeazzo requests you join his company.'

To tell the truth Tom was more than a little put out – after all he was meant to be in disguise. He'd shaved all his hair off and he was still dressed as a minstrel, and yet the Lord of Pavia had recognised him at a distance of several hundred yards.

'I don't think I'm going to take up spying full time

just yet,' he muttered in English to John, as he bowed to the messenger and nudged his horse to follow the fellow back to the main party. Squire John ran along beside him.

'Sir Thomas Englishman!' exclaimed Gian Galeazzo. 'You will join us on our pilgrimage to Varese?'

'I am honoured to do so, your lordship,' said Tom with as low a bow as he could manage on horseback.

'Ride beside me, Sir Thomas. So . . . you were returning to Pavia? Then you must have accomplished your mission astonishingly quickly!' Gian Galeazzo had dropped his voice to a whisper. 'You have scarcely been in Milan two days. How did you learn of my uncle's plans so easily?'

Tom felt as if his bluff had been called.

'Alas! Your lordship,' he replied, 'I have not been successful. I was forced to escape from Milan in order to save the life of my squire, John.'

Gian Galeazzo nodded at Squire John. 'You are lucky,' he said. 'It is not many who escape once they are in the grip of my uncle's cruelty.'

'But in the short time that I was there I did not hear of any plans by the Lord Bernabò against your lordship,' whispered Tom.

Gian Galeazzo clucked his tongue.

'Such news is worthless, my friend. It is like a blind

man saying there is no difference between night and day. You know very well I cannot sleep for fear of my uncle! Even on this holy journey I dare not set foot in my own city – for do not forget that I am co-ruler of Milan with my uncle! I have been forced to agree to meet him outside the city wall. Do you understand how humiliating that is? He treats me with contempt and . . .'

Gian Galeazzo suddenly checked himself – aware that his voice had risen enough to be heard by others. He smiled at Tom.

'It is not your fault, my friend. You have served me faithfully in this business and I shall reward you.'

At this point Gian Galeazzo turned abruptly away from Tom, and spoke in a low voice to the swarthy man of about the same age as Tom who was riding on his other side. Tom recognised the man as Gian Galeazzo's captain general, Jacopo Dal Verme. And, as Tom looked around the rest of the pilgrims, he realised that Dal Verme was by no means the only military man who had decided to go on pilgrimage. Tom was suddenly aware of Guglielmo Bevilacqua and Antonio Porro riding close behind the captain general. Gian Galeazzo was certainly taking no chances with his uncle's malevolence while he went to make his vows on the Holy Mountain at Varese. Tom shook his head.

It was as if the Lord of Pavia were afraid that the very trees were going to ambush him at every step of the journey. Little wonder if his uncle despised him . . .

As Tom was thinking all this, a murmur went up from the men surrounding Gian Galeazzo. Three riders were approaching from the direction of Milan.

Jacopo Dal Verme signalled to the troop to halt, and they waited there in the road for the riders to reach them. Tom glanced across at Gian Galeazzo. He seemed tense, as if he expected every moment to be his last, and he was watching the riders with such concentration that Tom was convinced he thought they might suddenly multiply into three thousand.

'My cousins!' called out Gian Galeazzo, and a smile replaced the nervous twitch to his mouth. The guards drew aside and allowed Bernabò Visconti's two sons, Ludovico and Rodolfo, to approach Gian Galeazzo, whereupon the three dismounted and embraced.

'You do me great honour to ride out so far to greet me,' said Gian Galeazzo. 'I thank you from the bottom of my heart.'

As the greetings continued, Tom turned to look at the third rider. He was dressed in black and his eyes were never still – darting here and there – forever assessing and calculating. They came to rest for a moment on Tom, and he shivered as he found himself under the penetrating gaze of Il Medecina.

The man did not show any sign of recognising Tom, however. He simply looked at him for a moment and then moved on to examine the rest of the company one by one.

By this time the cousins were slapping Gian Galeazzo on the back. It was obvious, thought Tom, that they shared their father's contempt for him.

'I see you've brought your entire army with you, cousin!' smiled Ludovico.

'I'm afraid not!' replied Gian Galeazzo meekly. 'I can't afford more than this small troop for pilgrimages'.

'Well, it's best to be on the safe side,' said Rodolfo. 'They can be dangerous places, these shrines!'

'You want to watch those crucifixes – some of them squirt blood you know!' Ludovico slapped his thigh as if he'd said something dreadfully witty.

The two brothers eventually remounted their horses. As they did so, Tom saw Gian Galeazzo nod to Dal Verme and the latter wheeled his mount around and rode off in a hurry, back towards Pavia.

Il Medecina, who had also been watching this with great interest, now also wheeled his horse around, and he too rode off, but in the opposite direction.

Tom frowned. He might not make a great spy, but he could tell when something was going on.

A flash of concern passed over Gian Galeazzo's face as he saw Il Medecina speeding off back the way he'd come, but then it was gone, and he was smiling and nodding at the banter of Ludovico and Rodolfo.

'Mind that horse of yours, cousin!' said Rodolfo. 'He looks like he might bolt!'

'I trust the Lord will keep me safe, for this is a holy journey,' said Gian Galeazzo, bending his head in a brief prayer, while Ludovico raised his eyes to heaven and tried to stifle a laugh.

'My astrologer says that Saturn, Jupiter and Mars are all in a most inauspicious conjunction in the house of Gemini,' Gian Galeazzo confided to Rodolfo. 'He tried to dissuade me from coming at all, since, he says, such a conjunction foretells of terrible disasters ahead – awful things will happen – dreadful calamities. But I was determined to come.'

'Well, let's all pray that there is nothing awful waiting for us around the corner,' said Ludovico, and Gian Galeazzo had bent his head to pray before he seemed to realise that his cousin was being ironic.

And so they set off once more, making their way towards the city of Milan.

At the Ticinese gate, where the road from Pavia

arrives at the great city, the entire party turned to the left, and instead of entering the city, it followed the path that wound around the perimeter of the walls.

The bonhomie between the cousins seemed to have subsided slightly as they circumnavigated the realm of Bernabò Visconti. It seemed to Tom that Ludovico and Rodolfo had become rather edgy.

'Perhaps it's the proximity to their father that makes the brothers nervous,' thought Tom. 'He'd make me nervous if I was his son. And Gian Galeazzo must feel a bit edgy too, since this is half his city and yet he daren't set foot in it.'

And then, as they rounded yet another part of the city wall, suddenly there he was: Bernabò Visconti, the great Lord of Milan himself!

And yet the great man didn't look at all like the tyrant of Lombardy he was. He didn't even look like someone Gian Galeazzo ought to be scared of. He was sitting unaccompanied, apart from Il Medecina, on a mule, outside the humble postern gate near the church of Sant'Ambrogio. It seemed so incongruous that Tom would have laughed, had he not suddenly realised what it was all about. Bernabò did not express his contempt for his weakling nephew by laughing at him in his face – although he was quite capable of that too – but on this occasion he was showing his contempt by his casualness, by his lack of retinue, by the absence of guards. There he was, just he himself: the most powerful ruler in the whole of Italy – in the whole of Europe – the crushing tyrant who kept his people in subservience and terror, who had ruled with his rod of heavy iron for thirty years, sitting mockingly upon a sorry creature as if he were selling onions. Only his baton of office, held in the crook of his arm, betrayed the reality of his power.

Nothing could be more calculated to show his utter disregard for his nephew – unworthy to be his father's son – who now approached him.

Gian Galeazzo took his uncle's hand in greeting, but at the same time he called out something in German. Jacopo Dal Verme had rejoined the group, and he too had now ridden up to Bernabò. There was a slight scrape of steel against scabbard and Gian Galeazzo shouted out: 'Now!'

And then it happened. The most extraordinary thing that anyone there had ever seen – or ever would see – happened in front of their eyes: Gian Galeazzo's captain general, Dal Verme, quietly leaned across to Bernabò Visconti and plucked the baton of office from the tyrant's hand.

There! That was the extraordinary, impossible thing that took place in front of the little postern gate, near the church of Sant'Ambrogio, on that May morning in the year 1385.

A shock vibrated through the air and hung there in a terrible instant of silence, as if nobody could believe what had just happened – least of all Bernabò himself. It seemed that the great tyrant – whose word had been life or death to his wretched subjects for thirty years and who, for thirty years, had been used to instant obedience whatever his command – could not quite take in the affront to his honour, to his person and to his power, that had just taken place.

And even as his sons tried to comprehend what they had just seen happen to their all-powerful father, they each found themselves silently surrounded by a dozen men-at-arms. It was all done so quickly and so efficiently that you would scarcely have noticed that anything unusual had taken place.

And before anyone had drawn another breath, Guglielmo Bevilacqua cut Bernabò's sword belt and thus disarmed him.

'You are a prisoner,' Dal Verme informed the tyrant.

'How dare you do such a thing!' Bernabò finally managed to splutter.

'It is my lord's command,' said Dal Verme, and Bernabò turned his ferocious gaze upon his nephew. But instead of being boiled away by that look, instead of shrivelling up into a burned cinder, Gian Galeazzo simply sat impassively upon his horse staring back at his uncle.

Perhaps he was amused by the turmoil of terrible thoughts that he knew must lie behind Bernabò's scorching gaze: 'How could this shrimp – this pathetic little nothing – this frightened schoolboy still wet behind the ears – how could he even attempt to do something against me – his formidable uncle? Well! He'll pay for it! He'll suffer such torments at the hands of the torturers that he will never, ever think of challenging his betters again . . . not that he'll get the chance of course! I'll make sure he dies the most agonising death that can be contrived! I'll do such dreadful things to him that . . .'

However, all that came out of Bernabò's mouth was this:

'My son!' he said . . . it was actually more of a whine. 'Why are you doing this to me? Everything I do is for your good! Everything I have is yours! Do not betray your own blood!'

Gian Galeazzo looked at the older man without emotion. 'You will have to remain a prisoner, since you have tried to have me killed so many times,' he said in a clear, formal voice, as if for his biographers to take note.

And before Bernabò could reply, the rest of Gian Galeazzo's modest escort arrived. From around the curve of the city walls over a thousand men-at-arms appeared. At the same time Dal Verme rapped out an order, and the troop pricked their horses and rode at a gallop to the next gate into the city: the Porta Giovia, which led directly into Gian Galeazzo's own palace.

Tom, who had fallen back to put his squire up behind him on his horse, arrived at the Porta Giovia in time to see the great tyrant of Milan and his two sons being put into manacles and then hurried down, presumably into some secret dungeon in the bowels of the palace.

There was one member of Bernabò's party, however, who was neither stunned into inactivity by the turn of events, nor there to witness this abrupt cessation of his master's power and glory. Il Medecina, Bernabò Visconti's closest adviser for so many years, the man who had steered the tyrant of Milan through many storms and tempests of his own making, had vanished from his side.

Time and again Il Medecina had warned Bernabò not to underestimate his nephew. Hadn't his constant refrain been: 'He is not at all what you see!'? How many times had he warned the tyrant: 'Do not let your nephew fool you into committing yourself to his power. He will not hesitate to destroy you!'?

But Bernabò had scoffed at him as often as he had warned him. And in those moments it was often only the restraining hand of Bernabò's wife, Regina della Scala, that had saved the tyrant from acting rashly with regard to Gian Galeazzo. Now she was gone, and Il Medecina had been unable to persuade Bernabò that the conjunction of Saturn, Jupiter and Mars in the house of Gemini boded calamity on a grand scale.

And this morning, when Il Medecina had accompanied Bernabò's two sons to greet Gian Galeazzo, and when he had taken stock of Gian Galeazzo's entourage and seen that it included no fewer than three generals, he had known that this was more than just a pilgrimage to Varese. And when he had seen one of those generals, Jacopo Dal Verme, wheel his horse around and gallop back towards the castle of Binasco, he had suddenly understood everything. He had suddenly realised, with the clarity of a conspirator's mind, that the seemingly puny Gian Galeazzo had, in fact, a large army following at a distance, and that he had come to Milan not on his way anywhere, but specifically to challenge his uncle.

He had therefore ridden pell-mell back to his lord and master, and begged him to go back inside to the safety of the city. But Bernabò would have none of it.

He was not scared of a flea bite like Gian Galeazzo. He was not about to run from the shrimp whom he was about to humiliate. And nothing Il Medecina could say would move the Lord of Milan to act with caution towards his nephew. So when the party arrived, and when that first move against Bernabò was made – when Dal Verme leaned across and snatched his baton of office – Il Medecina had turned his horse and vanished before anyone realised he had gone.

By the time the Lord of Milan and his sons were led off to their dungeons, Il Medecina was already well on the road to Padua.

Meanwhile the lances were pouring through the Porta Giovia, and as soon as they were within the city, they fanned out in every direction – galloping down the narrow streets of Milan, blowing hunting horns and shouting:

'Long live the Count of Virtue! Down with the taxes the tyrant extorted! Long live Gian Galeazzo!'

And the good people of Milan tumbled out of their beds and workshops to stand on the street and gape and wonder at what was going on. By the time the last of Gian Galeazzo's troops had passed under the sign of the serpent eating a man that hung above the Porta Giovia, the townspeople were cheering the fall of the man who had ruined them with his taxes, burdened

373

them with his dogs and tortured and executed their friends and relatives.

They stood on the streets and cheered the ruler of Pavia, whose very title, 'The Count of Virtue', gave them hope and seemed to reflect his reputation for clemency and benevolence. They would have been disappointed to learn that 'Virtù' was simply the district of France that Gian Galeazzo's mother, Isabella, had brought with her as her dowry. Her father, the king of France, had sold her for 600,000 florins to an Italian tyrant in order to raise the money to pay off his ransom to the English.

But to the good people of Milan, on that May morning, the young Count of Virtue could only live up to his title. The nightmare of Bernabò's rule was suddenly, unexpectedly and delightfully over. What is more, the new Count of Milan promised lower taxes and more benign rule.

It may be that not a single person in that entire city was sorry for the destruction of Bernabò Visconti – except for those within his own palaces, who now found themselves fair game for whatever revenge the citizenry wished to take upon them. For one of the first benign acts of the new Lord of Milan was to have it proclaimed in the public streets that all citizens were now at liberty to pillage and plunder the palaces and homes of Bernabò and his sons.

This offer, which was nonrenewable and a one-off, was calculated to keep the law-abiding citizens of Milan pleasantly occupied while their new lord and master set about reassuring the General Council of the city as to the benevolence of his rule. This he did by making donations to various charitable causes in which they all had a financial interest.

Tom and Squire John had meanwhile ridden to the southern palace, where Bernabò had resided until that morning. They found the place in turmoil. The occupants were desperately trying to get out, while the citizens were desperately trying to get in. The result was a sort of deadlocked scrum at each available entrance and exit.

'The servants' entrance!' whispered John.

'Good thinking!' replied Sir Thomas.

An unearthly howling had set up as they slipped round to the side of the palace. Instead of plundering the tyrant's home, some of the more civic-minded citizens had set about slaughtering his dogs. About a dozen of the strongest men – at no small risk to themselves – were going from kennel to kennel, cutting the animals' throats. Those animals still alive seemed to have a presentiment of their impending fate, and had set up a chorus of despair and outrage that swelled to fill the sunlit volume of the day.

Even the most enterprising citizens had not yet got round to the servants' entrance, and Tom and John were able to slip into the palace without challenge. The guards had made themselves scarce some time before. Many servants were still trying to put their worldly possessions into carryable packs, while others were already heading off with whatever they could carry in two hands.

Squire John led Tom up a staircase towards the series of interconnecting rooms where he knew the Lady Beatrice kept her residence. They had just reached the first floor when a door opened and a serving girl with a shawl wrapped round her head hurried out. She was carrying a bag and kept her head down. Two other heavily laden servants followed her and made for the stairs. John and Tom fell back to allow them to pass and then carried on their way towards the domestic living quarters.

They hadn't got more than a few yards however, before a voice stopped them.

'Gian!'

John span round and almost before he'd finished turning, he exclaimed: 'It's you!' and leapt across the landing. The next second he was holding the serving girl in his arms.

'I'm so scared . . .' Beatrice began.

'It's all right,' John replied, also in Italian. 'We'll protect you!'

'Well, let's hope we don't have to,' said Tom in English. 'The sooner we get out of here the better!'

A couple of looters had already appeared in the hall below, and from elsewhere in the palace the cries of the invading citizens could be heard above the noise of splintering doors and shutters.

John grabbed Beatrice's pack and Tom took some of the burden from the other two.

'Your lady certainly doesn't believe in travelling light,' he observed. But John was too preoccupied with providing a proper escort to the lady in question to even notice that his master had spoken to him.

They hadn't taken more than a couple of paces down the stairs, however, when a voice rang out above them.

'Stay where you are!'

For some reason they all froze. Perhaps the voice was so effortlessly commanding that they all thought for one moment that they must be doing something wrong. Tom looked up and there was the Lady Donnina de' Porri, standing at the head of the stairs as if she still owned the place.

'You are not going anywhere, young lady,' said Donnina de' Porri.

In the confusion, Beatrice had stumbled to her knees, and as John tried to lift her to her feet he could feel she was trembling all over.

'We are leaving here as quickly as possible,' replied Sir Thomas English in his most un-minstrel-like voice. 'And my advice is that you do the same.'

'I understand my Lord Bernabò is under arrest by his nephew. Is that correct?' Even Donnina de' Porri's questions sounded like a command, and Tom found himself obeying instantly.

'Yes. That is correct,' said Tom.

'Then it is my wish that I accompany him in his imprisonment. And I order you to come with me, Beatrice.'

'But she's only young and . . .' began Squire John.

'And I am half dead?' asked the beautiful Lady Donnina.

'No! Of course! I didn't mean . . .'

Tom was amused to see that the Lady Donnina made his squire as confused as she made him.

'My lady,' said Sir Thomas English. 'If you wish to accompany Lord Bernabò in his current plight, that is your decision and I shall honour it. May I be permitted to escort you to the appropriate authorities? I fear for your safety unless you accept my offer.'

More and more looters were pouring into the richly

decorated hall below them. Most of the newcomers paused for a moment to gape at the hitherto unimagined richness of the decoration, and then – as if inflamed by the ostentation of such a private display of wealth – they set to work tearing off as much of it as they could to carry back to their own humble homes.

'There!' shouted one of the law-abiding citizens of Milan. 'It's the Lady Donnina de' Porri!' And all eyes suddenly turned upwards to where he was pointing. There was a surge forward and suddenly Tom was half-way down the stairs with his sword drawn.

'The Lady Donnina is under my protection!' he shouted. 'Stand back and let us pass!'

The citizens fell back with a quite spectacular display of precision drill. There was always a satisfactory distinction, Tom observed to himself, between threatening armed soldiery and unarmed civilians.

So it was that Squire John rescued the Lady Beatrice from the mob and Sir Thomas English escorted the Lady Donnina de' Porri to the presence of Gian Galeazzo.

'As I have shared my lord's bed,' said Donnina de' Porri, 'so I shall share his imprisonment.' And that was that.

Tom never could quite understand how such a man as Bernabò Visconti could generate such loyalty in those around him. Hadn't he been a man of intemperate appetites and behaviour? Hadn't he treated his fellow creatures as if they were unfeeling blocks of wood? Wasn't he guilty of torturing and killing men on a whim? Hadn't he ruled arbitrarily and through fear for all these years? And yet there were those who were still loyal to him. Loyal enough, in the Lady Donnina's case, to endure his fate alongside him.

Yet though she insisted that the Lady Beatrice show a like dedication to her father, and join in her sacrifice, Gian Galeazzo would not allow it. The Lady Donnina was escorted down to the dungeons to join her dethroned lord and master alone.

Chapter 36

Milan 1385

The wedding was the talk of Milan, of course. How could it be anything else? For a start, the black mourning cloth that everyone had been ordered to hang out to mark the death of Regina della Scala had all been finally taken down and stored away. In its place garlands of flowers were hung across the streets and white and gold embroidered cloths were hung from windows. The fountain in the square of the Duomo ran with wine for the entire day, and musicians tramped round the houses blaring their trumpets and beating their drums and performing impossible cadenzas on their flutes.

And there were public feasts. Tables had been set up in many streets and the food was piled high upon them for all and sundry to join in. The new Lord of Milan wanted to ensure that the common people had no second thoughts about the sudden change of rule.

Then there was dancing outside the inns, with different bands competing at different street corners for the crowds who came to merry-make and get dizzy.

And of course there were rumours of the feasting that was going on – even now at this very moment – in the great Visconti Palace in the north of the city – the palace that had been empty for as long as Gian Galeazzo had not dared to enter Milan.

And now Gian Galeazzo was here to stay, life would be one long celebration – at least until the wedding was over. There were still guards at the entrances to the palace, of course, but even they had acquired a festive air, and had entwined garlands around their helmets and decorated their pikes with nosegays.

But inside those walls, so people said, a fabulous feast had been laid out. There was a swan, they said, complete with its signets, served up on a golden dish, and the swan had a golden crown around its neck. A wild boar had been led in – as if it were alive – and the cook had rushed in with his knife and cut it in two and inside were cooked meats and finely minced delicacies that the servants took up and distributed around the tables.

They said that even the sturgeon was served in a golden net – as if it had just been caught.

It was no wonder that the wedding was the talk of

Milan. But perhaps the aspect of it that was most talked about by the good citizens was the fact that the bride's father was absent. He was languishing in one of his own dungeons deep in the bowels of what had been his own palace in the south of the city.

Could he hear the merrymaking from down there? He must have been able to. He must have known that his own flesh and blood was being married without his being there. And many a law-abiding citizen shook their head in a gesture that lay somewhere between disapproval and high amusement. The new Lord of Milan must be doing it on purpose as a torture for his uncle, they said. That was the common opinion.

But even more, said others, the real torture for Bernabò Visconti must be that his daughter, the Lady Beatrice, was marrying a squire of low degree – a mere nobody without powerful connections in the courts of Europe. An Englishman who was neither a prince nor a duke, nor likely to inherit anything worth mentioning. It was exactly the sort of marriage that Bernabò Visconti himself would never have permitted as long as he could order a suitor to be put on the rack.

It was a love match. And the old Lord of Milan would have sooner had his daughter put to the stake than allowed her to make such an unprofitable alliance.

And many a head nodded wisely and said that it was all part of Gian Galeazzo's plan to show that his rule would be as different from his uncle's as is the hangman's rope from a daisy chain. And other heads nodded in agreement and added that it was really designed to torment the fallen tyrant. That the nephew took delight in authorising this marriage because he knew the anguish it would cause his uncle, deep in his black cell, would be worse than any physical torture he could devise.

However, such considerations were not apparent to any of the wedding guests that thronged the courtyard of Gian Galeazzo's palace, where the festivities and feasting had been set out under the sky of azure and over a carpet of rose petals that covered the entire magnificent enclosure.

'So, Sir Thomas Englishman,' said Gian Galeazzo, putting his arm around Tom's shoulder as he spoke. 'I said I would reward you for your services, and so I shall.'

'But, my lord, I fear I performed no useful service for you whatsoever!' replied Tom.

'But indeed you did!'

'I brought you no news of your uncle. No useful information. I found nothing out . . .' Tom could have gone on listing the ways in which he had been a truly hopeless spy.

'But I wanted nothing like that,' whispered Gian Galeazzo, as if he were teasing Tom in some inscrutable way.

'What?' said Tom. 'You asked me to find out about your uncle . . .'

'My dear fellow,' replied the new Lord of Milan in a low voice. 'I have plenty of spies at my disposal. What on earth made you think I should I need an outsider like yourself?'

'Then why did you send me back to Milan?' asked Tom.

Gian Galeazzo gave him a rather old-fashioned look, and then whispered in his ear: 'To help persuade my uncle to trust in my faint-heartedness and irresolution. I believe my Lady Caterina provided you with some tips on how to go about it?'

The look on Tom's face must have told exactly what he was thinking, for Gian Galeazzo dropped his bantering tone and sounded more sincere as he added:

'I am sorry, Sir Thomas. I was not as straightforward in my commission to you as I would have liked to have been. But had you known my real intention, you might have found it more difficult to perform your part.'

Not for the first time, Tom felt himself as helpless in the coils of the Visconti serpent as the wretched man whom the Visconti viper was forever in the act of

385

swallowing. But at least, he consoled himself, he would soon escape. There was nothing now to stop him setting off on the road that led out of Lombardy: not concern for his Squire John, not fear of Bernabò, or Regina della Scala or Donnina de' Porri . . . nothing could hold him here any longer.

'So,' said Gian Galeazzo, raising his voice. 'When would you like to start on acquiring new books for my library? It should be a pleasant enough task!'

The road out of Milan suddenly disappeared.

Tom stopped stock-still. There was nothing else the Lord of Milan could have said that would have made him even consider staying another week in the land of the Visconti, but to have the task of caring for all those books . . . to be able to go out and buy whatever he wished and build up a great library for the Lord of Milan . . . perhaps he would never be quite free of the coils of the Visconti serpent after all . . .

Some time later the bridegroom found himself cut off from his beloved by the press of ladies-in-waiting wishing to kiss the bride and tell her of their latest exploits. Squire John found himself sitting alone with his old master, Sir Thomas English, drinking a glass of sweet wine.

'Sir Thomas,' said Squire John. 'You never did tell

me what happened to you and Ann after you escaped from Peter de Bury and his men.'

'Ah! That's a story in itself,' said Tom.

'Indeed,' said Squire John, settling himself in his seat.

'But if you think I'm going to tell it to you here and now at your own wedding, you must be crazy! Why! There's your bride looking for you already!'

Squire John leapt up and the next moment he had his arm around the Lady Beatrice's waist as the minstrels struck up a galliard and the happy couple stepped out to start the dancing that would go on until dawn.

The End

Supporters

Unbound is a new kind of publishing house. Our books are funded directly by readers. This was a very popular idea during the late eighteenth and early nineteenth centuries. Now we have revived it for the internet age. It allows authors to write the books they really want to write and readers to support the books they would most like to see published.

The names listed below are of readers who have pledged their support and made this book happen. If you'd like to join them, visit www.unbound.com.

Moose Allain
Basil Alzubaydi
Carol Ames
Alan Andrews
Evelyn Andrews
Claudia Archer
Sandra Armor
Dan & Toni Arthur
Allison Ashley
Lynn F. Avery Jr.
James Aylett
Annette Badland
Christopher Ballard
Sophie Barbaro
Elizabeth Barrial
Josh Bartman
Greg Bauhof
Pete Beck
Thorhalla
    Gudmundsdottir
    Beck

Roberta Benson
Julian Benton
Ekaterina Berova
Zac Bettendorf
Canute Bigler
Zandra Bill
Brian Bilston
Holly Blades
Rebecca Liddle Blair
Jason C. Block
Elena M. Bloom
Jason Boggs
Dimitrios
    Bogiatzoules
Charles Boot
Ruth Boreham
Adrienne Kristia
    Pamintuan
    Brandao
Richard W H Bray
Philip Brennan

Mayer Brenner
Stefano Brentegani
Adrian Briggs
Ken Broman
Richard Brooderson
Derek Brou
Margarita Brown
Pendrick Brown
Ed Bruce
Stephen Bruce
Anthony Brun
Brad Bulger
Brian Burhans
Chris Butcher
Marcus Butcher
Daryl Butterworth
Mike Buttrick
Laurie Canfield
    Cameron
Anna & Tom
    Schwartz Canto

Paul Carlyle
Barry Carpenter
Diane Carpenter
William Carpenter
Sarah Carter
Carl Casinghino
Ricardo Castro-
  Torres
David Chamberlain
Greg Cheesman
Mary Chipman
Thomas Chubb
Jonathan
  Churchman-
  Davies
Bob Claster
Steve Cleff
Benji Clifford
Phil Clifford
Brian Cogan
Elliot Cohen
Leo Collett
Clodagh O Connor
David Cooke
George Coppinger
Andrew Cotterill
Steve Cox
Dawn Coxwell
Kim Craigs
Megan Crockford
Adrian Culley
Heather Culpin
Daniel Dadmun
Brett Danalake
Duncan Dawdry
Stoffel Dbls
Corey de Danann
Deadmanjones

Celia Deakin
Brian Defer
JF Derry
Mark Diacono
Diana
David Dickinson
Kylie Dickinson
Michelle Donald
Jenny Doughty
Yiannis Doukas
Katherine Draper
Nicole Drespel
Dan Duffek
Keith Dunbar
Sir Alexander
  Dutkewych, B.A.,
  K.G.St.J.
Nicola Edwards
Gerald Eggleston
Paul Mietz Egli
Matthias Ernst
Matthew Eve
Michele Farmer
Owen Fay
Ken Fincher
Gregory Fink
Sarah Forbes
Aaron Fothergill
Nate Fox
Adam Fransella
Mark French
Thomas Fries
Eva Fritz
Rich Frost
Jim Galbraith
Margaret Gallagher
Ulrika Gålnander
Amro Gebreel

Georgina Gedroge
Cynthia Geno
David Giangrande
Martin Gooch
David Gordon
David Graham
Wendy Gray
Mike Griffiths
Lina Grigaitis
Joe Grumbo
Mel Hall
Steven Hallmark
Nicholas Haney
Andrea Harms
Jody Harnish
Philip Harris
Elaine Harry
Caitlin Harvey
Joanna Haseltine
Brogan Hastings
Michael Heddlesten
Catherine Heege
Becky Heiskell
Christina Hellström
Simon Henry
Bill Heuglin
Catherine Heywood
John Heywood
Josh Hill
Ley Holloway
Mojmír Horák
Jeff Horne
Joanna Hughes
Nik Hurrell
Greg Hurst
David Hyland
Gregory James
Fred Jannin

Terry Jones

Darriel Jeffree
Iris Jeltes
Rob Jenkins
Kerensa Jennings
Andrew Jobbins
Wes Johnson
Helen Jones
Juanjo
Jonathan Judy
Lisa Kadonaga
Haruko Kaizawa
Alex Kania
Nobby Kash
Kathrin KD
Kevin Keller
Adam Kennedy
Dan Kieran
Patrick Kincaid
Simon Kingston
John Kittridge
Birke Knipping
Murray Knox
Richelle Kracht
Andrew Kristoffy
Daisy Lacey
Carrieann Lago
Mit Lahiri
Evelyn Laing
Gary Lamont
Kim Lawson
Bridget Caron Lee
David Lee
James Leeds
Andrew Leimdorfer
Béatrice Letutour
Ellis Lewis

Rupert Lewis
Claire Lindsay-
    McGrath
Tamasin Little
Katja Lokhoff
Lynn Long
Liz Lothian
Pil Lotze
Jess Loveheartley
A Loyd
Chuck Lucas
Kelly Luck
Gari MacColl
Andrea Mackenthun
Antonio Muñoz
    Maestre
Kerstin Maier
Philippa Manasseh
Cecily Marsh
Grant Marshall
Paul Marx
Hélène Masse
James Mather
Ruth McAvinia
Carol B McCollough
Clair McCowlen
Tom McDermott
Karen McDonnell
John McEwen
Daniel McGachey
Robert McIntyre
Wendell McMurrain
Ian McWilliam
Mike Melville-Reed
Pamela Michele
Jan Miller-Klein
Andrew Mills
Michael Minden

Mansoor Mir
John Mitchinson
Virginia Moffatt
Simon Monk
Jim Mooney
Nyck Moore
Jade Moores
Alison Morgan
Jenny Morgan
Raven Morgoth
James Morris
Carl Moss
Tim Munson
Nick Murza
Lynda Naclerio
Kathy Nagle
Carlo Navato
Jaime Nelson
Michael Nelson
Al Nicholson
Elisa Nicolai
Noims
Mark Nutter
Julian O'Donovan
Chatrina O'Mara
Paul Oakley
Kenichiro Obana
Alan Onions
Alan Outten
David Parent
John Parrett
Elwyn 'Slim' Parry
Lex Passaris
James Craig
    Paterson
Jay Payette
Russell Payne
Heather Pazmino

Viggo Pedersen
Gwen Pelletier
Jay Pennington
Clifford Penton
Robert Phillips
Paul Pick
Justin Pollard
Glenn Anton Polyn
Katie Pow
William Powell
Janet Pretty
Jonathan Pritchard
Katharine Purvis
Nick Quinn
Colette Reap
Gemma Regan-
  Mochrie
Corey Reid
Helen Reid
Louise Reid
Clay Renfroe
Stephanie Ressort
Olly Richards
Charles Richardson
Thomas Richter-
  Emde
Jem Roberts
Mr. Jack Robertson
Helen Rogerson
Igor Rogov
Wojciech Rogozinski
Sebastian Röhrig
Stephen Rooney
Nicky Roper
Ira Rosenblatt
Chana Rochel Ross
Nadine Rückert
Sven Rump

Benjamin Russell
Bonnie Russell
Gail Russell
Kate Ryan
Lisa Ryan
Yehuda Sadeh-
  Weinraub
Thomas Sandelands
Roman Sannikov
Arthur Schiller
Gerhild Schinagl
Manon Lynn
  Schürch
Jenny Schwarz
Anne-Marie Scott
Catherine Seeligson
Helen Selden
Jo Sharples
Kuniko Shoji
Julia Shortt
Shawn Sijnstra
Dave Sikula
Catriona Silvey
Mark Simpkins
William Slaughter
Peter Sleight
Jodie Sloan
Nigel Smale
Andrew Smith
David Smith
Michelle Smith
Nigel Smith
Christopher Sniezek
Anna Söderblom
Lili Soh
Pawel Somogyi
Martin Spencer-
  Whitton

Karen Steiger
Christopher
  Stephenson
Warren Stine
Toby Stone
Sheila Gibson
  Stoodley
Katie Stowell
Kathleen Strawder
Robert Two Sheds
  Stroud
Nina Stutler
Tristan Swales
Keith Tait
Alexis Taylor
Elaine Teenan
Alice Thacker
AJ Thomas
Emily Angharad
  Thomas
Martha Thomases
Mike Thompson
Rhys Thompson
Catherine Tily
Astrid Timonen
Pekka Timonen
James Tomkins
Gail Tomlin
Kev Toumaian
Anne-Marie Trace
Shinya Uehara
Shaun Usher
Olivier Vigneresse
Ana Vitorino
Tim Vivian-Shaw
Nicklas von Plenker-
  Tind
Robert Waft

Terry Jones

Susan Warlow
Olivia Watchman
Barbara Watt
Shannon Rose Alice
   Webber
Alexandra Welsby
Deb Werth
Don West
Chris Weston
Scott Weston

Wynn Wheldon
Pete White
Beata Wierzbowska
Emily Wilhite
Mark Williams
Randy Williams
Sean Williams
Derek Wilson
Sam Windrim
Andrea Wiskin

Thomas Ray Worley
Nicola Wright
Janice Yelland-
   Sutcliffe
Artur Zakalski
Adriana Zayia
Angelina Zayia
Christopher Zayia
Gregory Zayia